THE FINAL DRAFT

THE DECKER CONNECTION
BOOK 4

CHERYL CAMPBELL

ISBN: 979-8-9929865-3-2

2nd edition

Always remember these fundamental truths:
Know your worth.
Be brave and fight.
Love wins.

CHAPTER
ONE

HARPER

————

I never expected to see my life packed into a storage unit, but there it is. The container sits in the driveway filled with all my things. My memories. My belongings. My identity. My twenty-six years packed into totes and boxes.

It's been a week of ups and downs as I purged, sorted, tossed, and packed. I gave everything the Marie Kondo touch. Does it bring me joy? I kept it. No joy. Out it went. Now I stare at a bunch of totes that should be filled with joy, but in reality, is a hodgepodge of stuff that I don't know if I love anymore. I don't know much of anything right now.

I wipe the sweat from my brow as I look at it all stacked in this container that will ship to Raleigh tomorrow. Sweat trickles down my back, and I need another shower. Why is it so hot? Even after ten years of living in Atlanta, you'd think I would get used to the heat and humidity. Spoiler alert: I haven't. And moving in the middle of a sweltering summer heatwave was not on my bingo card this year, but yet, here I am.

Lawson adds a box labeled "stuff" to the container, and I shake my head, not really in disbelief, because I'm not surprised. Rather, it's acceptance of his lack of organizational skills. I wonder what he calls stuff. It could be anything from pictures to books to underwear. It's not hockey-related because that "stuff" is packed into his luxury Jeep Grand Cherokee. When it comes to hockey, he's got it. The other details aren't exactly his specialty. Besides, we both know he won't be the one unpacking these boxes when the time comes.

"That's the last of it," he says. He pulls the sliding door down and latches it. The sound startles me and punctuates the reality of this moment. He lays his arm across my shoulders as we stand side by side, looking at the closed container.

"Yep."

"I'm sorry, Harps. I know you don't want to leave." He pulls me in a little tighter, his brotherly love surrounding me. "I meant it when I said you can stay." He sighs, his regret filling the moment. "I hate that you're doing this because of me. It breaks my heart to see you look so sad."

I am sad, but not for the reasons he thinks. This house became my home after a drunk driver tragically killed my parents in Minnesota when I was a sophomore in high school. At twenty-two years old, Lawson's life took an extraordinary turn as he made his NHL debut and assumed the role of legal guardian for his sixteen-year-old orphan sister within months of each other. It was a hell of a year for both of us.

When I came to live with him, he bought this house in the suburbs and did his best to give me an excellent high school experience while balancing his new hockey career. He became a surrogate parent overnight. It was unconventional and not what either of us wanted, but we made it work. We had to. Lawson made Atlanta my home. And now, it's not. While I'm anxious about this next step for me, I'm sad for him. And angry. After ten years of playing hockey for Atlanta, six as captain, multiple playoff seasons, and one Stanley Cup, they traded him to the

Carolina Renegades. Gone are the days of loyalty and franchise players, I guess. With one phone call and a stroke of a pen, he lost another family: his team. Just like that. No warning. No idea it was coming. To say it shocked him is an understatement.

We were wrapping up a lazy summer and driving back from a beach trip in Charleston when he got a call from his agent notifying him of the change. No call from the team owner, his coach, nothing. It was like the call he got the night our parents died. Out of the blue, totally unexpected, and so unbelievable, the news had to be repeated several times for it to sink in.

He considered retiring, but I wouldn't hear of it. He loves hockey, and I won't let him quit because of me. I've impacted his life too much as it is. He's a damn-talented hockey player and can lead a team to Lord Stanley again. There's no question about it.

It's time for me to stand on my own two feet. I put on my strong facade for Lawson and reach up to take his hand draped over my shoulder.

"I'm not sad. We're going to be fine. We're Cartwrights."

He bends down and kisses the top of my head.

"Damn right we are."

We walk back into a shell of a house. Everything that made it a home is gone. We packed all our personal belongings but left the furniture for now. It feels sterile. Empty. We left the big stuff because it will look better furnished when we choose to sell. Besides, neither of us is going into our own place for now, and well, we aren't ready to say goodbye to this house yet. Moving out in stages is a slow goodbye, a kind of goodbye we aren't familiar with. I'm realizing I hate goodbyes all-together.

Lawson's phone vibrates on the counter, and he answers it on speaker. "Hey man, you calling to tell me you've changed your mind about having a roommate?" Lawson chuckles, but the full-on laugh coming through the speaker is all Chance Fuller.

"No way. Just wanted you to know I decorated your room in Golden Bears colors, in case you needed to coordinate your stuffie. You can make room for your shit around all my old trophies." They both laugh.

Chance and Lawson were high school rivals back in the day. We grew up in small towns that revolved around hockey. Texas might have Friday night football, but Minnesota lives for hockey. The mention of Minnesota is another reminder of everything we've been through.

Chance is the captain of the Carolina Renegades, Lawson's new team. Getting traded so close to camp didn't give Lawson much time to find a place to live and get everything in order. Especially when I'm part of everything.

Chance was the first person to call after the news broke. He welcomed Lawson to the team and into his home. They're going to be roomies for the foreseeable future. They played together their rookie year in the AHL and became good friends despite their previous rivalry.

"I hope Darcy doesn't hear about that room," I say. "She'll be up there so fast you won't know what to do." Darcy is a mutual friend and an amazing interior designer. She designed Chance's beach house and did work at our house too. I look around and another wave of sadness hits me because most of her touches are erased, packed in a metal container in the driveway.

"Maybe I'll bring her with me," Lawson teases.

"Like Matt would let her around you again," Chance says. "He changes the channel every time your damn Jeep commercial comes on." His laughter fills the room.

"Hey, I was nothing but hospitable to a friend of yours in need. Is this what I should expect this year - you busting my balls?"

"Sounds about right," Chance adds. "Hey, Harper, you set for your big move?"

"As ready as I'll ever be." I try to add excitement to my voice, but I fail, and it falls flat. Lawson looks at me warily. Tomorrow Lawson and I are going our separate ways.

I'm moving to New York to pursue my writing career. As fate

would have it, on the very day Lawson was traded, I received the incredible news of my acceptance into a prestigious writing program at NYU. It was like fate wanted to split us up with a one-two punch.

When news of Lawson's trade hit, all his current and former teammates reached out. It's a testament to the kind of leader and friend Lawson is. Hockey is a tight community, especially for guys like Lawson and Chance who have both phenomenal talent and character. Because they respect him, I've always been in their circle of protection. My own band of brothers, as it were.

As soon as Lawson mentioned my move to New York, Zac Burns insisted I stay with him. He's Lawson's former teammate and current goalie for the New York Havoc. Apparently, his ex-girlfriend and previous dog sitter recently moved to Brooklyn after an ugly break-up. Now he needs a new dog sitter, especially with the season starting soon.

Zac laid on the sweet talk of how much I'd be helping him out, insisting I'd be less drama than his ex and the deal was done. When I asked if his last dog sitter was just a roommate like me, he laughed and assured me he's better off with our arrangement. I don't know the entire story, but there's definitely more to it. In exchange for dog-sitting, I'll be living in a luxury New York apartment building with a doorman.

"You know Burnsy is a good guy," Lawson says. "And he'll barely be there. But if he steps out of line, you let us know. Chance and I will take care of him."

"You know he won't." I roll my eyes. There isn't a guy in the NHL who would step out of line with Lawson's little sister. A small smile breaks through when I think about my new roommates. "I can't wait to play with Noodle."

A choking sound fills the room as Chance tries to catch his breath. "You're going to play with his noodle? What the fuck, Lawsy? Where are you sending her?"

Lawson and I can't contain our laughter. "Noodle is his miniature dachshund, you idiot. You know me better than that."

Lawson sighs. "Listen, I'm headed to Raleigh in the morning after I drop Harper at the airport. Should be in around five, just in time for a cold one. Be ready to fire up the grill for our steaks."

"Absolutely. I'll have a welcome committee waiting for you. I invited a few of the guys that are around to meet the great Lawson Cartwright," Chance says with a twinge of humor in his voice.

Hearing this banter, I'm comforted knowing Lawson will be fine with his new team. It softens my anger on his behalf a little. Maybe this move is a blessing in disguise for him. But for me? Time will tell.

The rest of the move's logistics fell into place quickly after that first call. Our personal belongings are going into storage in Raleigh until Lawson gets a place of his own. I sold my car since I won't need it in New York, and Lawson insisted I keep the money for "pocket change."

I hope to make my own money someday from my first book. Or I'll get a job as a barista. Or a pet sitter. Either way, I can't live off Lawson forever. Sure, he makes millions, but those millions are precisely what got him traded. Apparently, Atlanta couldn't afford him anymore and needed money off their salary cap. Lawson doesn't have many playing years left, so I want him to save for his future.

I hope that this rigorous NYU course will hone my skills to become a published author, opening the door to my dream career. Then I'll be self-sufficient.

I've been writing since my therapist encouraged me to start a journal after my parents died. It became therapeutic for me, an escape from the tragedy in my life. I'd make up stories and use them to deal with my feelings, making sure my characters ended up okay.

The stories were full of fantasy, hope, and happily ever afters. Or at least happy for now. I'd had enough stories with tragic endings, like people dying in car accidents. Writing was my escape from a harsh reality, a place where stories always had happy endings.

Over time, my writing evolved into romance stories, something my life severely lacks. Maybe I should classify myself as a fantasy author at this point because romance and I are exactly that. A fantasy.

New city, new degree, big dreams... this change might be the perfect jumpstart for my career and a whole new life. And maybe New York will be where I find romance? After all, it is called the City of Dreams.

CHAPTER
TWO

JULIAN

————

I pace across the small office waiting for the professor to arrive. It's been years since I was in school, and it feels like nothing's changed, except I'm not in trouble this time. At least I don't think I am. The offices are still small, musty, and crammed full of old, dusty books. The decrepit wooden desk has probably been in this room since the 1800s.

I'm as anxious as a cat in a room full of rocking chairs. Fuck. I'm here to meet with the professor of an elite writing program, and that's the best analogy I can come up with? What am I doing here?

Turning to leave, I collide with a petite Black woman, and I instinctively steady her with a hand on her elbow. "I'm so sorry. Are you okay?"

Her eyes travel from my mid-chest, and her head tilts up as she takes me in. She gives an appreciative look I've seen on women before, and I chuckle. I love that she's not shy about checking me out.

"I'm just fine. And so are you," she purrs. It never fails to make me laugh. Women are shameless, and frankly, I'm here for it.

She composes herself and shifts into business mode. "You must be Mr. Decker? I'm sorry I'm late. I hope you weren't waiting long." She steps past me and enters the room.

"You're Professor Daniels? You don't look like your picture." I'm rarely caught off guard. As the top sports agent in the country, I pride myself on reading people. I can tell who they are, their wants and needs, often before they know themselves. I'm an easy-going, laid-back, allow-people-to-get-comfortable-with-me kind of guy. Couple that with my business acumen and viola, a successful business owner.

"You mean because you thought you'd be meeting an old white man?" She laughs. "I'm Professor Daniels's assistant, Ramona Spector. He's running late and asked me to hold your first meeting. You'll be working with both of us on this project." She gives me a flirty wink and motions to the chair sitting in front of the desk. "Come in, sit down. I've been looking forward to this all day."

I take a seat as she closes the door and moves behind the desk, clearing a space for her notebook. She looks out of place in this room, adding to her mystery and my confusion.

My anxiety is peaking, and for a guy like me, that speaks volumes. I'm rarely anxious. But right now, I'm on heightened alert. She called me by my name. My actual name. How did she find out? I'm racking my brain for a response. Great, no words.

"I'm going to cut through the bullshit, Mr. Decker. I've already gone off script with our meeting today, but then, you aren't a typical student. So let me lay it out for you." She looks at me without breaking eye contact. Her face is blank, but maybe a little amused if the lines around her eyes tell me anything. Her voice is sharp, businesslike, the playful flirting completely absent.

"In this program, people are pushed out of their comfort

zone to make them better. That's why you signed up. But you're different. We've never had someone like you in the program before, and I've decided to break the rules and do something unconventional. Before we proceed, I need to know if you're up to the challenge, Mr. Decker?"

My mind is reeling. I'm still speechless. She stares at me, waiting for an answer.

"How? How do you know my name?" I used a pseudonym for all of my submissions. She shouldn't know who I am.

"Mr. Decker, why are you here?" she challenges.

"Right now, I'm not sure." Was this a mistake? If she found my name, can others? My anxiety goes up another notch.

"Because I know your name?" she asks. "Or because you aren't up to the challenge?"

"Both."

"Mr. Decker, your submission fascinated me. A son of a billionaire, a successful agent to some of the top athletes in professional sports, named one of *People Magazine's* hottest bachelors in the country six times, and a closet romance author. Call me curious."

"But you weren't supposed to know all of that. How did you find out?" I'm still baffled that she found me. The real me.

"I always do a deep dive on the program's finalists. I know people in high places. They tell me things. But don't worry, Mr. Decker. Your secret is safe with me. I promise. Which is why I wanted to meet and discuss my proposal. I assume by your reaction you want to stay anonymous?"

"I'd prefer that, yes."

"And you'd still like to take part in the program?"

Do I? I think back to the day I opened the acceptance email. I jumped up and punched the air. My new assistant, Violet, heard me through the door and assumed I signed a big client. If I had that level of enthusiasm, then there's my answer.

"Yes. But I have to stay anonymous." My heart is beating hard and fast. I can practically hear it and worry she can too.

She silently nods her head at me. "I think we can do that. It will be challenging, given your assignment, but I will leave it at your discretion when to reveal yourself."

If word gets out that I'm JB Moore, a romance author, it could severely damage my reputation and my business. It's vital I keep control of this secret. For the first time since the meeting started, I take a deep breath and attempt to calm my racing thoughts. It's all been a mind-fuck. "Okay. As long as I have control, I'll make this work. What's the next step?"

"I've read your submission, and it's good. I like your style and perspective. However, you struggle when finding the female motivation and her voice, which makes sense, given your gender." For the first time since I sat down, her severe look eases, and we both become a little less guarded.

I nod in agreement. Ashleigh, my younger sister, and I have been reading romance novels together for years. I spend a good part of my life around women. But just when I think I have them figured out, I get thrown for a loop.

Take my sister-in-law, Dani. She claims that being assaulted was worth it because she met Alexander. She's the most glass-half-full, sunshine person I've ever met, and she fell in love and married my grump of an older brother earlier this year. I'm happy for them, but I don't claim to understand her perspective.

"I'd like you to cowrite with a new author. She has a lot of promise. The book will be a dual point of view, but I want you to write the female character. She'll write the male. It will sharpen your writing and spark interesting dialogue between the two of you."

"But how can we do that without her knowing my identity?" Once again, my anxiety builds.

"Emails, conference calls, you choose. Use technology, Mr. Decker. Hell, wear a mask or a furry costume. You make the rules. If you want to reveal yourself, then that's up to you." She sits back, crosses her arms, and stares me down. Our relaxed truce is over. She's challenging me. Again.

Write a book with someone? I've only shared my secret with my editor, Casey Samuels, and I had her sign an NDA. Now that we've grown to trust each other, it's probably unnecessary, but it's there as a precaution.

Am I up for the challenge? Do I want to do this? Yes. I want this more than anything right now. I'm bored with work, my siblings are happy and settled, and I need something that excites me. And this excites me.

I stand up and extend my hand. "Thank you for this opportunity. I'm up for the challenge."

A skeptical amusement plays across her face as we shake hands. "We'll see about that. Professor Daniels will reach out later this week and reschedule your introduction with him, but he didn't want to waste time." Her almost-cackle makes my anxiety spike. I need to leave this office. Now.

As I open the door, she calls out, "Good Luck!" I doubt she really means that. She's got my head spinning, that's for sure.

As I step out of the office, I bump into a gorgeous woman who's looking down at a notebook in her hands. She's dressed in a white blouse, unbuttoned just enough to let me know where her cleavage starts. Her breasts are the perfect size. Her fitted pencil skirt hugs her hips and hints at the curves beneath. Stilettos add several inches to her height, but also makes her unsteady on her feet. What they do for her legs is practically sinful. Black-framed glasses highlight her caramel-colored eyes. A neat bun holds back her dark blonde hair. I imagine with a strategic tug of a pin, it would fall down around her shoulders in a hot-as-fuck way. I can't tear my eyes away from her deep red painted lips and imagine where I'd want them on my body. Fuck. She's straight out of a librarian fantasy.

"Oh, I'm so sorry," she says. Her hands rest on my chest as she balances herself. What is it about this door that makes me bump into people?

"Are you okay?" I check her out from head to toe for injuries, but also because I can't resist. Her dark eyes look up at me, and her expression fills with panic. She blushes and appears embarrassed.

"I'm fine, I'm fine. I'm sorry." She pulls her notebook to her chest and hurries away.

"Hey, do I know you?"

CHAPTER
THREE

HARPER

———

My meeting with Professor Daniels was what I expected. Mostly. He's an older, white man with a Ph.D. in Literature and Creative Writing, like so many of my professors from my master's program. Typical. He told me I'd be working with him and his assistant professor, Ms. Spector.

But it's his description of this program that has me reeling. It's intense, which I knew it would be, but it didn't prepare me for the assignment. Write an entire book in twelve weeks? It took me almost a year to write one, and I'm still not happy with it. I'll need to treat this like it's my full-time job, and it's going to involve a lot of overtime. And focus.

The other part I hadn't factored in was a writing partner. I'm not sure how I feel about that, but Professor Daniels assures me it's necessary for my growth. For most authors, writing is a solitary, isolating process. They lock themselves away with their characters and write the story they want to tell. To collaborate feels unnatural, but I'm willing to trust the process. I want to improve my skills and create a story readers will love.

Overwhelmed by all the new information, I'm so frazzled that, while reviewing my notes as I walk, I slam into someone. This must be how Lawson feels when he's checked into the boards. Strong hands grab my arms to keep me from falling backward from the sudden collision. My hands land on his firm pecs as I steady myself and hold on to my notebook. I look up into a pair of familiar aqua eyes and gasp.

Julian Decker. I know he lives in New York, but what are the chances of me literally bumping into him? One in eight million, give or take. Maybe I should buy a lottery ticket today.

Shit. I feel my cheeks warm and heat creep up my neck and down to my core. He's one fine man. I need to get out of here before I die of embarrassment. Straightening my glasses, I do my best to look indifferent about this collision. I step back, turn, and take several quick steps down the hall, my heels clicking on the polished tile.

"Hey, do I know you?" he calls out.

I stop in my tracks. Moment of truth. Do I remind him we have mutual friends, including his sister, and we met briefly at a party last summer? Or that my brother and his best friend are roommates? Or should I act like we haven't met and go about my day?

Because, of course, he doesn't remember me. I'm a nobody compared to the circle he runs in. He always has a model or actress on his arm. He's met so many women, we all probably blend together.

Decision time. With a deep breath, I slowly turn around and take him all in. He's wearing fitted, dark jeans and a no-logo polo shirt, which means it probably costs a fortune. Casual but professional. His dark blonde curls are perfectly styled. The slight beard on his chiseled jaw gives an appearance like he forgot to shave, but I'm sure it's a totally intentional look. He doesn't forget things like that. His perfect lips curl into a smile as he notices me checking him out. But what's captured my attention are his captivating deep blue eyes, framed by thick, dark lashes.

"I know you, don't I?" His head cocks to the side, like a puppy trying to figure out why you're yelling at them. Granted, an adorable puppy that melts your heart and makes you forgive them for eating your favorite shoe, but still.

Apparently, he's decided for me. I wince before giving him my casual, I-do-this-all the-time-look.

"You probably don't remember me."

"I never forget a face." He studies me, his gaze noting my every detail as he tries to piece the mystery together. I'm so overwhelmed by the intensity, I could swoon. "But sometimes a name," he confesses. "Help a guy out?"

Despite my desire to remain aloof, I can't contain my giggle. "Your charm is unnecessary, Julian. I'm not one of your past conquests." He's taken aback by my comment and almost looks offended. I didn't mean to make him uncomfortable.

"I'm Harper Cartwright." He's racking his brain trying to place me. I give him the last clue. "Lawson Cartwright's sister."

Relief fills his face. "Oh my god, yes! Ashleigh's friend." He puts his hands to his head and grabs his hair, mussing it a little and making him sexier, if that's possible. "I'm so sorry. You look different. And out of context and I didn't put it together." His posture relaxes, and he drops his guard.

The fact he remembers me as his sister's friend warms my heart. I'm often known as Lawson's sister, Harper. It's rare I'm known outside of his persona, and I admit, I like he sees me this way.

"I heard about Lawson. Shitty move by Atlanta, but their loss. What are you doing in New York?" He shifts into casual conversation with ease. No doubt, his conversational skills make him a successful sports agent. His open posture is disarming, and I let my guard down too.

"Would you believe dog sitting for Zac Burns?"

He throws his head back and laughs, shaking his head in disbelief. "Damn, I need to talk to the Havoc management. He must have one hell of a contract if he can get Lawsy's sister to move across several states to be his dog sitter." As he chuckles at his own joke, his face lights up with a smile that's easygoing and friendly. He's casual and confident, but not cocky, and it's a seductive combination.

I shrug. "What can I say? I'm a sucker for Noodle. He's irresistible."

"Lucky Noodle," he mumbles. "Listen, let me give you my number, and if you need anything, reach out. I mean it. Ash would have my head on a platter if I didn't watch out for her friends."

He holds his hand out, waiting for my phone. Without consulting with my brain, I hand it to him. He holds it up to my face to unlock it, flips it around, takes a quick selfie, and enters his number. He sends himself a text, and now he has mine.

Well, today has been unexpected. Welcome to New York, indeed.

CHAPTER
FOUR

JULIAN

———

I stare at the contact information for my writing partner. Priscilla Jenkins. I wonder why she chose that as a pen name. Master's degree in creative writing. No big deal. I may not have a formal education in writing, but I can tell a story. Besides, my MBA from Wharton is nothing to sneeze at.

No published works - yet. Maybe she's trying to go with traditional publishing, which is hard to break into. I've published three books independently, and they've produced decent numbers, but I would like to see them grow.

Let's see what else I can learn about Priscilla. Prefers strong heroines. Good. Me too. Likes flawed heroes. Oh great! One of those women who prefers the male character on his knees, and not just in the bedroom. I bet she'll create our male to be some weak, soft, cinnamon roll kind of guy who won't even challenge my girl. I'm willing to put money on it.

I'm exasperated, and we haven't even started this yet. We're using software that allows us to collaborate and communicate with chat while maintaining anonymity. Apparently, we both asked for that. We also agreed to use our pen names for the duration. Hell, Priscilla could be a single guy with lots of cats living in his mother's basement in Kansas. I doubt it, but who knows?

I log into our secure portal and find our first assignment is preloaded. *Collaborate on an outline and create characters for a sports romance.* Fantastic. I can do sports romance. Sports are my thing. Any sport works for me. I'll let her pick.

I wonder which we should do first: the story or the characters. When I write by myself, I usually have the characters and come up with an interesting story. What's Priscilla's method? Only one way to find out.

JB: Hi Priscilla! Which do you do first? Character or plot? And what sport do you prefer?

She responds almost immediately.

PRISCILLA: Hi JB! This is wild, right? I can't believe we are co-writing a book. Still in a state of shock here. Professor Daniels eluded you're a man, but he never confirmed. Is that true? You never know when authors use initials or pen names. I mean, it's no big deal, but a male romance author is unusual. We agreed to pen names, but call me curious.

I was waiting for this, and even so, my anxiety creeps up a notch. I made it clear anonymity was essential, but maybe a gender reveal isn't that big of a deal.

JB: Ever hear of Nicholas Sparks?

PRISCILLA: OMG. Of course. I didn't mean anything by it. It's unusual. Different. And I like it. I'm hopeful we can make each other better.

While I'm figuring out what to say, she gets us back on track.

PRISCILLA: To answer your question, I'm not much of a plotter, so I focus on my characters and let them tell me their story. But I suppose we should agree on some basics. I can write a pro hockey player pretty well. What do you want the girl to do? I'm open to any trope but admit I'm a traditionalist, so no harems if that's OK with you.

HA! She thinks she can write about hockey players. I seriously doubt it, but that's where I can help her. My best friend is in the NHL, and I represent several other players. I know these guys better than most. But fine, she wants to take a shot, I won't stop her.

She poses a good question, though. What does my girl do? Work for the team? Do they meet on a dating app? A teammate's sister? I channel my inner Chance. He's busy with minimal time to meet people. How does he meet women? When he's on the road, girls hang out at the hotels, hoping to score with a player, but I can't have him fall for a puck bunny.

I appreciate Priscilla's traditional view. If I'm honest, I'm traditional too. It may look like I have a harem, but things aren't always as they appear. I'm a one-woman man.

I need to know more about the setting to narrow it down.

JB: In-season or off-season?

PRISCILLA: More time to be together in the off-season, but maybe dealing with the travel schedule is part of the conflict?

JB: True.

Well, maybe she understands the reality. Which do I prefer? What does my girl want? I let myself daydream and consider the girls I know. I scroll through my phone contacts for inspiration and quickly realize most of these girls aren't someone I'd want to be with long term. Good for a fun time, not a long time. That's why I'm still single at thirty-one.

I keep scrolling, looking for interesting women I could model my character after. Emma Jones, Ashleigh's best friend. She's a teacher. So is Xander's wife, Dani. Maybe my character could be a teacher.

Emma is a strong possibility for a muse, since she's single. She's tiny, feisty, and always reminds me of Tinkerbell. She's adorable, sexy, and nope. I'm too close to that subject matter and can't think of her that way. My character is not like Emma. I need to scrub my mind clean of those thoughts immediately.

I keep scrolling through my contacts. Let's see. There's Darcy Davidson, Ashleigh's future sister-in-law. She's interesting and endearing. A designer. That job gives her flexibility our hockey player might need. Maybe a designer.

Then I scroll to the newest contact in my phone. Harper Cartwright. She definitely checks all the boxes. Sexy, bold, funny, confident. I don't know much about her background, but I could work with this. I'm reminded how my body reacted when she was pressed up against me, and I'm liking where this is going. My character development starts to form.

JB: Let's make it the last half of the season. He'll have to work harder to see her. I'll complete on my character sheet and send it over shortly.

PRISCILLA: Great! I'll do the same. So excited!

The best way to work on my character? Get familiar with my inspiration better. I text Harper.

> Hey Harper! Julian here. Checking in to make sure you got home with no more incidents.

The bubbles start and stop for the next ten minutes. I can't remember the last time I waited for a girl to text me back. It's for research, I tell myself. Yeah, that's it. But is it?

I picture those ruby red lips and wonder what they taste like. What the fuck is wrong with me? I need to focus on this project, not Harper.

> Minor incident, but that's New York for you.

My heart stops and I feel a twinge of panic. My fingers can't move fast enough to text her back.

> What kind of incident? Are you ok?

> Fine. Just took the subway in the wrong direction. Only took me four stops to figure it out. 😅

She's taking the subway? Sure, millions of people do that every day, but it's not safe for her. Especially not looking like a cross between the sweet girl next door and a sexy librarian. I grit my teeth and exhale through my nose. I need to calm down.

> Where are you now?

> Don't start with me, Mr. Decker. I've got one overprotective brother. I don't need another.

I'm definitely not thinking brotherly things about her right now. But she's right. Where is this coming from?

> Besides, Noodle will protect me.

The image on my screen shows a little brown wiener dog, its long body relaxed in her lap. I shake my head at her ridiculousness and write that on my character sheet. She's naïve. But laced with a little sass.

Usually when I hear Mr. Decker, I look around for my father.

But I can imagine her saying it to me, and another fantasy involving my desk comes to life.

Maybe my girl takes care of the hockey player's dog when he travels. I add animal lover to her character traits. Kind, compassionate. A dog walker would have to hustle to make a living at it, so I add tenacious. Maybe even scrappy. Like a cuddly kitten that thinks it can scratch your eyes out but can't really do much damage. They think they're fierce, but they're actually cute and cuddly.

An idea takes root. The characters don't really see each other but leave notes for one another. The notes become flirty and suggestive. He comes home early, startles her, and she pepper sprays him in his own home. YES! I like where this is going.

> I wouldn't put all my faith in Noodle.

Noodle will take on anyone from the ankles down. I believe in Noodle power! 👊

> I'll be the judge of that. Let me take you to dinner.

Thanks, but I can't.

Not to sound cocky, but that's the first time a woman has turned me down in, well, I don't remember. Strangely, I'm intrigued. Is it really a can't or more like a no thank you?

> OK. Another time?

What does that mean? WTF does an emoji mean? I stand up and pace around my home office, clutching my phone.

I reach out to my friend Trevor, who owns the Savannah Pajamas baseball team. He uses emojis like they're another language. I only understand half of his texts most days.

Hey T, what does it mean when I ask someone to dinner, they say no, I say another time, and they respond with this 😊

I read his response, and have no choice but to concede defeat.

💩

Yep. 😔

Disappointment settles in, but I use it as motivation to complete my character development. Yeah, I'm disappointed. Not about the rejection. My ego isn't that inflated that I can't handle a little rejection. No, I'm disappointed because I'd like to get to know Harper more. Genuinely. I shake my head to clear my thoughts and get to work. I'll have to let my imagination create my character for now.

Professor Daniels said I struggle with female character development. Watch me knock this out of the park.

CHAPTER
FIVE

HARPER

———

I stare at my laptop, hoping inspiration will jump out at me from my screen. No such luck. I scroll through TikTok to get ideas, and nothing. This is why it took me a year to write my book. Now Professor Daniels thinks I can do this in twelve weeks. He's a crazy person.

Noodle snuggles in my lap, and I absently play with his floppy ears. His body relaxes, and he turns his head more, granting me better access. "You need to work on subtlety, my friend." He's so damn cute, I give him what he wants. I'm a pleaser and apparently that applies to people and dogs. "Come on buddy, time to earn my keep." I give Noodle one more scratch behind the ears and put him down. "And find inspiration for my hockey player hero."

As a small thank you to Zac for a place to stay, I offered to cook for him and his friends tonight after their first pre-season game. The guys are adjusting to in-season living again, and while they can eat at the arena, sometimes they like to kick back and relax without trainers looking over their shoulders and watching their plates. With amped-up workouts, they are burning serious calories. Some call it hockey season, but it's really pasta season. IYKYK.

Zac and I had a showdown over my insistence on this dinner. He doesn't want me to do anything for him, adamant I'm his roommate with zero expectations besides Noodle. I can't help it. I like to do things for people. It's how I show I care, say thank you. Besides, surrounding myself with hockey players will help me create my character and hone in on those nuances that will make him three dimensional. It's a win-win.

When I threatened to call Lawson, Zac backed down and said I could cook tonight's dinner. My brother may not be his captain anymore, but he still has influence, and I'm not above playing dirty to get my way. The Havoc are playing the Renegades in a few weeks, and Zac doesn't want to be the reason his team gets special attention in the corners.

Once he agreed to let me do things for him, like occasionally cook, he asked for my infamous chicken parmesan. In Atlanta, Lawson often brought the younger guys home with him under the guise of feeding them and team bonding. His ulterior motive was to keep them out of the bars and out of trouble. Lawson failed to realize the guys enjoyed visiting our house because it was a welcoming home, something many of them deeply desired. Most would rather get a home-cooked meal, kick back around the video game system, or perfect their dart game on the back porch, then go back to a nondescript apartment. Didn't he notice them always calling their moms at our house?

And now here I am, in New York, living with one of those guys a few years later. It may be a fancy apartment, but it still doesn't feel like a home. Maybe I'll help Zac there too. I'll reach out to my designer friend, Darcy. She'll know what to do. Lawson and I aren't so different when it comes to taking care of people. It's our Minnesota values and a Cartwright family trait.

I'm up to my elbows cooking when a text from Julian Decker

comes through asking me to dinner. Talk about blown away, and admittingly, I'm confused about his motivation. Maybe it's at his sister's request. Maybe his latest actress or model is unavailable. Whatever. I'm sure he's just being nice, friendly, brotherly even. While I'm appreciative, I don't have time to daydream about a sexy sports agent. There are hungry hockey players to feed.

The door bangs open, and the Havoc have entered the apartment. Zac and his teammates come in, dropping their bags and shoes at the front door. I can hear the keys hit the bowl on the entry table.

"Hi honey, I'm home!" someone calls out. There's a muffled "umph" and laughter coming from the foyer.

Someone quietly says, "Dude, that's Lawson Cartwright's sister. Watch it." Another sound of tussling and laughter further announces their arrival.

Noodle comes out of hiding to greet the visitors, but at the sound of a loud thud, he makes a U-turn and lays across my feet. I pick him up and go nose to nose with him. "Hockey boys," I say, like he understands.

"Hey, Carty Junior. Smells great," Zac says in greeting as he enters the kitchen. Hockey players love nicknames, and several years ago, Zac stuck me with this one. Sometimes he calls me CJ for short. This affectionate moniker makes me part of the team, I guess, and I'm honored. When I meet new players, I usually have to look at rosters to figure out their real names. I'm not sure who will be here tonight, but I'm willing to bet I won't get government names from any of them.

Zac reaches to take Noodle from me, and the dog snuggles in. "Guess I know who he likes better." The missing front tooth makes his grin almost childlike and disarming. Zac uses his boyish charm to give him the innocent boy-next-door persona. He's intense on the ice with pucks flying at him, but off the ice, he's a kid at heart with a tiny dog that he adores.

"He knows I'm a softie."

Three other guys enter the kitchen, making it feel smaller,

because the four huge hockey players take up all the space. They watch our exchange with amusement. I'm not sure what they think's going on, but I can assure you, it's not. Zac's a nice guy, but he's a friend. This isn't a forced-proximity, one bed romance trope, so they can squash that idea. I have my own room and don't even feel the need to lock the door. I'm safe with Zac.

"CJ, this is Harvard, Jetsy, and Mac. Boys, this is Harper Cartwright." They don't even question my nickname.

"Thanks for doing this," Mac says. "I'm starving." It takes me a beat to understand him because of his heavy French accent. He steps closer to the stove and takes the lid off the marinara. "Ohmygod, this smells incredible."

"Can you be my dog walker too?" Harvard asks as he eyes the food. Bruises cover his ruggedly handsome face, and his eye is swelling shut. It's an occupational hazard of a defenseman.

"You don't even have a dog," Zac replies.

"I'd get one if she'd cook for me like this," Harvard answers.

"Enjoy your time in the sin bin?" I ask. The game was on in the background, and I caught a few highlights. His eye shows exactly how his night went. I hand the spoon to Mac to stir the marinara and make an ice pack for Harvard's eye.

"He knocked Burnsy on his ass." He shrugs like it was just another day in the office, and knocking down the goalie explains everything. Which it kinda does. "I'd do it again if I had to."

"And you will next game and the game after that," I tell him as I hand him the baggie with ice and point to his eye. No one touches your goalie. It's a cardinal rule in hockey.

"Boys, give me two minutes. Grab beverages and head to the table. And there's plenty, so don't be shy." They rummage through the refrigerator for beers and sodas and leave me to dish up their food. "Off you go," I say to Noodle, and he waddles over to his bed and curls up. He's clearly over this excitement.

I deliver the plates, and after a round of heartfelt thank yous, they quickly devour their food. I'm still making my plate, and Jetsy returns to the kitchen.

"Whatcha need?"

"That was the best chicken parm I've ever had, and that includes here in Little Italy. Can I have some more, please?" He's already finished. Did he inhale it?

"Sure." I beam at him. I love it when people enjoy my cooking. "More spaghetti?"

"No ma'am. Just the chicken." I quirk my eyebrow at him. Ma'am? While I'm all about manners and politeness, I'm twenty-seven and not old enough to be a ma'am. I feel old when the players call me ma'am. Then again. Is he even twenty-one yet? He blushes under my scrutiny.

"Anyone else need anything before I sit down and join you?" That's always been the rule. Once I sit down, they are on their own.

Various forms of no thank yous come from the dining area. I grab my plate, extra cheese, and join the boys. Jetsy is behind me to pull out my chair. This boy is adorable. I make a mental note to include manners and charm as traits for my character.

With seconds and thirds devoured, everyone's full. Then the banter really kicks in. Laughter ensues, and I do my best to keep up with all the inside jokes. It's one of my favorite things about hockey players. I've witnessed hours upon hours of relentless teasing using their unique hockey slang. The comradery fills my heart. It reminds me of my Atlanta home, but maybe it's the people, not the place, that I truly miss.

My phone buzzes, and Harvard snatches it up. Yep, reminds me of home. It's taken one meal and assurances I'm not involved with Zac, and I'm practically the team mascot now. New city. New team. Same result.

"Gentlemen, a new player has entered the game," he announces.

"Give me my phone," I say with gritted teeth. I grab for it, but he keeps it out of reach. Defeated, I slump in my chair, cross my arms, and put a pout on my face. I've played this game too many times and never win. These guys, with their long arms and relentless spirit for teasing, never work out well for me.

I look to Jetsy for some help. He's the polite one, but the twinkle in his eye says I'm done for. "Who is it?"

My phone gets tossed to Zac. "Julian Decker?" He cocks his head to the side, questioning me.

"Isn't he some billionaire, playboy, sports agent that dated that pop star?" Harvard asks with a grin.

"Yup," Mac adds, wiggling his eyebrows and making kissing sounds.

"And Chance Fuller's best friend," Zac adds sternly, all boyish charm gone. He's staring at me like I'm coming at him with a penalty shot.

"Wasn't there a thing with him and that princess from Sweden?" Harvard asks, like he's reporting on TMZ.

"And Lawson is Chance's roommate," Zac says to me like I don't know that. What's he getting at?

"You sure keep up with gossip," Jetsy says to Harvard. Exactly what I was thinking. "But I remember something about that." Jetsy is smiling while he pulls out his phone, probably looking up Julian's Wikipedia page.

"I think she was a hockey player's cousin," Mac says.

"Why is Decker texting you, CJ?" All playfulness has left his voice, and he's in full protector mode. I know that tone because Lawson is the over-protective world champion. He could give master lessons to helicopter parents.

The other three quiet down and wait, all eyes on me. This text and Zac's serious tone sucked all the joviality from the room. Even Noodle comes and sits beside me to investigate what's going on.

My emotions swirl with annoyance and excitement, each fighting for dominance. Now doubt and curiosity tag in. I don't know how to feel, but I certainly don't want to sort it out in front of this crew. I bite my bottom lip while I consider how to respond. Hearing his history, I'm asking myself the same thing.

Why is Julian Decker texting me? Looks like curiosity and excitement are winning the emotional wrestling match.

"I'm friends with his sister, and we bumped into each other earlier today." I shrug like that explains everything. And I wish it did. But I'm not sure it does. Pop stars? Actual princesses? Me? One of these things is not like the other. But then again, he asked me to dinner tonight. I'm intrigued. For my book research, of course.

I act cool so I can get my phone back, eager to see what he wants. In reality, I want to grab it, run to my room, lock the door, and scream into my pillow like a sixteen-year-old girl. But I don't. I take a calming breath, hold my hand out, and wait for Zac to give me the phone. I try to return his stern face, but unfortunately, it's not on my list of expressions. He's reluctant, but he sets it on the table next to me. Not in my hand.

"Be careful, Harper." Using my name alerts me to his level of concern. Message received.

Zac's warning can't dim my excitement. I'm practically giddy. Between tonight's hockey player inspiration and Julian Decker, my male main character is taking shape. I'm ready to bring Gavin Snow, star NHL forward, to life. He's an incredibly sexy, oozing-with-charm rogue, with a sordid dating past who scores on and off the ice. I'm falling in love with my book boyfriend already.

CHAPTER SIX

JULIAN

———

My calendar is relatively light tomorrow. A quick message to Violet and now it's all clear. It's times like this that I relish being my own boss.

It's late, but now that I have a free day, I want to keep my momentum going. The only way to do that is to get to know Harper better. After all, she's my muse and if I want to nail this character, then I need to know her inside and out.

> Coffee with me in the morning?

Twenty minutes later, she responds.

> I don't drink coffee.

Who doesn't drink coffee? I can't imagine starting my day without my morning caffeine.

How do you function without coffee?

I manage.

Can I take you to breakfast then? No coffee, but maybe some orange juice?

I only drink orange juice if there's champagne in it. 😜

I can't take it. Her texts are coy and maddening. This is why I prefer old-fashioned verbal conversations. Texts require interpretation. I don't know if she's serious or teasing me, but I find myself smiling despite it all. Maybe it's her sass? It's not often I find a woman who challenges me. It's contrary, and I kinda like it. But she hasn't said yes to meeting me tomorrow, either.

I know this magnificent cafe that serves the best mimosas in the city.

Oh, do share.

I will. Get ready for an awesome breakfast tomorrow!

Sorry, I've convinced Zac to try yoga with me, and his first class is tomorrow. I need to be a good role model.

She does yoga? My dick appreciates the vision of her in the perfect downward dog. Bet she's flexible and bendy, and I picture how that translates to other parts of her life.

I didn't realize dog walker job descriptions included yoga consultations. I may have to get a dog.

> Not the first time I've heard that tonight! 😅
> Harvard wants a dog so I'll keep cooking
> for him.

Harvard? Cooking? It's like she's talking in code, and I need the key. Was she on a date tonight? Is that why she said no to me? But she cooked? All I know is I want to keep her talking. Texting. Whatever. I want more Harper.

> I have an unexpected day off tomorrow. Let's
> drink champagne and I'll show you around the
> city.

The dots appear and disappear for the next five minutes. The anticipation for her response rivals sitting through a draft with my clients. I don't get it. Why is she indecisive when it comes to me? And why am I one hundred percent certain about her?

> You had me at champagne.

Yes! I do a fist pump in the air. My yell echoes in my penthouse and catches me off guard, acutely aware of the quiet. I want to change that.

> Should I come to you to avoid another subway
> mishap?

If I had it my way, she wouldn't ever ride the subway again, but I can't be overbearing. I've learned that from my younger sister, Ashleigh. Girls with overprotective brothers don't see protection as an attractive quality. Keep them safe without them being acutely aware of your intentions. It's a difficult balance that I've worked on for years with Ash.

> Sure. I'll send you the address. I have yoga and
> work to do in the morning. Noon?

> Great! Noon it is. See you then.

I'm not surprised her Tribeca apartment building has a doorman. Lawson would prioritize her safety because she isn't affording this place on a dog walker's salary, that's for sure. I give the doorman my name, and he informs me I'm not on the list. Harper probably isn't used to building protocols, so I shoot her a text.

> I'm here. You didn't leave my name with the doorman.

The phone rings at the desk, there's a quick conversation, then I'm directed to the elevators and the sixth floor. I knock, the door opens, but it's not Harper's sexy smile and painted red lips greeting me. Instead, I'm facing a scowling, shirtless hockey player.

"Um, I was looking for Harper Cartwright?" I lean back and look over at the apartment number, checking to make sure I'm in the correct place. I am.

"CJ, it's for you," he yells into the apartment. This must be the right place. She's living with Zac Burns? CJ? Is she more than his dog walker? So many questions race through my mind as I attempt to piece the puzzle of Harper Cartwright together.

He looks me up and down, doing the bro assessment. We're both about the same height, and while he has a little more muscle than me, I'm no slouch. He probably knows who I am, but I'll be polite.

I extend my hand. "I'm Julian Decker. It's nice to meet you, Zac. The Havoc look like they've got a good team this season."

He hesitates for a split second before he shakes my hand. His grip is a little harder than necessary. "I know who you are." Yeah, I thought so.

"Be right there." Her voice floats from down the hall. This place is nice, great location, but like many New York apartments, it's not huge. How many bedrooms are in this unit? I'm hoping for at least two.

"Come on in," he says. I hear the click-click of nails on the hardwood floor and am greeted by a light brown, floppy-eared dog whose body is extremely disproportionate. His stubby legs come to a stop, his long tail wagging furiously, the rest of his cylindrical body swaying back and forth. He's pretty cute.

"You must be Noodle." I squat down to pet him, and his entire body shakes, practically convulsing. I look up at Zac with concern. "Is he supposed to do that?"

"Yeah, he's in protection mode." I smirk as Noodle licks my loafers. Apparently, this hockey player is in protection mode too. Why, I'm not sure. I'm harmless. Mostly.

Harper rounds the corner from the hall and comes to a stop. She's a vision with her hair down in soft waves over her shoulders, looking more blonde than I recall. Her hair was up when I saw her yesterday, and it was sexy. But now. Wow! Breathtaking.

The jeans she's wearing hug her curves in all the right places, and the cropped burgundy sweater hints at the soft skin peeking out from below. She looks like a fashionable New Yorker ready for fall.

My eyes scan her from head to toe, and I appreciate what I see. As I check her out, there's a low grumble coming from Zac. I do my best to keep my facial expression neutral since I'm unsure about this living situation.

"You look great." Wordsmith of the year right here, ladies and gentlemen. "Are those shoes comfortable? I thought we might walk today." She's wearing those boots girls wear with a little heel. Harper is probably five-ten or so, and I love the extra few inches bringing her closer to my six-three frame. Women often pick fashion over function, but today, I prefer function for Harper's footwear. I figured she'd enjoy a stroll through the city, taking in the sights, sounds, and energy of the streets. Unfortunately, I don't get to do it enough because I'm always in a hurry. My driver is on standby if we need to change our plans and skip the walk.

"Yeah, I'm good as long as we aren't running a marathon." I appreciate her sensible fashion sense. It's probably her practical Minnesota values shining through. Her smile has a tender, heart-warming effect on me, and I'm already willing to give her anything she wants. This girl. Damn.

"What are you guys doing?" Zac asks. His scowl betrays his attempt at acting cool. I almost forgot he was here, all of my attention focused on Harper.

"Going to lunch," she answers quickly. "Tell Harvard to keep icing his eye. He's too cute to look so broken."

He gives her a side hug and kisses her temple. Shit. She's more than a dog walker to him and he's obviously marking his territory.

She grabs her crossbody bag and slings it over her shoulder, the strap falling between her breasts. I've never been more jealous of an accessory in my life. She gives Noodle a head scratch and motions to the door. "Shall we?"

"Lead the way, gorgeous." Sorry Zac. I just call 'em like I see 'em.

CHAPTER
SEVEN

HARPER

———

He called me gorgeous. I stutter a little, processing that term of affection. Or does he say that to all the girls? He's a first-class charmer, after all. And what in the hell was that hug and kiss from Zac? There is absolutely nothing between us. Was he claiming me? Hockey players are a strange breed. You'd think I'd understand them by now, but then they do things like kiss my head, and I'm back at square one.

Deep breath, Harper. You've got this. It's only lunch with one of America's hottest bachelors. Your friend's brother. Yeah, that's it. He's simply being kind to a new girl in town. His sister's friend. That's what this is.

We make our way downstairs, and I practically get trampled exiting the building's front door. Julian pulls me back by the elbow and I'm tucked into his side. I keep forgetting to check before I merge into this busy sidewalk of fast-paced New Yorkers. The pace is certainly different from suburban Atlanta.

"Stick close to me, gorgeous. I can't lose you before we get to lunch." He laces his fingers in mine and holds my arm close to his. I'm captivated by his panty-melting smile and I forget to breathe again.

"You okay?" Concern fills his expression as he looks at me. We stop and the pedestrians go around us like he's a boulder in the middle of the river, the water parting at his will. That's the thing with guys like Julian. The water bends for them.

I shake my head, clearing all the negative and confusing thoughts. I run through a few of the mantras my therapist and Lawson make me recite when I have thoughts of self-doubt. *Enjoy the day. Live in the moment. You are a woman of worth.*

"Yeah, I'm good. Still getting used to the New York pace." I smile up at him, and his cool blue eyes light up with amusement. As he leads me down the sidewalk, he matches my shorter stride, adjusting to my slower pace. For reasons I can't explain, I get butterflies.

"How long have you been in New York?" His tone is light, friendly. Inquisitive even.

"I moved here a few weeks ago, the same day Lawson moved to Carolina." He nods, processing my timeline. "I hated the suddenness of it, but honestly, I couldn't ask for a better scenario." My smile brightens as his fades.

"That's, um, good. I'm glad it worked out." His voice has a tinge of sharpness and his mood seems to dim.

We walk another half block in silence when I stop walking. He takes another step before turning to me, realizing I've stopped. Worry sets in.

"Was it something I said?" I hope I didn't tick him off, but I'm clueless about this sudden mood change.

He looks at me, and he transforms in a split second. His eyes glitter with mischief, and a playful grin slowly stretches his lips. "No, no. Sorry. Had an errant thought. I'll turn off everything in my head and focus on welcoming you to New York."

We walk two more blocks, and he stops near a plain glass frosted door that has a worn, cardboard sign that says *Back in 15 minutes.* Not much help if you don't know the start time I mumble under my breath. Yellowed newspaper clippings from a decade ago, with faded ink, cover the windows. Someone painted "Mitchie's" in a loopy script, but chipped the M as if they tried to scrape it off and gave up. Pink bubble gum fills a crack in the glass.

"Um, this place looks like it's closed. Like years ago, closed." I scrunch my face at this rundown storefront, thoughts of murder and darkness running rampant through my mind.

Julian gives me a full-bodied laugh. He puts his arm around my shoulders and leans down to whisper in my ear. "That's what they want you to believe. Remember, not everything is as it appears. Come on." He steps toward the door, and I stay put.

"I swear, if there's plastic on the floor and you Dexter me," I mumble.

"Noted." He's holding back his chuckle. "I promised you lunch and champagne, and Mitchie's won't disappoint." His eyes drink me in. "Do you trust me?"

"I did until ten seconds ago. I mean, I might be a little over-dressed." As we stand on the sidewalk discussing murder scenarios, a celebrity actress and her husband approach us.

"Jules, so good to see you," she says casually. He leans down to give her a kiss on the cheek. Obviously, she's more than an acquaintance. This reminds me of Julian's elite social circle, and the jarring contrast makes my presence here feel even more surreal.

"Lettie, good to see you. Colin." He acknowledges her husband with a nod. They're holding hands, so casual, no paparazzi around. Are they hiding in plain sight?

Her eyes meet mine, and the warmth of her smile chases away any lingering nervousness. "You eating lunch at M's?"

"M's?" I'm truly confused. And star-struck. She's stunning in jeans and a fisherman's sweater, her blonde hair in a messy bun. This is a far cry from the glamorous world depicted in magazines.

"I'm trying to convince Harper I won't murder her." Julian winks, and my face turns crimson.

She wraps her arm around mine. "Harper, I can promise he won't murder you. If he so much as hurts your feelings, you let me know, and I'll avenge you." With a determined nod, she pulls me towards her husband, who tugs the door open. She leans in close to say, "I swear, he's one of the good guys." She lightly squeezes my arm and lets me go once we cross the threshold.

"Enjoy your lunch," Colin says to me. He puts his hand to the small of her back, and they walk over to a table with Iron Man and his wife, who are waiting for them. They greet one another, and I stand there watching in shock. Avengers assemble, indeed.

Julian leans over, puts his chin on my shoulder, and his breath tickles my cheek. "I take it you're a Marvel girl?"

I'm on sensory overload and I'm slow to process it all. His voice pulls me out of my daze, and I look around the brightly decorated restaurant. It's cheery and modern, a stark contrast from the outside. I do my best to keep my jaw from hitting the floor. Is this real life? I'm dumbfounded, but in a good way. I need to keep my head on straight. Approach with caution. Act like I'm used to this. Despite my lack of acting talent, that's my plan.

The hostess at the podium smiles at Julian. "Mr. Decker, your table is ready. Right this way."

He takes my hand, and we walk through the small restaurant filled with people I've only seen in movies and magazines, all enjoying their relaxing lunch. A long, black marble bar adorns one wall. Behind it, expensive bottles of alcohol fill the glass shelves, glistening in the light. It's understated and simple. The white tile walls bring a brightness to the room, as well as the pops of color in the modern art hung throughout.

I manage to put one foot in front of the other until we are at the back of the room. The wall is a glass garage door that, when up, opens to a brick courtyard filled with flowers and trees. It's stunning. And surprising. Who would've suspected that this place existed beyond the shabby, covered windows? The heaters take away the slight chill from the air, and the inside and outdoors effortlessly blend.

"Is this okay?" the hostess asks.

"Of course." It's more than okay.

Julian holds my chair, and I stare at him as he takes his place across from me. The hostess hands me a simple menu printed on bright white cardstock, and there are ten items listed and no prices.

"We'll have a bottle of Ace, please." Julian looks across at me. I snap my jaw closed because I'm sure my mouth is hanging open. A bottle of Ace of Spades? Jay Z's champagne? That bottle costs several hundred-dollars, maybe more. I'm not a big drinker and was kidding about only drinking champagne. I'm good with a ten-dollar bottle of wine from the grocery store for special occasions. What kind of alternate reality did I enter?

"Oh no, that's okay. I was kidding about the champagne, really."

Concern fills his face. "Do you like champagne? Or would your rather have something else?"

"It's just, I don't." He has me flustered. It's too expensive. Too much. Too everything.

"Tell me what you want, Harper." His teasing tone is gone, and he looks into my soul as he asks me that question. I need to keep my wits about me because what I want will freak him out.

"I like champagne. I'm not a big drinker and usually only drink on special occasions," I confess.

"Well, in that case," he turns his attention to the hostess. "We'll have that bottle of Aces. And two glasses of water, please." She nods and leaves our table and his focus is all on me. "This is a special occasion, worthy of champagne, wouldn't you say?"

"It is?"

"It is." His voice, strong and confident, fills the air as he reaches for my hand.

"Why is that?" I'm overwhelmed by this. By him.

"It's your welcome to New York." His dazzling smile makes me lightheaded, and I'm grateful I don't fall out of my chair. My insides are all fluttery, and I'm so turned on I may not make it through lunch. Julian Decker should come with a warning sign—may cause spontaneous combustion.

CHAPTER
EIGHT

JULIAN

———

"Well, in that case, we'll have that bottle of Aces. And two glasses of water, please." She nods and leaves our table. Harper is adorable. And sexy. Watching the surprise on her face when we entered this speakeasy cafe will be a core memory for me. The blush of her cheeks when I whispered in her ear is my new favorite color. The way our hands fit together perfectly, the innocent touch of her skin to mine, makes me crave more. I've never had a reaction like this, and while it should scare me, it doesn't. It's different. Harper's different. And I want to get to know her more.

"This is a special occasion, worthy of champagne, wouldn't you say?" Anything she wants. It's hers.

"It is?" Another surprised look. I'm making it my mission to surprise her as many times as possible today because I can't get enough of that expression. She looks innocent, thoughtful, playful, and fucking delicious.

"It is." I reach for her hand because I need to touch her. Today's a special occasion, at least for me.

"Why is that?" She tilts her head, cautious, waiting for my answer. There it is. Those eyes sparkle with curiosity. What's going through her mind right now? I try to come up with an alternate response to the truth.

Because today is when I started falling for you. I almost say it but think better of it. Talk about freaking this poor girl out. Dial it back, Decker. Give her time to adjust. But there's no doubt what I want, and it's Harper Cartwright.

"It's your welcome to New York." It's lame, but I don't want to scare her off with a declaration of love on our first date.

I'm only kidding myself if I think I'm here to learn more about her for my book. I want to learn more about her for me. Taking a breath, I compile the list of questions I use when developing a new character. It's a perfect starting point to uncover the unique traits and characteristics that make Harper so special.

She looks up from her menu. Her amber eyes dance with delight. She's enjoying herself. And I did that. One point for me.

"So, are you living with Zac?" I blurt this question instead of casually slipping it into conversation. Smooth. What is it about this woman that leaves me befuddled? I had a plan, but one glimpse of her happiness, and she scattered my thoughts and sent me off-script.

I'm a brilliant conversationalist. One of the best. I built my career, hell, my whole agency, on my ability to talk to people, learn their motivations, get them what they want, or convince them they need what I have. Earning trust through communication is one of my greatest skills. With Harper, I'm literally at a loss for words.

A new surprised look graces her face. This time, her deep red lips form a perfect O, and I think of places I'd like to see her mouth. While her makeup is subtle and natural, she seems to like bold lip colors. I'm practically feral at this point thinking about them. Grinning shyly, she contemplates her response.

"Yeah, we live together. He'll be traveling a lot with the season starting. Noodle and I will miss him, but as long as we have each other." She shrugs.

The pop of a champagne cork interrupts us, and her face fills with happiness. The waiter pours a small amount for me to taste, but I nod no and direct his attention to Harper. She takes a sip and smacks her lips. It's not sensual, but my dick doesn't seem to notice the difference.

"Ohmygodthisissogood." She holds her flute out for a refill, much to the waiter's delight.

"I'm glad you like it." He's enamored by her giddiness and pure joy. I'd hate for him to lose his job, but he needs to dial down the friendliness. He pours me a glass and directs his attention back to Harper. Yes, he's doing what I asked, but still. "Are you ready to order?"

Harper looks indecisive. She twists her mouth and bites her bottom lip. Holy hell, this woman is killing me.

"I'm sure it's all good. Surprise me?" Her absolute delight brightens the room and scorches my heart. It's a privilege to watch her face light up with enjoyment. I love how she's focused on the moment, the experience. I admire her ability to be wholly present.

The gleam in the waiter's eye is off the charts. He's charmed by her too. "Any allergies, dietary restrictions, or foods you don't like?"

"No, nothing. It all looks fantastic." He nods his head. "Got it."

He turns his attention to me. I take a page out of Harper's playbook. "Surprise me too, but with something different. That way you can taste me, I mean, mine too." Around her, I turn into a bumbling fool.

She snickers at my faux pas. Embarrassed, I down my champagne in one gulp. I'm not a fan of the bubbles and wish I had something stronger to calm my nerves, but I also need to stay sober. I'm acting like a prepubescent boy on his first date. Get it together, dude.

"Can I ask you something?" She's timid, her tone shy. Her confidence waivers a bit, and I don't like that at all. Her confidence and boldness are attractive, and I never want to see that wane.

I drop my shields and give her my genuine smile, the one I reserve for my family. "Ask me anything, gorgeous."

"What's the story with the Swedish princess?" She winces slightly, obviously embarrassed to ask the question.

I laugh so loudly that a few of the other patrons look our way. "How do you know about that?"

"Well, when you texted last night, the boys being boys took my phone and played keep away. They saw your name, someone mentioned a princess, and I was curious."

"The boys, huh?" Who the hell are they, and why are they teasing her like ten-year-olds?

"Yeah, I cooked dinner for Zac and some of his teammates last night. I should have known to not have my phone at the dinner table. Rookie mistake." Her confidence returns when she's talking about the boys. She said no to me last night to be with Zac and his teammates. Interesting.

"Do you like to cook?"

"I love it. It's relaxing, and when they ask for seconds or thirds, it's the ultimate compliment." She likes praise. Got it.

"What's your favorite meal to cook?"

"Depends. I can make cooking for two more complex, really spend the time a good meal deserves. When cooking for a group, especially hockey players in season, it's protein and pasta. Regardless, I rarely get complaints."

"Good to know. What would you request for your last meal on earth?"

"I don't know, maybe this place? Are you planning on killing me today, Julian?" The gleam in her eye is all sass.

My laugh is boisterous again. I can't contain my composure

with her, and I don't care. "Not today, not tomorrow. Seriously, your favorite go-to meal?"

She looks around the room and leans in conspiratorially. "The number one combo at Chick-fil-A."

I laugh again. She's killing me. "Beverage of choice?"

"Oh, sweet tea, to be sure. It only took six months of living in Atlanta to fall in love with that nectar of the gods. Zac scowls when he sees it in the fridge, but he'll get over it." She beams at the mention of his name. Fuck.

Back to Zac. "Yeah, sweet tea is hard to find in the city, but if you behave, I'll let you know where the spots are. Are you and Zac..."

"Are we what?" The playful way she avoids the question is charming, but the uncertainty of his involvement is intensely frustrating. I can get him traded, but I'd rather not cash in chips unnecessarily.

"Are you a thing?"

"A thing?" She sips her champagne, eyeing me. A slight tip of her lips tells me she's enjoying this way too much.

"In a romantic relationship? Friends with benefits? Room-mates? You know, a thing." The thought of her in his bed gets my blood boiling, so I work hard to push it out of my mind.

The waiter interrupts when he brings our food. Her eyes light up, and her hands come together in a quiet clap. "Oh my gosh, this looks amazing. Thank you." She has a roasted pear salad with salmon, and I have a grilled apple and chicken salad. I've had both and agree the salmon is the best. He's earning his tip today.

"I hope you like it. Let me know if you need anything else." He tops off her drinks and leaves after a quick appraisal of the table.

She eyes my salad, debating which one looks best. "Here." I slide my plate to the middle of the table, offering my meal to her. I want her to always have a choice.

"Oh no, don't do that. I don't want to take your food."

"Try both, and tell me which is the best. I'll order another."
I'm enjoying watching her eat more than I should. Her face is
expressive, all of her feelings right there for me to see. She
takes bites of both and decides she likes the salmon with the
apple. Of course she does. She likes things off the menu.
Check.

We continue mixing our plates through lunch, her combining
flavors to create a new and arguably better meal than the original. She's always on the search for the perfect bite. She's creative
and adventurous. Check. Check.

As lunch winds down, getting to know Harper takes center
stage. "Tell me about yourself, Harper Cartwright." I stare at her
beautiful face and she's positively glowing. While I'm very
attracted to her, I want to know the details that make her special.

"What do you want to know?"

Everything. "Let's start with the basics. Age, birthday,
favorite color. That kind of stuff."

"You mean like my dating profile kind of thing?"

"You're on dating sites?" The thought of her meeting random
guys sets me on edge. I clench my jaw and attempt to dial back
my displeasure. There's no way Lawson would approve of her
having an online profile. Dating is hard for women, but dating in
New York City is absolutely brutal. I'd rather have her with Zac
than on the local dating scene. My thoughts are some kind of
fucked up. I need to focus.

"Not anymore." Shit. Is it because of Zac? Always comes
back to that, doesn't it?

"Okay, but only if you reciprocate." She tries to quirk her
eyebrow at me, and I laugh.

"Deal." She looks exactly like Lawson with that expression.
Only a hell of a lot prettier.

"I feel like I'm auditioning for *The Bachelor*," she mumbles.

"Well, if you were, you'd get a rose every single time," I
confess. "They keep hounding me to do that show. Every
Thanksgiving it's a standing conversation if I'll ever say yes."

"Seriously? Would you consider it?" She seems genuinely curious.

"Absolutely not. I'm a one-woman kind of guy." I get another surprised look, which morphs into disbelief. "What? You don't believe that?"

"You seem to have a different woman on your arm every week."

"Why Ms. Cartwright, are you stalking me?" I love teasing her. She blushes and gets flustered for a moment before she composes herself. It's endearing. And it's totally Harper.

CHAPTER
NINE

HARPER

———

"Why Ms. Cartwright, are you stalking me?" I can feel the heat rise in my face. Do I admit I stayed up way past my bedtime cyberstalking him? Hell no. I'm taking that confession to my grave.

"You're hard to miss, Mr. Decker. You're all over my social media. I can't get away from you." Okay. Only slightly true. More like I googled him until my algorithms assumed he's all I wanted to see. Stupid computers.

"Well, for your information, you can't believe everything you see on the internet. While I often go out in the company of beautiful women, I haven't had a relationship in the past four years. Contrary to popular opinion, the internet does not know all." He seems sincere. "So back to your audition, as you called it. Hit me with thirty seconds of Harper."

I take a big gulp of champagne, and he goes to refill my glass to find a few drops left in the bottle. Did I drink most of that?

Oh, I'm feeling tipsy and giggly. So yes, it's possible. He casually slides my water toward me, encouraging me to hydrate.

"Okay. First, I'm not usually a day drinker, so this is already out of character." At the mention of day drinking, I hiccup. He holds back his laughter, and I roll my eyes.

I shimmy in my chair, sit up straight, flash my pageant queen smile, and try to compose myself. I'm going to pull out my Southern accent for this audition. Although I moved to Atlanta in high school, it's difficult to replace my Minnesota accent. I'm going to try anyway.

Julian pulls out his phone and starts the timer.

"Hi, I'm Harper Cartwright." I hesitate for a second. I recently had a birthday, but with the move and everything, it was just another day. "Twenty-seven, a fan of most things hockey, except the smelly gloves. I enjoy reading, love animals, would like to get a kitten, but don't think Noodle would appreciate that. Oh, and I adore otters. Love them! I want to take a cooking class in Italy. Huge fan of anything banana flavored but don't particularly like bananas. Enjoy live music, but I've never been to a big concert venue like a stadium or arena. I want to be good at line dancing, but I'm quick to get offbeat and out of step. Oh, and I'm double jointed." I reach over and stop his timer. Thirty point two seconds. I sit back and cross my arms, damn proud of that performance.

"Did I pass this round?" Is that what he wanted? Did I share too much? I'm sure I'm boring compared to his life. But based on the growing smirk on his face, I think he's amused.

"With flying colors, but I have so many questions. A little concerned you stumbled on your age, though."

I giggle at that. "Yeah, my birthday was last week. With everything going on, I kinda forgot I've made another rotation around the sun."

"Well, we'll do a belated birthday celebration to make it memorable."

"Unnecessary. Now it's your turn." I reset the timer and hold up his phone. I can't wait to hear the insight he'll share. "Go."

"Julian Barnett Decker, thirty-one, Gemini. Perpetual bachelor, but fine with changing that status. Middle child. I like most sports but grew up playing baseball. Favorite animal is a tortoise. Favorite food is Tex-Mex because I like it spicy." He wiggles his eyebrows and I roll my eyes at his innuendo. "Not a fan of flying, but I do it anyway. Broadway musicals are dope, and I can't pass up a good-natured prank. I can't sing for shit, but that doesn't stop me from singing in the shower. I'm loyal to a fault, and I'd take a bullet for my family or friends. And you are the sexiest woman I've ever met, and I want to kiss you so fucking bad it hurts." He reaches across the table and takes his phone from my hand, stopping the timer. He then takes a finger, places it below my chin, and closes my mouth.

All playfulness is gone, and he's gauging my reaction. Which is stunned. I reach for my glass and knock over my water, breaking the spell. The waiter is at our table in an instant, mopping up my mess.

"I'm sorry, I didn't..."

"It's okay, ma'am, I've got it," the waiter says. Second time I've been ma'amed this week. Ouch. That's more cold water thrown on me, bringing me back to reality. Because Julian wanting to kiss me is not my reality. It can't be.

Julian stands next to me, holding out his hand. "Come on, let's continue this conversation as we walk off lunch." His care-free, easy-going smile is back, making me wonder if I imagined what he said. And this is why I don't drink alcohol. Granted, it's been a while since I've been with anyone. And he's incredibly hot. I can't stop my overly horny brain from daydreaming about what it would be like if this were real.

We walk out of the café's back door and find ourselves in a sketchy alley, but as I look around, is actually clean and well kept. Not what it initially appears to be. Like this day.

He takes my hand and leads me to the main street. Our

hands fit perfectly, like two puzzle pieces. His light squeeze gives me a warm tingling all over. I mean, all my bits are tingling. If he makes me feel this way holding hands, I can't imagine what else his hands can do to me. I'll have to save that fantasy for later.

"Did we dine and dash?" I never saw a bill come to the table.

"Which answer would make you more surprised?" The twinkle in his eye is back.

I shake my head in disbelief. Julian keeps me on my toes. He also doesn't treat me as off limits or a girl who needs to be protected. I like it. More than I should.

We walk to a subway entrance, and he stops and takes a deep breath. "Look Harper, I'm not a fan of you taking the subway, but you're a city girl now, and it's part of this life. Let me show you all the right things to do, so you're not easy pickins." The butterflies go crazy in my chest as his eyes look me up and down. Those baby blues are filled with a hunger lunch didn't satisfy. Between his subtle signals and his slight Southern accent, I can't hide the grin that forms on my lips. Maybe he is the protective type, but hides it well. Points for trying. I assumed that bossy, protective trait was in there somewhere. His restraint in not telling me what to do is another point in his favor.

"Deal. You tell me where we're going, and I'll figure it out." Honestly, maneuvering the subway has been my one roadblock to exploring the city, and I'm grateful for the tutorial. We go down the stairs, and his grip on me tightens. He's nervous, but for me or him, I'm uncertain.

"Let's head to Central Park, upper west side," he says. I pull out my phone, and I hear a slight "tsk, tsk" from beside me. Okay, so don't use my phone. Got it. I glance at the map and find a line traveling uptown. I head down to find the right train, Julian never letting me go.

He shows me the best places to sit/stand, explains how to hold my bag, and insists I use plenty of hand sanitizer. I snicker at his gentle reminders when I'm not doing something right. Makes me want to be wrong if only to watch him squirm. Teasing him is fun and I'm getting more enjoyment than I should from his reactions.

He's also peppering me with questions. Favorite color? Favorite book? Sweet or salty? Clothing brand, music genre, last movie I watched, the list goes on. I try to ask him questions, but he won't have it. This getting to know one another is pretty one sided, as far as I'm concerned.

When we make our way above ground, he visibly relaxes. His constant state of high alert lessens and the wrinkles on his brow recede. Dropping his shoulders, a cocky grin spreads across his face. His disdain for the subway couldn't be more obvious.

"Do you mind if we duck into my place to freshen up?" I look around, well aware it's a typical tourist move, and take in my surroundings. Central Park is on one side of the street and beautiful old buildings on the other. He lives here? Not some tall, glass, phallic-looking building. Another assumption corrected.

"Um, are you going to kill me in there?"

"Gorgeous, I'm not sure why you're so concerned about me killing you when you've been killing me all day. Come on." He tugs my hand toward a building that isn't tall or shiny. Instead, it looks historic, distinguished. An older gentleman opens the door for us, like he knew we'd be arriving at this exact time. While my building has a doorman, this building feels different, more upper crust.

"Mr. Decker." He gives a stoic nod.

"David, this is Harper Cartwright. Please ensure she's on my guest list and has access to my place, even if I'm not home." David gives a small salute, and I gasp at his request. He looks at me and shrugs. "In case you find yourself lost, need a place to rest, or hide your shopping bags." The corners of his mouth turn up, and the butterflies in my stomach scatter like they're drunk on champagne too.

We head to the elevator, where we're greeted by yet another doorman, or maybe he's the concierge. The building is in a pricey neighborhood and has more security and staff than I'm used to. "Frankie, did you catch the game last night?"

"Sure did. You were so right about Kline. I don't know how you do it, but you're always right." He shakes his head in awe.

Julian laughs it off. "Frankie, this is Harper. She's a good friend, new to the city. She's got open access to my place anytime she needs it."

He clicks his heels together and gives a slight bow. "Yes, sir." He tips his hat to me in greeting. "It's nice to meet you, Harper. Welcome to New York." He pulls out a business card and hands it to me. "Please call me if you need anything. Transportation, restaurant recommendations, theater tickets, you name it. I'm your guy. Unless you want sports tickets." He points his thumb at Julian. "Then he's your guy." They both laugh. Clearly, Frankie has profound respect for Julian and will go to any lengths for him. While it speaks highly for Frankie, to me, it says more about Julian. It's the way he treats people. They aren't beneath him or employees, but friends.

"Thanks, Frankie. I appreciate it. I can't have enough friends in this city." While tucking his card into my purse, the elevator doors open. We step in and are alone in the quiet, and it puts me on edge. I've gotten used to the city noise now, and silence is almost painful. So is the tension. Being alone with him is a bad idea, especially with my lowered inhibitions. Julian pulls out a card and the elevator rises. We both look straight ahead, lost in our thoughts.

When the doors open, we step into a brightly decorated foyer. Julian guides me into the apartment, and I'm amazed once again. First, that the elevator opens directly into his apartment. Second, the open, relaxed vibe is not what I expected at all. The white, modern kitchen opens into a central sitting area. The large denim sectional is casual, hip. Shelves overflowing with books cover one wall. The fireplace is in the corner, and there's an oversized chair and blanket waiting for someone to curl up with a cup of hot chocolate. There is one hall to the left of the room, another to the right.

"The guest bathroom is down that hall. I'm going to freshen up and need to make a quick call. You okay for a few minutes?"

"Yeah, fine. Thanks." I'm still fixated in one spot, taking it all in. Julian is not what I thought at all. I'm not getting playboy vibes. He's kind, thoughtful. Unexpected. Just like this day.

Julian goes down the other hall and calls out, "Feel free to look around. I know you want to." His laughter fades as he gets further down the hall.

I find the bathroom and freshen up. Under the guise of getting to know him, I snoop in the guest bedroom, and it's nice, cozy, almost feminine. The framed photos that adorn the dresser catch my attention. Julian's family and friend group is tight and elite. Lawson and I call it the Decker Connection. It's like six degrees of Kevin Bacon but with Deckers. I can see the group evolution in these pictures. As time passes, new faces are added in each picture.

I lift the first framed photo and examine the details. It's Julian, his brother Alexander, and sister Ashleigh as kids. I assume it's their parents with their arms around them, embracing them with love and protection. They seem to be at a beach with the dunes filling the background. Everyone's attention is on Ashleigh and they're in various stages of laughter. They all look so happy and carefree. The image resonates deeply, reminding me of a similar family photograph I've packed away in a storage container. I wipe an errant tear and place the picture on the dresser and scan the others.

There are the college pictures with the addition of Chance, and Alexander's best friend, Trevor Lewis, owner of the Savannah Pajamas Baseball team.

The most recent picture appears to be from Alexander's

wedding. The Decker Connection is much larger now and includes Cole Davidson, Ashleigh's fiancé; Cole's sister Darcy; her boyfriend, Matt Hartman; Alexander's wife, Dani; and their son, Tyler. Julian and Trevor have their arms around Emma, Ashleigh's best friend. There's another Decker wedding coming up, and I'm curious about the new Decker Connection picture. Who will be in this one?

I continue my snooping and sneak a peek in the closet. It's filled with women's clothes and I noticed girly stuff in the bathroom. Yep. Figures. Julian would have women here all the time. The idea of Julian and me fades and I'm filled with disappointment. I need to get real. Of course we can't be a thing, not with his constant stream of women. He says he hasn't dated anyone in four years. Doesn't mean he's living the life of a monk, now does it?

I'm not a one-night stand kind of girl, although I wish I was. Others make it seem easy. Just sex. No strings. I tried it once and was a total basket case afterward. The constant post sex analysis and emotional torture I put myself through was too much for me. I promised myself never again. I'm a relationship girl through and through, even though there haven't been many. One thing I'll say about my brother and his friends, they've taught me I'm a woman of worth, and I deserve all of a man, not merely the parts he wants to share, especially his penis. But call me curious, because I can't seem to stop my mind from wandering to all of Julian's parts.

Like any red-blooded woman with eyes and a libido, I'm drawn to Julian. You'd have to be dead to be immune to his magnetism. I need to shut down my foolish imagination. I'm not living in a romance novel where the playboy changes for the small-town girl. But a girl can dream, can't she? Sure, but she ends up devastated in the end. Oh, what am I thinking? He's not really interested in me. Is he?

We'd never work because he'd need to drop the facade and

be completely honest with me. I'm convinced he uses his charm as a defense mechanism. Call it my intuition, my Spidey sense. Something's off. I don't know what he's hiding, but he's not telling the whole story.

CHAPTER
TEN

JULIAN

———

I needed to call Chance about an endorsement deal that required an immediate answer, and he talked my ear off. He's a chatty bastard, and I love him for it. Just not today.

At least I gave Harper plenty of time to look around, get comfortable. I need to practice patience with her. While it may be a virtue, it's not one I have.

I hope she's up to hitting the zoo. It's usually feeding time in the early evening and my favorite time to visit. I figure she'll enjoy it too. Her face lit up talking about Noodle and otters. I picture us walking hand in hand, laughing, and then I'll kiss her. I can't wait to taste those lips. Damn, the anticipation is killing me.

I enter the room and seeing her in my space makes me feel strange. Content, maybe. "I see you found the best spot in the place." She's curled up in my reading chair, her hands under her cheek, her legs tucked underneath. I snap a quick picture because I need to capture this moment.

She doesn't respond. A few steps closer and I realize she's fast asleep. Champagne for lunch probably wasn't the best idea, since she isn't much of a drinker. I stand staring for longer than is proper, deciding if I leave her or move her to a bed. And if I put her in a bed, is it mine or the guest room? Fuck. I'm befuddled. Again.

Ashleigh sleeps in that chair the same way, and she's fine. Leaving her is probably the best decision. I cover her with the throw and grab my laptop to set up shop at the kitchen counter. Close enough to watch her, far enough away it won't seem creepy.

Having my muse here gives me the inspiration I need to finish my character sheet and send it to Priscilla. Harper gave me great insight and amazing little details to include as I flesh out Charlotte Jackson, New York dog walker to the stars. She's beauty and brains, wrapped up in kindness and sweetness with a dose of sass.

My fingers fly across the keyboard as I begin my opening chapter. I've never knocked out so many words this fast. I might keep Harper hostage until this project is done. As Charlotte comes to life on the page, I'm not sure I want to share her with the world. I'm feeling fiercely protective. And possessive.

I consider Charlotte hooking up with a hockey player and glance at Harper. What's the deal with her and Zac? If I ask Chance, it may open Pandora's box for him and Lawson. I don't want to put him in that position. She wouldn't flirt with me if she's in a relationship, would she?

I open my writing app and send a message to Priscilla.

JB: Here's my first chapter and character sheet. Meet Charlotte Jackson. Your hockey player is going to love her. He's going to fall fast. I'm not a typical fan of instalove, but this girl will do that to him. Let's touch base tomorrow morning and plot out the next few chapters.

I hit send. Harper's phone buzzes sharply, breaking the kitchen's silence. It must be in her purse, which she left on the counter when she checked out the kitchen. The buzzing serves as a reminder to me. Should I wake her? She's been out for a few hours.

I text Frankie and send him on an errand for dinner. As soon as it arrives, I wake up sleeping beauty.

"Hey gorgeous," I whisper. I brush the hair away from her face and trace her cheekbones with the back of my knuckles. Even asleep, with a little drool at the corner of her mouth, she's stunning. I lightly kiss her cheek, and her eyes flutter open. I get another surprised look, but this one is laced with panic.

She sits up quickly, and our heads collide. I hope I don't get a black eye like Harvard. Does she think I'm too cute to look broken? I can only hope.

She lets out a little yelp and pulls her legs into her chest. She buries her face in her hands and is mumbling to herself. If I wasn't worried that I'd frightened her, I'd say she's adorable.

I reach out to brush her hair away so I can see her sleepy eyes. "Hey Harper. I didn't mean to frighten you. I thought you might be hungry and, well, I didn't want it to get cold."

She splits her fingers and peeks out a little.

"I fell asleep?"

"Yeah, you looked so peaceful, I left you alone for a bit."

She sits up and pulls herself together. It's amazing to watch. I witness a transformation from a sleeping zombie to a fully in control woman. She rolls her shoulders, runs her fingers through her hair, and tugs her sweater down. She puts on a forced smile, and she's even more amazing.

"While I appreciate the effort, it's unnecessary. You're beautiful. And I'm glad you feel at home here." I hold my hand out to help her up. "Come on sleepy head, I've got dinner for you."

She looks at me, uncertainty filling her expression. "Is that?" She motions to the kitchen counter where I've been working.

She's beaming from ear to ear. This is the most unfettered

expression I've seen yet. She brushes past me and heads straight to the counter where a white and red bag waits for her. As she wraps her fingers around the large Chick-fil-A sweet tea and takes a long sip through the straw, all is forgiven.

We eat in relative silence, only broken by Harper's moans of ecstasy over her chicken sandwich. Those moans are making me want more of her. She reaches into her purse and scowls at her phone.

"Everything okay?"

"Hmm, yeah, fine. Work stuff."

"Dog walking?"

"What? Oh, no. It's nothing." She looks at it one more time and tosses her phone back in her purse.

"This was incredibly thoughtful. I'm sorry I ruined your afternoon plans."

"No apology necessary. I've learned to cut off your drinking a little earlier, that's all." I tease her. "So before you Rip Van Winkled in my chair, find anything interesting while you were snooping."

She blushes. "I was admiring your pictures, perhaps, but not snooping. I love the beach picture. You have a beautiful family."

I know the exact picture she's talking about. I put it in that room because every time I look at it, I get choked up. "Yeah, that was the summer before Mom got sick. Ash was ten, Alexander was in college, and I'd just graduated from high school. It was a magical summer and I'm grateful we had that time."

My mom died seven months later. It hit us all hard, especially my dad and Ashleigh. I was away at college and missed a lot of her illness. Alexander and I were in the middle of baseball season, and they insisted we stay in school, be there for our teams. Then we got the call to come home because she didn't have much time left. We were home for two weeks before she died. Two weeks to say goodbye.

Harper silently wipes a tear from her cheek.

"Hey, I'm sorry. I know you lost both your parents when you

were in high school. That had to be rough." I take her hand in mine, trying to comfort her. I can't imagine what she went through, having her entire life turned upside down.

"No, I mean, yeah, it was. At least I had more time with them. I was sixteen. I miss them every day, but poor Ashleigh was so young." She sniffles. I hand her a napkin, and her kind eyes tug at my heartstrings.

"She was young, but then I got injured the next season and had to have surgery. I spent a lot of time at home recovering, and we got close. Well, more like evolved from siblings to friends. We watched rom-coms, read *Twilight*, and did all the teenaged-girl things. It's when I really developed my love for reading." I wave my hand around the room to the shelves full of books.

"Have you read all these? Or are they only here to impress the ladies?"

"I've read most of them. I have a TBR shelf in my bedroom. And for the record, you're the first woman I've ever brought up here."

She looks at me in disbelief. To the comment about women or the books, I'm not sure. "There are more books?" There's that surprised look I'm excited to see. "It's like you live in a library." Yeah, I suppose it is like a library. But sometimes it's the quiet I don't like. What I do like? Having her here.

I beam. "Yep. I have some of your favorite authors around here somewhere." She told me she likes romance, so I admit I have those to gauge her reaction to my book selection.

"Seriously?"

"Harper, I'll never lie to you." I put my hand to my heart, sealing the vow. Okay, so if she doesn't ask, I don't have to tell. That's still being honest, right?

CHAPTER
ELEVEN

———

"Harper, I'll never lie to you." He seems sincere, but there's no doubt he's had women here. The closet has women's clothes in it.

"Um, hmm."

"What does that mean?" He sounds a little hurt.

"Don't bring women here? I mean, it's fine, it's your place. Do you and all, but don't say you never bring women here and you won't lie when...." I shrug my shoulders and say it as nonchalantly as possible. Although I'm not upset, I intend to challenge him on his dishonesty.

I get one of those full-bodied laughs, and it echoes in the large room. "You did snoop! I knew it." He snaps his fingers. "Are you jealous?"

"Why would I be jealous?" My defenses pop up, and I'm not sure why.

"Harper, the only women that have ever breached this threshold are Ashleigh, Emma, Darcy, and Rosie, my housekeeper. Oh, and maybe Mary Kate, my former assistant now and then for work stuff. And you. Don't believe me, ask Ash. It's all hers. She lived here for a while and leaves stuff all the time. Besides, if I had a woman here, why would she be in the guest room? That's not where I'd want you."

Heat floods my cheeks, and his flirting knocks me off balance. Does he mean it, or is it to tease me? Keep me flustered? Because it's sure doing that.

"Julian Decker, shame on you. Is that why you lured me up to your lair? To have your way with me?" Two can play at that game.

"This is a lair? And you've gone from murder to sex. I like where this is heading." His tone is seductive, and it's working. The automatic lights switching on, startling me and interrupt our flirting.

I step closer to the windows and admire the beauty of Central Park. This green space in the middle of this concrete jungle fills me with a sense of peace. I can't believe Julian gets to see this view all the time. Today, the gold and yellow hues highlight the trees as they transition to autumn. A warm, magical glow envelops the park, mirroring my current feelings. I hate for it to end, but I need to get home.

"I'm sorry I ruined your plans, but Zac has a game and…."

"Are you going to his game?"

I still haven't answered his question about Zac, but he hasn't answered my question about the Swedish princess, so we're even.

"No, I'll watch it on TV, but I need to take care of Noodle. Can you point me toward the subway? I'm ready to put your lessons to the test."

"Oh, I left out the part about not riding the subway after dark. Ever. Especially alone." He swipes his phone from the counter, sends a quick text, and reaches for my hand. "Come on gorgeous, I'll take you home."

Frankie greets us in the lobby. "Going to the Havoc game tonight?"

"Not tonight, Frankie. Taking Harper home."

"Kat was here a minute ago. She's downstairs waiting for you."

"Kat?" Here's a new name. I wonder how many names are in Julian's harem.

Julian shakes his head at me. "Unbelievable," he mumbles.

We get back in the elevator and go down a level. "Now we're going to the murder place?" I tease.

We step out into an underground parking garage where a black Range Rover with tinted windows is idling. A striking raven-haired woman dressed in black jeans and a fitted white button-down gets out and opens the back door.

"Harper, this is Kat. Kat, Harper. We're taking her home, please." I stand there, mouth open. Again. "Get in." I get in the back seat and slide over. Other than prom in a ridiculously large limo filled with teenagers, I've never experienced being chauffeured around before. This feels different and way out of my league. The elaborate control panel in the back seat is lit up like a Christmas tree. This can't be my life.

As Kat drives out of the underground garage, my address pops up in the GPS. Julian pushes another button to turn off the music, and a corner of his mouth turns up into a half grin. The twinkle in his eye is becoming unmistakable. He's about to tease me. "Hey Kat, how long have you been working with me?" He knows the answer, so why is he asking her? What point is he trying to make?

"Six years, give or take. Why? Thinking about getting rid of me?"

Their relationship is interesting. I noticed it with Frankie too. Julian treats everyone with the same respect, regardless of their role, making sure each person feels valued. He pointedly uses "with," and not "for," when referring to employment. Maybe it's a carry-over from his baseball days, where players understand the concept of team. Julian appreciates people and the role they play. It speaks volumes about his character. It's an exceptional quality not everyone, especially those with money, exhibit. Maybe Julian isn't the playboy but a man of character. I can't stop the warm feeling wrapping around my heart and giving a little squeeze at that thought.

"Never. Without you, I wouldn't be anywhere on time. Just wondering if you ever remember me taking women to my place. I mean, if anyone would know, it'd be you, right?"

She glances at me in the rearview mirror and grins. "You don't have to answer that, Kat." I turn to him and swat his arm. "Do not line up your loyal witnesses to testify. It's none of my business, anyway." I do my best to act uninterested, but I'm not fooling him.

"Suit yourself. Remember, things aren't always what they seem."

"You sure say that a lot."

"Because it's pretty much the credo to my life."

Kat pulls along the curb in front of my building, and Julian opens his door, gets out, extending his hand to me. "Can you get home okay, or should I walk you to your door?"

"Oh, no, I'm fine. I'm going to get Noodle and come back down for his evening walk."

Concern crosses his face. Not again. I stifle a sigh, hold back an eye roll, and give myself a mental pat on the back for keeping it together.

"I do it every night. I'm fine. We walk to the park one block over, do a lap, and get back quickly." I challenge him to mention safety.

"Do you mind if I walk with you? I'm not ready to call it a night."

"Sure. Will you wait down here? I'll be right back." If I invite him upstairs, I might not send him home. He's pure charisma, and I'm certainly not immune to his charm. I'm not prepared for that tonight. For him.

Even though we live together and my having guests is probably fine with Zac, I don't think he'll be happy if Julian's here when he gets home. His behavior was weird when I left and we need to talk about that too.

Upstairs, Noodle greets me at the door, his entire body wagging with excitement. His rope toy hangs from his mouth.

"Hey buddy, I'm sorry I've been gone. Did you miss me?" I stoop down and scratch his head and wait for an answer. When he doesn't respond, I release the enormous sigh I've been holding in all evening. Noodle snuggles into my arms when I pick him up. That's response enough, I suppose.

In my room, I freshen up and open the document JB sent. Reading through his character sketch, my breath hitches. The physical description could be any average blonde. But she feels familiar. She's the dog walker for New York's elite. She loves strawberry ice cream, but not strawberries? That's a bit specific. It's like my banana thing. Strange. I laugh at my overactive imagination. Julian has my brain so scrambled, for a moment I wonder if he could be my writing partner.

There's a note on the counter in a barely legible scrawl that catches my eye.

> CJ,
> Going out with the guys after the game. You're
> welcome to join us. Text me for deets. It must have been
> a really long lunch.
> Z

Since when do we leave notes? I shake my head and grab the leash. Noodle sits at my feet, his butt shaking on the ground, waiting patiently for me to clip it to his collar. No more time to worry about writing partners, roommates or the sexy sports agent downstairs. The dog is ready to go.

"Come on Noodle. You're the only guy I understand these days."

CHAPTER
TWELVE

JULIAN

———

I take a moment to check my messages. Nothing major work wise. It's not like I'm a doctor saving lives or anything. Most things can wait a day or two. Priscilla messaged back that she did a quick read of my first chapter and likes it. That's promising. Harper is promising.

I see Noodle before I see her. He's pulling on his leash as he comes around the corner, Harper following behind, laughing at his antics. He gets to me, stops, sniffs my shoes, and plops down, his burst of energy exerted.

"Hey, fella. I understand. She takes my breath away too." I rub his head and look up at her, smiling down at me, clearly amused. "Is he going to make it to the park?"

"He's fine. He got the zoomies upstairs. I'll give him a minute to recover." I reach out and take the leash. If restraining a six-pound dog is how I can help, I want to show her I'm here for her.

I put my hand on the small of her back and guide her to the

door. The foot traffic outside her building isn't as bad as this afternoon, so we're safe, but just in case, I take her hand. Her fingers wrap around mine and I'm encouraged by the slight gesture.

Noodle takes off to the left, and I assume he knows the way, so I let him take the lead. I worry he'll get trampled, but he's staying directly in front of us. He's different from Alexander's English Bulldog puppy, Hank, who is larger than Noodle but not as street savvy. Noodle is a New York City dog, tough, scrappy, and apparently street smart.

It's the golden hour, the sun dipping down below the horizon. The lighting illuminates Harper's aura, and she's stunning. We walk in silence until we reach the small park, her focusing on Noodle, me focusing on her.

Dog-walking neighbors, playing kids, and parents on benches fill this busy park. I'm relieved it seems safe at this time of day.

"You walk here every evening?"

"I do. We go for longer walks in the morning, but our evening walks stay local."

"How did you get into dog walking?"

She looks at me and smiles knowingly. Whoops. My line of questioning isn't as subtle as I thought.

"Noodle came with the apartment." Yep. Still not answering my question, and she knows it.

"What else keeps you busy besides cooking for the Havoc and caring for Noodle?" I want to know everything about her.

"I'm taking a class at NYU. I finished my master's this spring, so this is like a fall internship. The timing was right, with Lawson's move and all." That explains running into her on campus. It still doesn't explain her relationship with Zac and that's where I focus my energy.

"Is New York where you want to be?"

"Is it where you want to be?" I've noticed she loves to answer questions with questions. I'm well-versed in that tactic and wonder if I've met my match.

"It's where my company is, so it's where I am. I'm lucky I travel and try to move around to avoid the New York winters. I don't mind the city, but I prefer to be closer to friends and family." I've lived here for the better part of the last eight years. I'm a Southern boy in a Northern world. I enjoy New York, but it's a necessity, and I live by the motto that I'll bloom where I'm planted.

"I can see that about you." She thinks she's figured me out. I doubt she's done that in a day, because I've barely scratched the surface when it comes to her.

"How did you get into sports management?"

"You could google me to get that."

"Yeah, but I want more than the Wikipedia page. Tell me something I couldn't find on the internet." She's challenging me to trust her. To go deeper. If I want her to keep this going, I have to do this. Without an NDA. I take a deep breath and set my resolve. She's worth the risk.

"I was a baseball player in college at Michigan. Pretty decent stats. I blew out my elbow, and after a lengthy recovery, I knew my chances of going pro were shot. If I couldn't play at the highest level, what was the point of playing? My mom had died, and I was at home recovering. I was lost. I fell into a pretty deep depression. It was a dark time for me, considering I'm generally an optimistic guy. Ashleigh and her romance books helped."

"Yeah, I've heard about your smutty book club." She giggles and blushes and playfully bumps into me with her shoulder. Several of her favorite authors are steamy, and I wonder if she likes to do more than read about hot, steamy sex.

"It's not smutty. Are you shaming fellow readers?"

"Oh, not at all. I find it interesting you're into spicy romance novels."

I chuckle at her sass. "I tell men if they want to understand women, read romance novels. Women write most of them, and it's practically an instruction manual to their wants and desires. Tell me I'm wrong." My response is a challenge. I need to know if her favorite books are what she wants. I'm more than willing to read up on her preferences.

"You're not wrong. But I love that romance novels are as unique as women. There's something for everyone."

"That's true."

Her pursed lips signal she has more questions. "So, who was your first client?" I admire her tenacity. She isn't giving up easily.

With a slight nod, I continue the story. "When I went back to school, Chance was about to get drafted and was getting courted by several agents. He asked me to rep him because he wanted someone he could trust and would have his best interest at heart. Truth is, he knew I needed a purpose after so much loss. My mom. Baseball. I wasn't in a great place. He saved me."

I swallow the lump in my throat. I'll never be able to repay my best friend. He pulled me back from a dark place. I shudder at the memory of those days. I owe him everything.

"So I studied how to be an agent. Took more finance and law classes than I cared for, but if my best friend trusted me with his career, then I was going to be the best damn agent he deserved. A few of my teammates also signed on with me. And it started there. Friends trusted me, put their faith in me, and I took care of them. I was a twenty-one-year-old playing in a world of billionaires and savvy lawyers. Luckily, I knew a billionaire team owner and his friends, and they gave me decent advice." I'm proud I created my agency on my own, but my ego isn't that big to not recognize my mentors for their advice and guidance.

"My dad was skeptical and wanted me to work with him as part of the Reapers organization, but I needed a job without the traditional confines. I wanted to be self-made and do it on my own. It was important to me, as I figured out who Julian Decker was supposed to be without baseball. I minimized my commission in the beginning, wanting my friends to fully enjoy the fruits of their labors and to express my gratitude for their trust. Their success was my reward. I owe everything to those guys. Eventually, my business grew, I started repping non-friends, and well, it took off. Because when I do something, I don't do it half-assed. I'm all in." Does she hear what I'm trying to say? With her, I'm coming at her full force.

"Wow. That's impressive. I didn't peg you as a type-A driven businessman, but clearly, I was wrong."

"What gave you the impression I'm not driven?"

She bites her bottom lip, hesitant to share her thoughts. We stop our walk at the park entrance. I turn to give her my full attention and encourage her to say what's on her mind.

"You seem, well, never mind." She shakes her head, trying to change the direction of this conversation. Oh no. She doesn't get off that easily. I want her assessment of me.

"What do I seem, gorgeous?"

The wind blows her hair across her face, and I reach up to tuck it behind her ear. If I was writing a scene in a romance novel, here is where I would kiss her. My lips are desperate to taste her, devour her. I stop myself from leaning in to take that kiss, the scent of Harper's perfume filling my senses. She's not ready for that. Besides, life is not a romance novel, and rarely that simple.

Noodle walks around us, wrapping our legs up in his leash. See? Even Noodle is getting into the act. I want to know what's on her mind. What she thinks. Why she thinks that way. And yeah, tasting those lips. But her mind first.

"You're not who you portray to the world. There's more to you. And I want to know why you keep the real Julian Decker hidden." She lowers her head at her admission.

I gently put my finger under her chin, tilting her face until our eyes meet. "You want something else not on the internet?" She nods her head. I'll share a safe and probably pretty obvious fact. "I have trust issues. There are people out there who manip-ulate the narrative, are selfish, and just fucking mean. Internet trolls are the worst. I spend half my time bailing out clients, not because they did anything wrong, but because the media likes to spin a story. I intentionally keep my public image shallow and clean. They haven't earned the right to know me. You want more? You earn it."

"How do I earn it?" She bites her lip, the corner of her mouth in a slight upturn, as her eyes search mine. I think of several ways she can earn it, but that's not Harper's style.

"You already have, so ask me anything. I'll do my best to answer."

Her eyes glimmer with excitement. "So I heard something about a Swedish princess," she says conspiratorially. Add persistent and cute as hell to the list of her adorable qualities. I untwist us, step out of Noodles' leash knot, and take her hand.

"You going to tell me about Burns?" I counter.

She laughs and swings our clasped hands on the short walk to her place. Before I'm ready, we're back at her building. This game we're playing is awkward. I want to take her upstairs and kiss her until she forgets everything else. But she hasn't invited me, and I doubt she will. At least not tonight. Harper isn't falling at my feet, and it's sexy as hell.

She gives me a hug that doesn't last long enough and stretches on her tiptoes to give me a peck on the cheek. As I watch her walk away, I have an undeniable desire to see her again. Soon. I'm enraptured and intrigued. Until we meet again, gorgeous.

CHAPTER
THIRTEEN

HARPER

———

I'm sitting at the breakfast bar with a cup of tea and writer's block when Zac comes stumbling in. "You're home early." I glance at my watch. "Or is it late?" The sun rose about twenty minutes ago.

Noodle glances at him from his spot at my feet, and I swear he shakes his head at him in disappointment. I can feel the judgment from up here.

"I thought you'd text me last night. Come out with us." His bloodshot eyes tell the story of his night, and I'm grateful I didn't. Besides, I'd met my monthly alcohol consumption at lunch.

"Nah, long day. I fell asleep before the game was over. Congrats on the shutout, by the way. Good game." I conked out on the couch and woke up a few hours ago. A little hung over, but more from the company than the champagne, if I'm being honest. None of which my roommate needs to know about.

"What did you and Decker do all day?" He looks around the apartment, stretching his lean body to peek down the hallway.

"Looking for something?" Or someone is more like it. I suspect he's checking to see if I'm alone.

He stumbles down the hall to the bedrooms and is back a few seconds later. He dramatically drops to the couch and moans. "I shouldn't have done that last round of shots."

I make a tray of hangover supplies and set them on the coffee table. "Gatorade, ginseng, a bagel, and a shot. Should probably be of penicillin, judging by the hickey on your neck, but tequila will have to do."

"Are you judging me?" He sounds a little incredulous, and I'm not sure why.

"Nah, Noodle has enough judgement for both of us." He uses his ramp to get up on the sectional, sniffs Zac, and walks over to me at the other end.

We both laugh at his snub as he curls up next to me.

"I can't believe you stole my dog," he mumbles. I throw a pillow at him. "Ow!"

"Seriously?! You blocked twenty-eight pucks flying at you going ninety-miles-an-hour and you're complaining about a pillow? You're deranged," I scoff.

"Thirty," he mumbles under his breath.

"Whatever." I roll my eyes and focus my attention on Noodle. Without another word, he pops in the ginseng, washes it down with the shot, and drains the Gatorade. He picks at the bagel, looking at me.

"So Decker?"

Is there something he knows that I don't know? Even more worrisome is if he's talking to Lawson about me. His question bugs me because I don't think I know how to answer. What are we?

"What about him? Are we sharing stories now? You first. What was her name?"

"Don't remember. Daphne, Velma, Shaggy, something like that."

I laugh so hard Noodle judges me too. "Did you have sex in the Mystery Machine?"

He chuckles and throws his arm over his eyes. "Hell, I don't know. She was with some guy named Fred who wore a scarf, and it went downhill from there." He squeezes his eyes shut to block out the light or the memory.

"I bet she went down." Now I'm the one making comments under my breath. I can't believe the antics of these guys. "You really don't know her name?"

"Nope." He gets up and grabs another Gatorade and sits next to me to pet Noodle. "You know whose name I know? Decker. What did you guys do yesterday?"

"Why? Are you reporting to Lawson?"

"No, I promised not to. What you do here is none of his business. He's only checked in once your first week, and I told him you were fine. That's all he gets. But since I'm your roomie and all, I'm entitled to a little more scoop than him, don't ya think?" He wiggles his eyebrows and winces at the movement.

It's not like I'm keeping secrets or anything. I want to live my life under my terms without Lawson having to worry about me. But it would be nice to hear why Zac's hackles are up about Julian.

"We went to lunch. He took me to this super cool cafe that looked like it was closed from the street but was filled with celebrities. I drank too much champagne, and we went back to his place."

I watch his shoulders tense and his jaw tighten. Noodle notices too and crawls into his lap, serving as his therapy dog.

I shake my head in disbelief. "Where I fell asleep for a few hours. He drove me home, we walked Noodle, and he left. The end." My irritation seeps through with the way I emphasized those last words.

He stares at me like I'm a player coming at him on a break-away. "The end?"

"Yup. The end. What's your problem with him? He's a nice guy."

"He's too good lookin' for one. It's not natural."

"Are you serious? Have you seen his siblings? That entire gene pool is unreal." My stomach does a little flip as I recall his family's pictures. "But you can't hold that against him. Why don't you like him?"

"Honestly, I don't know him. I asked Rhino since he's repped by The Decker Agency, and he has nothing bad to say about him."

"You asked around about him?" I stand over him with my hands on my hips. "Incredible." I groan in frustration and sip my lukewarm tea and go back into the kitchen. I put the kettle on the stove to heat more water, slamming it around more than I should.

Zac's behind me, his hands on my shoulders. "Don't be mad at me, CJ. Please." He's begging, which is funny coming from this burley hockey player. I'm surprised begging is even in his playbook.

"Just don't." I raise my shoulder, and he drops his hands. "Nothing happened. I'm not his typical type of girl." He's just being nice to me, I remind myself. He's not interested in me as anything more than a friend. It's the chase he enjoys.

"Exactly."

I spin to face him and he takes a step back. "What does that mean?" I snap back. While I agree, I'm not a model or actress, I'm also a bit offended.

"You're different, CJ." I glare at him and wonder how he will finish that thought. With a sigh, he says, "You're the kind of girl you marry."

I'm confused. Is this a bad thing? "What's wrong with that?"

"Because girls like you make guys like us do crazy things. And I'm worried what kind of crazy Decker has in him, that's all." I'm shocked by his candid response. It's not what I expected him to say, and I'm even more confused about Julian's intentions.

And there it is, ladies and gentlemen. My ultimate problem. I'll never understand how men think.

So me, writing a male character? I'm sunk.

CHAPTER
FOURTEEN

JULIAN

———

Sleep eluded me last night. Harper was all I could think about. What her lips would feel like on mine. How her body would fit when her legs were around me. How her soft hair would feel wrapped around my fist. Fuck. Thinking about her is creating a situation I'd rather not have as Mrs. Dilworth joins me in the elevator.

"Good morning, Julian, dear." She greets me with an aristocratic air while her pug, Digsby, pokes his head out of her oversized Birkin bag.

"Where are you and Digsby off to so early this morning?"

"Today is our spa day. Isn't that right, Digsby?" I swear, the dog rolls his eyes at me. I don't want to guess what a spa day entails for either of them. She arches her eyebrow, staring at me, sizing me up while I try not to laugh. Nothing deflates my cock faster than Mrs. Dilworth's glare.

"Sounds like a well-deserved day of pampering." I'm always polite, at least on the outside. Another neighbor enters the elevator and they lean their heads together to share the latest building gossip. I have no doubt it includes me.

"You ladies have a fabulous day." With an "after you" motion, I sweep my arm out. I have a lot to think about, so I texted Kat to let her know I'm walking to the office today. I need to sort out my next steps with Harper.

When I arrive, the office is buzzing with excitement. Of course, it's always full of energy. It's an open workspace with desks scattered throughout. Lots of conference rooms line the walls for meetings. Since my agents are on the road eighty percent of their time meeting with clients and potential clients, they don't have offices. This office primarily serves as a place to house our support team and meet with clients when they're in New York.

The Decker Agency has forty-three agents and several are here today preparing for the NFL draft. We also employ thirty-nine support staff, seven accountants, and four lawyers. We represent athletes at every level, spanning fifteen sports from the NBA to bowling. Most agents specialize in a specific sport and have multiple players in their portfolio.

I only represent a few players now, transitioning most of my clients to highly trained and motivated agents. The few clients I carry are my friends, not forgetting the guys that got me where I am today. I still charge them minimal commission.

"Good morning, Mr. Decker." Violet, my new assistant, pops up to follow me into my office. I drop my messenger bag on the couch and grab a water from my fridge.

"Morning, Violet. Anything DEFCON-one this morning?" I crack the top and guzzle the entire bottle. Walking from the Upper West Side to Midtown was a great way to clear my head. I decided I only want to handle crises. Everything else can wait. I have other things to deal with besides work today.

"I'm sorry, I don't know what that is," she fumbles. "Josie

didn't tell me about DEFCON status." She scrolls through her phone like it holds all the answers. God, I miss Mary Kate. She was my assistant for years, and we practically started this agency together. Then she fell in love and moved to London. I still blame Ashleigh for playing matchmaker. I've had seven assistants in the past year, and I feel like it could be eight sooner than later.

"It's okay, Violet. Anything about to blow up or need immediate attention?" I give her my patient expression, remembering to not spook her. I can be a bit much, so I try to cut her some slack. She's definitely better than the last two assistants I've had.

"No, sir. I don't think so. But Mr. McCoy," she starts and is interrupted.

"Wants to know what the fuck is going on. You didn't come in yesterday, you come in late today. What's her name?" Patrick makes himself at home on my sofa and gives me an intense glare, raising the tension in the room.

Patrick is my Chief Operating Officer and second in command at The Decker Agency. Honestly, he runs the place. He was the first agent I hired to help me, and we've been together for seven years. He's great at the business side of things. Everyone is aware when they talk to him, it's like talking to me. We operate with absolute respect for each other and total transparency. Well, with work, that is.

Patrick still carries some of his original clients, like I keep my friends. We're both sentimental that way. He's a few years older than me, and his premature salt and pepper hair gives him a distinguished look. Many assume he's older than he is, which works well when people are hesitant because of my age. He's a huge football guy, and when I landed Logan Swindell, top quarterback in the NFL, he was here to stay. After that, we couldn't hire people fast enough to keep up with the demand.

Athletes want the level of service we offer. We treat you like family, and that's hard to find in this business. Just like family, we look after our clients, but we're also honest and direct, even if it's difficult. We've had to tell guys it was time to hang up their cleats, focus on their health, or put their family first. Yeah, we love the money they bring in, but we care about them as people. That's why several of our agents are previous clients. They want to keep the cycle and culture going. I'm proud of what we've created.

"Why do you assume there's a woman involved?" Of course it's true, but I can't let him think he's got me all figured out.

He quirks his eyebrow at me, not even giving me a verbal response.

"Thanks, Violet. Will you close the door on your way out? And let me know when someone calls so I can kick this man out of my office." She gives me a hesitant smile and leaves. She's sweet, but we aren't a good match. Speaking of matching, I picture Harper's dark eyes and flirty smile. I run my hand over my face and put my forehead in the palm of my hand.

"Shit. This isn't good. You've got that look."

"What look?" I mumble. I can't make eye contact with him.

"Like a man that's totally fucked because she's got him under her spell."

"I don't have a clue what you're talking about." I silently count to three, take a deep breath, and put my game face on.

"Can you find out who represents Zac Burns of the Havoc?"

"So that's how you're gonna play this?" He shakes his head in disapproval.

"Yep." For now, that is. "Don't you have some work to do?"

"Yeah, I hear you. Don't forget, we've got that meeting with Tyler Kingston and his family this afternoon to help them navigate the pre-draft drama. It would be nice if you showed your face. He's the top contender for the Heisman this year. His father is already talking shoe deals."

"We should charge a high maintenance parents fee. I swear, they make these draft negotiations ten times harder than they used to be." Fuck. I sound like a grumpy old man when I say that.

"Okay, Boomer." His laugher hits me where it hurts. "But, unfortunately, you're right." Patrick leaves, but stops in the doorway. "Hey, I'm glad you've found someone that makes you rather be somewhere else but here." He raps his knuckles on the door as he walks by, startling an already nervous Violet.

I've got a few hours before my meeting, so I focus on my fun project. I pull up my chat with Priscilla because I want to test the waters on a potential trope. The green dot shows she's online, so I'm excited we can work through my latest idea.

JB: What are your thoughts on love at first sight?

PRISCILLA: Instalove? Not the biggest fan. Why?

JB: Do you think it's real, or something that only happens in romance novels?

PRISCILLA: Are you talking about love or lust? Two different L words.

JB: True. Attraction is part of it. Can it be both?

Her responses have been quick, but now there's a pause and the silence is deafening. It's driving me nuts. Maybe she's thinking about a response. Or she had to answer the door. The waiting is killing me. I get so worked up wondering what happened to her, I imagine all sorts of crazy stuff. Almost twenty minutes later, she responds.

PRISCILLA: I think men are more visual than women. Not to say we don't appreciate a hot guy. Men confuse attraction for love. At least at first. That's why so many romance novels are slow burn, and so many women hate the instalove trope. Convince me I'm wrong.

Is that what it is? Is that what I'm feeling? Sure, I'm in lust with Harper. My god, she's beautiful. Captivating. Funny. Sweet. Confident. Bendy. But I want more than a roll in the sheets. Yes, I want that too. I want, well, more.

JB: Can't it be both? I've met a woman that's making it very hard to concentrate on anything because I'm thinking about her all the time.

PRISCILLA: But will she still consume your thoughts once you sleep with her?

Well, that certainly gives me something to consider. If I fuck her, will my attraction fade because the itch was scratched? And if that happens, how will it impact her relationship with Ashleigh or Chance and Lawson's? This is unfamiliar territory for me and I'm venturing into the great unknown. I'm all confused and doubting myself.

JB: I don't think so, but there's only one way to find out.

PRISCILLA: Ugh. You're such a guy. All about the chase.

JB: I'm not.

PRISCILLA: Because you never have to chase?

Damn. She's got me there. Not to sound like a douche, but I rarely have to chase. I'm the one turning them down. And when I ask someone out, they say yes. Quickly. Unlike Harper.

JB: Okay. I get it. Gavin's gonna have to work for Charlotte's affection. Let's do this.

CHAPTER
FIFTEEN

HARPER

———

"That yoga class kicked my ass," Harvard declares as we return to the apartment. I needed it to clear my head after that chat with JB this morning. I convinced Zac and his hungover friends to go with me. I'm better now. Balanced. They're a little better too.

"Our trainers practically did backflips when I told them I've done a few classes. They're ready to sign you up as a life coach, CJ," Zac adds. He gives my head a knuckle rub and goes into the kitchen to make smoothies.

"I'm not sure what kind of life coach I am, but I'm glad it's helpful." Zac seems lighter after our session. The hangover is a thing of the past. I yell over the sound of the blender. "And don't think I didn't see you get that girl's number," I tease.

"There's something about those yoga pants that just, yeah. But she seems smart, too." Zac shrugs. For him, getting a woman's number comes natural. Like playing hockey. It's a thing.

"And how, pray tell, did you assess her intelligence in a yoga class?" Jetsy asks.

I give him a low-five because I was thinking the same thing. Jetsy is freaking adorable. I'd like to see him find a nice girl.

"She goes to Columbia."

"And Henry went to Yale," Mac adds, and they all crack up. "Doesn't mean he's smart."

"True," Zac says.

"Who's Henry?" I ask. I'm so confused.

Harvard looks at me in disbelief. "Harper, do you really not know my name? I'm hurt." He clutches his heart and pretends to be wounded before he hits the button on the blender.

I look around at the four hockey players in confusion. "But you call him Harvard?" I assumed it's because he went to Harvard.

"Yeah." Jetsy responds. I'm still very confused. He sighs and shakes his head. At me or Harvard, I'm not sure. He reaches over, stops the blender, and everyone focuses their attention on me. Jetsy speaks slowly as he explains it to me like I'm dense. "Because in the big Yale-Harvard rivalry game, he lost control of the puck and scored the game winning goal for Harvard. Funniest thing I've ever seen." He swings an invisible hockey stick like that explains everything.

"Seriously?" I look around, and they're all laughing, even Harvard. I mean Henry.

"Mind if I use that in my book? It's funny," I ask Harvard.

"Be my guest. Make sure you give me a big dick, and I'm happy." He pours the smoothies, and Mac brings me one.

"Then it would be a fantasy," Mac says to another round of laughter.

I hope Lawson is vibing with his new team like this. The camaraderie and ball busting are my favorite aspects of this sport, and I want to ensure there's an accurate representation in my book. My character is a guy who plays hockey, but it's not his entire identity. His team is a brotherhood.

"Tell us about this book, CJ," Jetsy says. "Would it make me blush?"

"Everything makes you blush, asswipe," Zac yells from the kitchen.

I shake my head at their antics. "Well, my main character is Gavin Snow, a professional hockey player. I'm writing the male character, and my partner is writing the female character. We haven't gotten far yet: still creating the backstory, basic plot, that sort of thing."

"Is it a smutty romance?" Mac asks. "I've gone out with girls who like those kind of books, and can I tell you, total freaks in the sheets."

"Seriously?" Zac asks.

"Yeah, man."

"No, I meant you went out with girls who could read."

They all crack up. "On that note..." I get up and head toward my room.

"Nooooo," they all moan.

Jetsy grabs my hand and gives me puppy dog eyes. "Please don't run off. I'll make them behave." Zac scoffs. "I really want to hear about your writing."

"Really?"

"Yeah," Harvard says. "It's cool you write books."

I sit on the floor and go into a yoga pose.

"What the hell is that?" Zac asks. He's pointing at me, and I shrug.

"It's a gomukhasana pose. Or a cow face pose. Want to try it?"

He looks at me and does mental gymnastics, figuring out what goes where. "Nah, I'm good."

I chuckle at his dismissal. Zac's not a bad guy. None of them are. These ice gods live a lifestyle very different from us mere mortals. They aren't how they're portrayed in the media or romance novels. Not really. Fuck boys, yes. Goofy and immature? Also yes.

"Tell us more about Snowflake," Jetsy says.

"Who? Oh, is that what you'd call him?" Do I need to give him a new name? Hockey players never call anyone by their actual name. Case in point. Jetsy, Harvard, Mac, and Burnsy.

"Don't know him," Jetsy says. It's that simple.

"Well, he's a busy hockey player with more talent than sense. He wasn't looking for love, but he meets a girl that turns his world upside down. But his travel schedule and trust issues are a barrier to making it work."

Mac leans back on the couch and stretches his arms across the back. "Sounds about right on both accounts."

"Is he handsome like me?" Jetsy asks. He turns his head and makes a model pose.

"Is he smart like me?" Harvard asks, tapping his temple.

"Is he a hockey legend like me?" Mac asks, cracking his knuckles.

"Is he great in bed like me?" Zac asks, giving me that classic head nod that says it's fact.

They're so ridiculous that my eye roll could be a contender for a world record.

"Honestly, he's a little of all of you. He has Jetsy's charm and manners, Zac's humor, Mac's accent, and Harvard's adorableness."

Zac gets up, jumps on Harvard, gives him air kisses, calls him adorable, and pulls him to the floor. I transition into a child's pose.

"And you're writing this with another person you've never met. Isn't that hard?" Mac asks.

"Surprisingly, it hasn't been bad yet. I'm sure once we get to the plot, we could have creative differences." Like our discussion of love at first sight. I'm fearful we may have several disagreements before we finish this.

"What's the plot? Or is it just sexy time all the time?" Harvard asks.

"Those books have plots?" Zac asks.

"You don't think our girl writes porn, do you?" Mac sounds offended on my behalf. Our girl? Am I living in a harem novel?

"Of course not," Zac snaps back. "CJ has a master's degree, for fuck's sake. I'm just saying what kind of love story do hockey players have? We meet a girl, if she's exceptional in bed she's our girlfriend, if she gets pregnant, we marry her. Where's the story there?" To him, it's that simple.

"For argument's sake, let's say that's the storyline. How did you meet her? Did she fall into your bed?" They all smirk at that stupid question. Yep. Instalust is a real thing. "What makes her exceptional in bed and in life? And pregnancy is not the only reason to get married."

"True," Jetsy says. "But if I got a girl pregnant, my mother would kill me if I didn't marry her."

"Facts," Harvard adds.

I shake my head in disbelief. "What about when you meet the kind of girl you marry?"

"And she's not a buddy's younger sister?" Zac stares me down. He's reviving our conversation from this morning.

"Yep."

"Then I'll go scorched earth to get her to say yes."

"Exactly. There's your story. The push pull of it all. The motivations. The insecurities. See?"

"I guess," Zac shrugs. "But I'd rather bang it out." The guys all laugh at Zac's ability to bring it all back to sex.

"I'm sure you would." I should have known better. It's silly of me to expect anything different from them. They haven't met the one yet, but when they do, I'm curious what Zac's scorched earth looks like.

My phone buzzes on the coffee table. I stand up to take it into the other room. They're all watching me.

"What?"

"Be careful," Zac says in a serious tone. My imagination must be going wild because I swear his voice dropped two octaves. All playfulness is gone from his expression. His abrupt change of demeanor—the way his easy-going smile vanishes, replaced by a stony glare—throws me completely. I feel a pang of worry, wondering what I've done.

"With writing a book?" I'm beyond confused. We went from fun banter to a hard stop faster than a slapshot hitting the crossbar.

"With Decker," he says, like this turn of conversation makes sense.

"What?" I look around the room for an assist and get none. They all have their game faces on.

He tosses my phone at me. The text is on the home screen for all the world to see.

Hi gorgeous! Dinner tonight?

Obviously, there's only one thing I need to do. Turn the text preview off my phone immediately.

CHAPTER
SIXTEEN

JULIAN

―――

I knock out a few items at work, my focus lacking. Normally, when I'm at work, I'm at work. Always have been. But not today. I'm torn in three different directions. Making the circuit around the office, I connect with as many teammates as I can. Agents tell me about their challenges and their new clients or clients they're recruiting. After two hours of catch up, I'm reaching out to legal about putting a no-Vegas clause in all our contracts. They want to be represented by this agency, then Las Vegas is off limits. It's rare these athletes get out of there unscathed. It's called Sin City for a reason. I heard more stories that started with "while in Vegas…" than I feel like dealing with today.

Back in my office, I pull up the writing portal. That's what I want to focus on. I stare at a blank screen for far too long and do the only reasonable thing to loosen the writer's block.

Hi gorgeous. Dinner tonight?

I tell myself I need my muse. But deep down, it's more than that. I'm inexplicably attracted to Harper. Yes, she's gorgeous. But she's more. She's funny. Sassy. Independent. Bold. Gah.

And here I am again, waiting for a response to a text. I find it refreshing that her phone isn't an extension of her arm. I loved that during our lunch she didn't even have it on the table. She focuses on what's around her, not the next best thing. She was with me, in the present. So sexy. But now? It's not my favorite quality. I'm desperate for her answer.

I pull up my chat with Priscilla in the meantime. Our characters are mostly fleshed out, so it's time to write. I review our chat from earlier. Slow burn it is.

JB: I liked your chapter. You set up Gavin for a shit season, but other than that, it's good.

PRISCILLA: What does that mean?

JB: Well, if he's going to win the cup, Charlotte can't distract him. And trust me, she'll be distracting.

Of course, she's distracting because my muse is incredibly distracting. I check my phone for the fifth time. Nothing.

PRISCILLA: HAHA, I get it. You don't think men can do two things at once? Focus on their job and have a relationship? Sounds personal. Still thinking about that girl?

I love that she's giving it back to me. My mind wanders to Harper again, and hell, maybe she's right? I'm distracted, and I'm not even in a relationship.

JB: For your information, I'm not in a relationship, and I'm excellent at my job. I'm pursuing someone and honestly was a little distracted this morning. Still excellent, by the way.

PRISCILLA: I'm sure you are. Just like Gavin.

I chuckle to myself. She's got my number.

JB: Just like Gavin.

And that's where we leave it. I place my fingers on the keyboard to continue our thread when my phone buzzes. It's a FaceTime from Chance. I welcome the reprieve.

"Hermano!" His face fills my screen. His lopsided grin signaling all's right in Chance Fuller's world today.

"Glad to see that Duolingo subscription paying off," I chuckle.

"Yeah, shooting for trilingual this year."

"Dude, knowing how to curse in Russian doesn't make you anything."

"Fuck you. I can have a conversation with Ivan now and even make him laugh."

"He's laughing at you, not with you." Chance always brightens my day with his good-natured attitude and love of life. We've been best friends for over a decade, and it's a rare day we don't touch base.

"Yeah, maybe." There's a brief pause, and I hear the familiar sound of plates clanging in the weight room. "You catching a game soon?"

"I watched last night. What was with that fight with Batesy? He hit a nerve? You got more penalty minutes than usual." I chuckle at my friend who is the kindest man on the planet, but when he hits the ice, it's like the cold activates a superpower where he flies on skates, says curses that would make a sailor blush, and becomes so aggressive I worry he's possessed by demons. That's what makes him one of the top players in the league.

"That bastard always hits a nerve. Anyway, we'll be playing the Havoc and Demons games soon. That means more time than a quick dine and dash, amigo. I expect to see you earning your agent money by wining and dining me."

"You know I don't make a commission from you, right? So you're buying." He responds with a full-belly laugh.

"Deal. Hey, hold on." As he turns his head, his ear fills the entire screen. I can hardly make out what someone is saying to him through his earbuds. "Aww, give Harps my love."

He must be talking to Lawson. My mind goes awry. She has her phone near her because she's talking to her brother, but she hasn't returned my text. I remind myself I have to be careful with my flirting in front of Lawson. It's going to be difficult because it's so natural, like breathing air. Maybe I can use this to ask about Harper and Zac without sounding interested? And why hasn't she responded to my text?

"Jules, are you listening?" Chance breaks through my wandering mind when he yells at me.

"Sorry, work thing," I mumble.

"I get it, man. I'll let you get to it. Make sure you have time for me when I'm in town. I am your numero uno, after all."

"Still not bilingual," I tease.

"Not yet, but with hard work, I can get there. You taught me that, you know." I've always been Chance's biggest cheerleader. He doesn't need my encouragement, but appreciates it. He works hard but loves even harder. But I'm not sure languages are his thing.

"Stick to hockey." A call from Chance always turns my frown upside down. I check my phone again for a response from Harper. Nothing. He's right. A little work on my part, and I can get there with Harper. Hopefully.

CHAPTER
SEVENTEEN

HARPER

———

After my call with Lawson, I'm distracted. He reminded me he'd be in New York, and we'll have an entire day to spend together between his games. I can't wait to see him. He brought up the idea of having dinner since they will be in town for two games: New York and New Jersey, back-to-back. I suggested inviting Zac, which Lawson thought was a fantastic idea. Then he said we'd include Chance and Julian, and I seized up. That dinner has the potential for a colossal disaster, and I would be the catalyst.

I'm trying to focus, but mostly staring at a blank page on my laptop and scrolling TikTok. Social media is my go-to for inspiration when I need ideas for a story. People put their whole life out there for the world to see, and I'm not ashamed that I watch those videos. For artistic motivation, of course. I'm trying to work out what Gavin Snow's motivation is with Charlotte, when there's a light tap at my door.

"Come in," I call to Zac. I'm sitting on my bed with my

laptop across my legs, every pillow propped behind me. Noodle is curled up next to me, his steady breathing morphing into a light snore.

Zac enters my room with an absolutely gorgeous, to the point of obscene, display of flowers. I assume he's behind them somewhere because it's so large it blocks his entire upper body, and surely, they aren't floating on thin air.

"What's this?" I ask. He sits them down on my dresser with a firm thud, and the movement of the flowers gives off an overwhelming fragrance, making me feel like I'm in a field of wildflowers on a spring day. It's bordering on obnoxious.

Zac sneezes. "God bless you," I say, but my blessing doesn't erase his scowl. "What are these for?" Zac shrugs his shoulders, pulls the card from the center of the monstrosity and thrusts it at me. "I was talking to Lawson a little while ago and told him I was having writer's block. Maybe he sent them to cheer me up." Zac continues to scowl, not a word spoken. I'm not sure what's gotten into him, but he needs to dial it down a notch or three. Then he tosses a white bag from the Apple store my way. Now I'm completely baffled.

He stands there and crosses his arms over his broad chest, waiting. "What?" His head nods toward the bag he gave me. He wants to know who the flowers are from, but I don't want to do this in front of him. I'm fearful if they aren't from Lawson, I'll be getting more than the silent treatment from my roommate.

"I take it they aren't from you?" His scowl deepens. "Have I told you peonies are my favorite flower?" Based on the grunt he makes, Zac obviously doesn't care about my botanical preferences.

I swallow my nerves and open the card, sliding it out of the sealed envelope. It isn't a standard issue florist card. It's hefty. Expensive. I unfold it to find a handwritten note. It's not the kind of card you get when you order over the phone. This is the kind of note you write in person, and they deliver with the order. I close my eyes and take a breath before I read, keenly aware my every movement, expression, word, is being scrutinized by the hockey player studying me.

The handwriting is neat and masculine.

> *Gorgeous,*
> *I wasn't sure if there was a problem with your phone or if you were ghosting me, so I thought I'd contact you another way. Dinner with me tonight?*
> *Julian*
> *PS- I got you a new phone because, clearly, it's option one. Fingers crossed its option one.*

I pull the note to my chest and giggle, my nervousness forgotten. I wasn't ignoring him. Not really. I'm conflicted about how to answer. I need to focus on my writing project. But based on these flowers, there's no way I can ignore this man. I pull the box from the bag and find the latest iPhone. The lock screen is Julian on his knees, hands together, begging. Even when he's goofing around, he's incredibly sexy. I want to thread my fingers through his hair and tame those waves. But when it comes to Julian, there's no taming him. And do I really want to? His spontaneity and fun personality are super-hot.

The new phone has one text notification.

> DINNER?

I can't hide my amusement at his over-the-top gesture.

It reminds me of JB and his instalust thrill of the chase. Is that what's going on here? Is it the chase? If that's the case, he'll have to work for it. I don't want to be easy prey. After all, the chase is fun for me too.

Zac clears his throat. Agh! I forgot he's still in the room. It's really sweet that he's concerned but also none of his business what I do. Another conundrum.

"What's wrong with you?" My attempt at leaving it vague, maintaining a cool demeanor, is difficult considering I'm as giddy as a Swiftie on a new album release day.

Zac responds with another grunt.

"Sorry, I don't understand caveman," I respond with a little edge in my voice. "Speak now or forever hold your peace." I throw his attitude right back at him. Two can play at this game. He needs to either tell me what's on his mind or move on.

"I told you, CJ. I don't trust him." He's told me that, and I don't understand why.

"Is it him or anyone I might go out with? Just trying to figure out the context here."

Zac comes over and sits on the edge of the bed, keeping one foot on the floor, the other tucked under him as he turns and looks at me.

"Look, I know how guys think. Remember what I told you about you being different? You're a beautiful, sweet girl, and trust me, this is the tip of his level of crazy." He looks at the flowers and shakes his head.

"It's not like that," I mumble.

"CJ, it's exactly like that. I'm not going to be around much now that the season's starting, and well, promise me you'll be careful. I can't pick up the pieces of your broken heart when I'm not here."

Zac is a sweetheart, and I swoon a little at his concern for my heart. His stoic hockey-player persona put aside as he worries for me. I put my hand to his cheek, the scruff of his soft beard tickling my hand. The unease fills his eyes as he watches my face for a sign of distress. I peer into his deep brown eyes, offering a hesitant smile as my cheeks flush slightly. Hopefully, it's enough to ease his apprehension about Julian.

"Thank you. You don't have to worry about me, but I appreciate it. Worrying about me isn't in the roommate agreement." I'm touched by his concern, but I'm a big girl. I can handle this.

He nods quickly and leaves. I need to respond to Julian, and

I'm trying to be logical and not spiral into overthinking this. Julian's pursuit has my brain scrambled.

I open my laptop and stare at the chapter I've struggled to finish. Would Gavin Snow make an elaborate gesture like send a humongous display of flowers or buy a phone because Charlotte didn't respond to a text? I'll test the waters. Is Julian a typical man when it comes to the chase? I'll ask JB.

PRISCILLA: Would Gavin do something outrageous to get Charlotte's attention? If so, give me an idea.

Noodle moves to my lap while I wait to see if JB is online.

"I know, buddy. I'm curious what he'll say too." My hand rubs his ears, the soft fur calming my anxiety.

The floral arrangement on my dresser is so captivating that I can't help but be drawn to the beauty and intricate details. I focus my attention on the flowers while I wait for JB to respond. There must be at least two dozen peonies in this monstrosity of an arrangement in every shade of pink. Flowers that vary from exotic to simple surround them, but they all come together to create the most elaborate and beautiful display I've ever seen. It doesn't look like it should work, but it does. It's interesting, layered, complex, and I wonder if that's the point. Sometimes it's not supposed to work, but it does.

My computer dings, and Noodle and I startle at the sound. He gets up and moves to the foot of the bed, forgoing the snuggles for peace and quiet. I'm eager to read his response, my heart racing with anticipation.

JB: Depends on the definition of outrageous. He gets paid to play a game that involves a hard piece of rubber flying at a high rate of speed while having sharp blades strapped to his feet balancing on a sheet of ice. What Charlotte might see as outrageous, he might see as reasonable. Perspective and motivation are everything, don't you agree?

I let out a little exhale. Not the answer I was expecting, but a thoughtful one. Maybe my imagination is getting the better of me. JB isn't Julian, after all. My author brain is taking over my reality brain. There's no way Julian would write romance novels. I chastise myself for thinking life is like a romance book. It's not. I need to reign in my crazy a bit.

Time to get back to work. Perspective and motivation. What is Gavin's perspective and motivation with Charlotte? What's Julian's perspective and motivation with me? Zac seems to think it's because I'm different. Is it about the chase? Is the playboy ready to change his ways? Perspective. Motivation. I close my eyes and contemplate what would motivate a man to send such an extravagant arrangement of flowers because of an unanswered text.

My computer dings again, breaking me out of my confusing thoughts.

JB: But maybe he'd send her a new phone because she doesn't respond to a text. He's desperate for her to say yes. Is that outrageous?

I close my eyes and count to ten.

PRISCILLA: Yes.

CHAPTER
EIGHTEEN

JULIAN

———

PRISCILLA: Yes.

Not the yes I'm looking for right now, but I'll take it. Professor Daniels was right. This writing partner thing is making me put more thought into my character development. Priscilla is good for me. She's funny, challenging, intriguing. And her honesty has me questioning my delivery to Harper this afternoon. Was it over the top? Priscilla has me reconsidering my approach.

How would Charlotte react to Gavin's attempt to get her attention? What did Harper think? Did I freak her out? Did I cross a line? Did she get them? Maybe she's not home? Yeah, that's why she hasn't responded to my text. But she has her phone with her because she was talking to her brother earlier. Well, fuck. Maybe it's me. I tug at my hair and put my head down on my desk. I'm at a loss when it comes to Harper, but I'm not giving up.

I still have a lot to learn about Harper's background, but I know more than a stranger, thanks to our six degrees of the Decker Connection. I consider what I know. When you lose your parents as a young teenage girl, how does it affect your dating life? Lawson is a solid guy, but how would he influence her dating expectations and experiences? I can only imagine.

I open a new document and write my thoughts out. It's the best way for me to work out issues. Usually when I do this, it's about my characters. This time, I'm the main character. Am I coming on too strong? Am I scaring her off? Was the phone too much? Does Harper think the flowers I sent are outrageous?

She told me she liked Peonies, but never said they were her favorite. It was difficult to get her favorite anything. To avoid exclusion, she chooses not to decide. She stays open to possibilities. She doesn't like one thing. Like at lunch. It was fun to watch her make new combinations, unexpected pairings. So with the flowers, I told the florist to make it unusual. Unique. Like Harper. The florist's eyes bugged out at the request because she said it would be an over-the-top arrangement. I didn't care. From my perspective, it's worth it. Not outrageous. Because I need to see her again tonight. I'm drawn like a moth to a flame. Perspective and motivation.

Another message pops up in the chat.

PRISCILLA: I think we'd make more progress in person. Are you open to that? I'm in NYC. You?

Meet? She's not wrong. We'd make faster progress working in person. Am I willing to take that risk? She's signed an NDA, but those are only as strong as the integrity of the person who signed it. I'm asking Harper to take a risk with me. Probably a little hypocritical of me to not take risks too?

JB: I'm in NYC too. I'm willing to meet, but anonymity is essential.

PRISCILLA: We both signed NDAs. You can trust me. This program is important to me, and I won't do anything to mess it up. Tonight?

Tonight? I check my phone for the hundredth time for a response from Harper. Nothing. I'm still holding out hope.

"Mr. Decker." Violet appears in my doorway.

I've been staring at my screen and practically forgot I'm still in the office. The hum and chatter of The Decker Agency is white noise to me these days.

"What is it, Violet?"

"John Waters scheduled a call with you in two minutes."

"What's he want?"

"Mr. McCoy asked me to reach out to him on your behalf about a Havoc player?" She's so nervous around me that almost everything she says sounds like a question. I think I'm pretty easy to be around. Do I make Harper nervous? She's got me questioning everything.

Waters must represent Zac Burns. Great. Now I have to figure out quickly how to ask his agent if Zac has a girlfriend. This story better be good because this is seriously petty shit. What the hell am I doing?

My computer comes to life with a video call, and I'm facing a grinning John Waters.

"You trying to poach my goalie, Decker? I thought we called a truce after that Fuller incident years ago," he chuckles. John reps a majority of the east coast hockey players. He was naïve enough to try to steal Chance from me years ago. The operative word: try.

"I forgave you, but I'll never let you forget," I tease. Being a sports agent is lucrative and, typically, there's a level of competition with agents all vying for the big stars. Rule number one with the Decker Agency: We don't poach. Ever. We get our clients by reputation alone. Most seasoned athletes come to us because we put them first. Oh, our fees are at the top of the scale because you pay for service.

"What's up with Zac Burns? He leaving me?"

"Nah, you know goalies are too weird for me." We both laugh. "Listen, can we have this conversation off the record? It's more of a personal inquiry."

His jovial demeanor shifts to serious. "Shit, yeah. Everything okay?"

"Yeah, yeah, fine. Ashleigh was interested in him, and I want her to have realistic expectations, you know?"

"I thought your sister was engaged to Cole Davidson." He's going to let me take this as far as I want, but he's questioning it.

"She is." I shake my head. I don't need rumors about Ashleigh and Cole going around. It would be detrimental for him with the Liberties, and I won't have my sister's name tarnished. Ever. "No, nothing like that. This is for a friend of hers."

"Well, it's not like I'm in charge of his social calendar or anything, but he's a typical hockey player."

"What does that mean?" I know what it means, but I need him to spell it out.

"He plays hockey and fucks. Occupies his time with an occasional video game to break the monotony. Not a lot of drama. I think he has a thing with his dog walker. You know, typical hockey player." Well, fuck. Harper.

"Yeah, I get it. Good guy, though?" Tell me she's safe, at least. Then again, Lawson wouldn't let her be in a bad situation, would he?

"Yeah, a decent kid. His team's leadership likes him. Teammates like him. On the goalie weird scale, he's closer to normal."

"Thanks, John. That's all I needed. If I can do anything for you, just let me know."

We hang up, and I pace as I think about what he said. If I was smart, I'd step back, but I can't. Not until she tells me to, that is. I'm definitely not smart when it comes to Harper. She's got me taking risks and doing stupid things like pursue a relationship when I need to be focusing on this writing project.

My phone vibrates with a series of texts, breaking me out of my over analysis.

> Phone is fine. Thanks for checking. 😊
>
> The flowers are incredible, but unnecessary. Thank you. 🌸
>
> Dinner sounds great. Pick me up at 7:30. 😊

Yes! I spin in my chair and do a fist pump in the air. My worrying immediately vanishes with her response. She used a laughing emoji. She's amused. I'm good with that. One more thing to do before I head home for the day and get ready for my evening. I need to respond to Priscilla.

JB: Can't tonight. I have plans with my muse. Later this week?

CHAPTER
NINETEEN

————

I blink once. Then twice. Did I read that correctly? No. Certainly not. I tilt my head in confusion.

> JB: Can't tonight. I have plans with my muse. Later this week?

Muse? Is that what I am to him? He's using me for inspiration. All his flirting was to get reactions so he can create a character. My stomach sinks when that realization hits me. I feel foolish because I fell for his charm. Now my defenses are up, and I remind myself to keep my heart under lock and key.

It's fine. Really. Totally my fault for having expectations. He warned me more than once things aren't as they appear. His pursuit of me included. Damn. It stings, but I'll work through it. Turnabout is fair play. No reason I can't use Julian for character inspiration too. After all, Gavin is a charming playboy who needs to change his ways if he's going to get his girl.

You know what? This is good. I needed this reminder of

what's important here, and that's the book we're writing. If he needs a muse, I'll be his muse because his success is my success. With that resolved, I look at my clock. Crap. I need to hurry to get everything done before he gets here. Tonight, he'll meet the "fuck around and find out" side of Charlotte Jackson.

―――――

I zip up my boot when I hear Zac and the boys come home. Perfect. I want to get the most bang for my buck with this makeover. I went for shock value. Julian wants a muse for Charlotte, then I'll give him one.

Luckily, if you want a new look, then New York is the place to make it happen. After a few brief hours, I don't even recognize myself. I needed a little me time, and this afternoon checked that box.

The new outfit is tasteful but hella sexy and not my typical conservative look. But I'll own it because I'm pretending to be Charlotte. I convince myself it's a costume in my real-life drama. I'm playing the part.

My white bodysuit is low cut in both the front and back. The blousy sleeves and pleated front, with their delicate fabric, subtly soften the harshness of the overall design. The black leather miniskirt is a little shorter than I'm used to, but the thigh-high boots give me the confidence to pull it off. When the makeup artist saw my clothes, she understood the assignment. I feel like a Taylor Swift lyric come to life with my perfectly drawn cat eye. I'm ready to slay. At least I hope so. My blonde tresses are down in sexy, fuck-me waves. He wants a muse, I'll give him a muse. A confident, kick-ass version of Charlotte Jackson stares back at me from the mirror.

I touch up my ruby red lips and tuck the lip stain into my studded clutch. I'm ready to take the stage. There's a commotion in the den, and I hear a light knock on my door.

"Hey, Harper, it's Connor." He sounds timid and afraid, and I can't help but smile at the thought of this big hockey player afraid of bothering me. "Um, Julian Decker is here, and he and Burnsy are, well, you might want to come out here and... I dunno. I thought I'd come and let you know." His voice trails off as if he's questioning his actions.

I open the door, and he gasps and clutches his pearls. I reach up and pat him on the cheek. He really is adorable. "Thanks, Jetsy. I've got it from here." With a little wink, I walk past him, as he stays frozen in place. My heels click on the hardwood floor, a cadence for my grand entrance. Unfortunately, no one is paying attention to me except Jetsy. Zac and Julian are standing near the door in some kind of standoff. With arms crossed, they stare at each other in utter silence. It's ridiculous. I'm about to end this male posturing by resetting the game.

Mac sees me, does a double take, drops his game controller, and his mouth falls open. Harvard catches his reaction, looks at me, and does the same thing. The voice from the TV says, "game over." I can barely contain my pleasure. Yes. Yes, it is. It's the perfect soundtrack for my entrance. I walk up to the two men locked in a pissing contest and act badass as I struggle to contain my grin.

There's absolute silence in the apartment, adding to the tension. Even Noodle is in his bed.

I kiss Zac lightly on his cheek, leaving a perfect set of lips. After all, he started the goodbye kisses.

Zac and Julian disengage their stares at one another and finally notice I've entered the chat. "Don't wait up," I say to Zac. Without a pause, I glance at Julian and say, "Let's go." I'm out the open door before either of them reacts. I'm halfway to the elevator before Julian joins me. He doesn't say a word as he pushes the button, giving me a quick glance but focusing his attention on the doors. He can't even look at me, and I'm confused about how to interpret that. I worry I've taken this too far, but I'm committed now. I can't overthink this. It's go time. No regrets.

The elevator arrives quickly, and we step in, and he pushes the button to the lobby. He finally turns to look at me, and his eyes drink me in from head to toe and back again. He practically makes me come from his eye fuck. A quick lick of his lips betrays his nervousness. His eyes are a mixture of lust and panic. He might be short circuiting, and I can't hide my smirk. I'm doing my best to stay in character here. Whoops.

"Is this okay? I forgot to ask where we're going." I tuck my hair behind my ear, playing innocent and coy. He goes through several emotions in a few seconds, and if I wasn't in character, I'd double over laughing. His Adam's apple bobs, and he licks his lips again.

"If I didn't know better, Mr. Decker, I'd say you're at a loss for words," I tease.

He finally finds the ability to speak. "To be sure, it's a first."

We step out of the elevator, and he walks me to the front door, where Kat is waiting by the car. She sees me and gives an appreciative grin.

"Good evening, Ms. Cartwright." I'm thrilled she's with me on this adventure. She's abiding by the universal mantra: Chicks before dicks.

"Hi Kat. Great to see you again." She opens the door, and Julian gets in and slides over. He extends his hand to me, and Kat wiggles her eyebrows at me as she holds back her laughter.

Once we're secured in the car, she pulls away from the curb. "Where are we going for dinner? I'm famished." I'm doing my best to act like everything is normal, like I do this every day.

Julian shakes his head a little, like he's clearing an etch-a-sketch, trying to reset the page. I thought I'd shock him, but this reaction is even better than I could have imagined. An afternoon well spent, for sure.

"There's this French restaurant you might like, but if you're in the mood for something else…" He trails off and looks away. Kat catches his eye in the rearview mirror and laughs.

"There's that new place in SoHo Madelyn Reynolds was telling you about," she suggests.

"Madelyn Reynolds?" I turn, giving him my full attention and cleavage. Although my cleavage will never compare to the Hollywood starlet who apparently gives him restaurant recommendations. Another reminder of the circle he runs in. Insecurity rears its head, but then I remember the character I'm playing and push it down.

"Um, that's a great idea, Kat. Why don't you call ahead and take us there?" Julian pushes a button, and a partition goes up between us and Kat.

He clears his throat and looks at me again, clearly rattled. It's the first time I've seen his confident, charming, cheerful personality crack, and I feel guilty. I drop my character a little, feeling the weight of his hand in mine, as genuine concern washes over me. I wonder if I've broken him.

"Hey, you okay? If you don't want to do this, I can go home." I want to give him an out. Or a chance to tell me his secret.

His hand squeezes mine. "No, I'm sorry, Harper. I've had an out-of-body experience. But I'm back, I promise." And like that, Julian's eyes lock on mine, and his charming smile fills his face. "You look incredible, by the way. I should have told you that. I mean, you always look incredible, but this? This is hot."

Even with my tough persona, I feel the heat rise in my cheeks. "Thanks. Can I be honest with you?"

His eyes lock on mine. "Always." He takes my other hand, and his thumb slowly brushes the top.

"Zac doesn't trust you. Why is that?"

He takes a moment before he answers, his thumb continuing its path across my skin. That simple touch is turning me on. I focus on keeping my walls up. This is his chance to tell me I'm his muse and nothing more.

CHAPTER
TWENTY

JULIAN

———

"Zac doesn't trust you. Why is that?"

Her question hangs between us. There it is. Zac. I need to tread lightly and not scare her off, but I'm not a home wrecker, either. Plus, I don't respect a cheater. And I definitely do not share. I'm playing with fire here, and tonight she is red hot. I'm navigating my way through this to minimize the scorch marks I'll get.

When I first saw her at NYU looking like a sexy librarian, I was intrigued, enchanted, even. Tonight's look is beyond sexy. It's provocative and a little confusing. Not to say she's not hot as fuck, because it's taken every ounce of my willpower to keep my hands off her each time I've seen her. But that's not the issue at hand.

Why doesn't Zac trust me? He shouldn't. I want what's his.

"What made him say that?" I'm hoping she'll tip her hand, give me a clue.

She shrugs. "Should he trust you?"

"I don't care what Zac Burns thinks of me. It's you I care about. Do you trust me?"

Another shrug. "What are we doing, Julian? What am I to you?" She's lowered her shields. She's vulnerable, and it contradicts her tough-girl appearance tonight. I'm having a hard time reconciling the two. But this is Harper. A sweet, caring, funny, interesting woman hidden behind leather and makeup.

"I like you, Harper." Leaning closer, I tuck a strand of hair behind her ear, watching the blush bloom on her cheeks. "I like you a whole lot, gorgeous." Pulling back, I study her eyes, searching for any hint of her reaction. I'm this close to kissing her luscious red lips, but I resist the temptation.

"What am I to you?" she repeats. This time, she finds her confidence, demanding an answer.

"Someone whose company I enjoy immensely. A gorgeous woman who I find incredibly sexy. Harper, you are so many things to me, and I want to keep adding to the list."

"Tell me a secret." Her voice is low, seductive.

I respond without thinking, telling her exactly what's on my mind. "I want to kiss you."

Her lips morph into a wicked smile. "That's no secret." Boldly, she leans into me, and her soft, painted lips meet mine, a feather-light kiss that teases me. But it's oh so promising. There's the answer I wanted.

Excuse me while I have another out-of-body experience. Her lips on mine are heaven, and it takes a fraction of a second to react. I bury my hands in her hair, pull her closer, and take control of her sweet kiss. My tongue sweeps out, tasting her, seeking entrance into her mouth. I want to devour her. I'm hungry for Harper and lose myself in her. Her reaction says she's hungry for me, too.

Kat's voice comes over the speakers, announcing our arrival at the restaurant. We pull apart, and Harper's smoldering eyes contradict her giggle. She reaches out and wipes at my lips, her lipstick on her thumb.

"I like this color on you, Mr. Decker."

I press the intercom button on the door. "Kat, can you circle the block once for us, please?" The car pulls away from the curb. I pull a tissue out and hand it to Harper and pull down a lighted mirror. Her smeared lipstick is sexy as fuck, but no one gets to see it but me. She fixes her make-up and is ready when we arrive back to our destination.

Kat opens the door and helps her out, a knowing smile on her face. Even with her edgy makeup, Harper's happiness is unmistakable - her face practically shines with joy. It's a complete contradiction, and Harper Cartwright is making me question everything I thought about her.

The gap between that leather skirt and those boots is calling to me, but we're in public and going to dinner. I put my dirty thoughts away. For now.

Seated at our table in a cozy booth, I hear the gentle hum of conversation and the clinking of silverware in the intimate restaurant. I deliberately took a seat opposite her, my eyes fixed on her, enchanted by her presence, and curious to unravel her mysteries.

"Champagne?" I ask while perusing the wine menu. She bites her bottom lip as she debates the angel-devil sitting on her shoulders. She's conflicted. Where's that confident, sexy, kick-ass woman I picked up earlier?

"What's the signature cocktail here?" she asks the waiter.

"We make the best Old Fashioned in the city," he answers with a touch of pride.

"Oh, I've never had an Old Fashioned, but I'll try it. And a glass of water, please." Her eyes sparkle with excitement. She likes adventure, new things. Good to know.

"Make it two." The thought of tasting the whiskey on her lips makes mine curl upward into an amused grin.

"Let's play a game," I suggest.

"What kind of game?" Okay. Adventurous with a side of caution.

"Another round of Q and A, but more like Truth or Dare." She looks away while she debates the pros and cons.

"Okay. But dares are within reason." There she goes, changing the rules. She bends the world to her, and it's incredibly sexy.

"Of course. Consent, always."

The waiter returns with our drinks. She takes a sip, her lipstick marking the rim of the glass, and it's a total turn-on. This foreplay is killing me, but I'm here for it.

"Do you like it? Because if not, we'll get you another drink."

She twists her mouth a little while she considers the question. "It's different. I want to sip on it before deciding. Is that okay?"

I nod to the waiter. He'll return when we pick up our menus again.

"Of course. Truth or dare?" I challenge her.

"Truth." She's playful.

"Zac Burns?"

"Swedish Princess?" she teases in return.

"NDA." I shrug. That's all I can say.

"Do you like NDAs or just hide behind them?"

"I respect NDAs. In my line of work, they're necessary. But remember, things aren't aways what they seem." I give her a little wink. Let's get back to the original question. "Zac Burns?"

She takes another small sip. "Things aren't always what they seem." Her sassy mouth turns up, and she winks back, flirting with me. Her giggle is music to my ears.

"Good, because let me tell you something, gorgeous." She leans in a little. "I don't share." My voice is low and serious.

Her eyes widen in response, as she leans back in the booth. I hope I didn't come on too strong and frighten her away. As she takes a sip, I intently watch her, hoping to glean some insight into her thoughts. Determine if she has a tell. She puts her drink down, her fingers wrapped around the crystal glass, spinning it slowly. She squares her shoulders and boldly says, "Good thing, because I don't either."

CHAPTER
TWENTY-ONE

HARPER

————

Before I know it, I'm completely charmed by Julian. I can't help it. I fight it, try to act tough, put my shields up, and one seductive, growly comment destroys my resolve. I don't even care about the princess. I enjoy teasing him.

"Good thing, because I don't either," I say. His eyes track my lips as I sip on my drink again. I don't particularly like it, but at least I'm not chugging it and getting tipsy.

I need my wits about me or I'll kiss him again. If he's going to use me as his muse, then I'll use him for, well, my pleasure. Hell. I still haven't recovered from that kiss. It was the most sensual thing I've ever experienced or even imagined. I don't have words strong enough to write a kiss that hot. Every nerve ending was awake and on high alert. It was electric, and I want to do it again. But I exercise control. Look at me. I deserve an Olympic medal for the level of restraint I'm showing because I really want to climb over this table, straddle his lap, and kiss him again. I squirm a little thinking about it.

"My turn, truth or dare?" I tease. I secretly hope he goes for the dare. Julian has been the star of my explicit daydreams, and I'm open to the idea of bringing them to life. As I think about him, I cross and uncross my legs. I'm sure his name will be on my lips the next time I come.

"Truth." There's no hesitation. He said he'd never lie to me. Is now the time to test that vow?

"If you weren't a sports agent, what would you do?"

He takes a sizable sip of his drink, purses his lips while considering his answer. "Probably work with the Reapers is the realistic answer. Help in the family business. But if you're asking me if I could do anything in the world, I'd say work in publishing, you know, books."

Interesting. His answer was honest, although a little vague. I go for a follow-up, but he beats me to it.

"Truth or dare?"

I gently shake my head, chiding him for cutting me off. "Truth."

"You don't like your drink, do you?" Okay, so maybe my acting skills aren't what I thought.

I giggle and wince. "Not really."

He moves it in front of him. When I reach for my glass, he holds my hand. "Never drink something you don't like because you think you should." His eyes smolder. When I read about smoldering eyes, I obviously never fully understood the term. But I do now. All his attention is on me. If I'm reading him correctly, he'd rather be somewhere private. The next words he speaks are slow, intentional, and laced with innuendo. "Gorgeous, life is way too short to not enjoy it." He waves the waiter over and orders another bottle of Aces and four entrees for dinner. The way he shifts from sex to casual conversation with the waiter seems effortless, and a little frightening.

"I thought you could mix and match for the Harper special," he answers my unasked question.

"That's pretty extravagant, Julian. Truth or dare?"

"Truth."

"Is this how you treat all the women you pursue?"

There's no hesitation this time when he answers. "Nope. This is a first for me. Truth or dare?"

I put my hand up to stop him. We're going to go a little deeper on that one. "Why?"

"Why what?"

"Why am I getting this special treatment? I'm serious. Is it about the chase for you? Some macho competition with Zac? What is it about me that warrants this behavior from you, Julian? Truth, please." My teasing and flirting are gone, my vulnerability front and center. I convince myself I can handle anything he says as long as it's the truth. I wait for him to tell me I'm his muse.

He takes another sip of his drink as the waiter returns with the bottle of champagne and two glasses. He pours while Julian watches me. I take a sip, and damn, this is good. A small smile escapes as the bubbles dance on my tongue.

"Truth?" I nod. "Okay, the truth is, I don't know, Harper. From the time I bumped into you looking like sex on a stick in that skirt and those fuck-me heels, I was done for. It's not about the chase, although, admittedly, you've made it fun. I like you. Every conversation we have, I want more. It's like an invisible string, pulling me back to you. You're different, and that's hot as hell."

Well. Wasn't expecting that. There's that word again. Different. I bite my bottom lip to ensure my mouth isn't hanging open. I gulp the rest of my drink, dab my mouth with a napkin, and excuse myself. I need a minute.

If it's possible to orgasm from words alone, that would have done it. I'm so turned on right now I want to ride him like Seabiscuit. I lock the door to the private restroom and take a deep breath. Yeah, not helping. I feel my core heating, pulsing, demanding satisfaction. What the hell? I reach between my legs and I'm wet, aching. I've never had a physical reaction to anyone like I am with Julian, and if I don't do something, I'm going to demand he fuck me in the booth before our dinner arrives. I close my eyes, picture his lips on mine, and touch myself. I've never done this outside of my bedroom, but I've never had a fantasy come to life right in front of me. It doesn't take much until I'm holding on to the sink as I come on my own hand. It takes the edge off, but it's not what I want.

I freshen up and return to our table to find Julian visibly troubled. "Something wrong?" I slide in next to him this time instead of across the table. I can't take the distance anymore.

"Are you okay? You look flushed." His hand palms my face, his eyes searching for a hint of my distress.

"I'm fine." After dismissing his concern, I take in the amazing food spread on the table and my stomach growls in response. "Let's eat." I lean over to kiss the corner of his mouth, my lipstick a reminder of where my lips were. I raise my napkin to wipe it off, and he stops me.

"Leave it," he says under his breath, putting his hand on mine, pushing the napkin away. Apparently, he enjoys being marked by me. I store that information away. For later.

He's pleased with himself as I take the best parts of each entrée to make a perfect dinner plate for each of us. Indulging me is risky, but he evidently finds it amusing. I should warn him it's like feeding the gremlins after midnight. Dire consequences ahead.

We eat in silence, the clinking of the silverware the only sound coming from our table. Sexual tension permeates the air and holds a promise of what's coming. My champagne glass remains consistently full, thanks to the attentive waiter, causing me to honestly lose track of how much I've had to drink. Again.

The silence serves a purpose. I've been having conversations with myself, sorting through my feelings about being his muse, his secret, and how I feel about him. *How much grace do I give Julian before I call him out? On a scale of one to ten, how much does it mean to me he hasn't shared? Should I sort this out before I fuck his brains out? What's his motivation and perspective? What's mine?*

Should I drop the badass persona and give him a taste of being vulnerable? Would he return the gesture? When I've finished, I push my plate away and turn to Julian. His full attention is on me.

"Zac told me I was different too." At the mention of Zac, he stiffens. I smile softly and run my palm down his freshly shaven cheek. "I struggle with that word because as women, we're taught different is wrong, not cool, whatever. In theory, we tell people to embrace uniqueness, but when it comes to self-talk, well, it's a little harder to accept. All that to say, I feel like I can be myself around you. It means more to me than you know and, um, well, thank you."

His hand lands on my thigh above my boot and tugs on the hem of my skirt. His fingers trail a lazy circle right below the hemline. "Is this another part of you, or were you making a point? Because if so, I'm paying attention."

"Can it be both?" I ask playfully. "Truth or Dare?"

His stormy blue eyes sear into my soul as his hand moves a few inches under my skirt. "Dare."

"Dare it is." I dare him to rock my world. But then again, he already has, and the night is still young.

CHAPTER
TWENTY-TWO

JULIAN

———

Her hooded eyes look at me as she says, "Dare it is." I swear my dick stands at attention, hoping he's part of this dare. Down boy, or it's going to be an awkward walk to the car. I've barely recovered from the kiss that totally rocked my world. I've tasted heaven, and I want more.

"You name it, I'm doing it, gorgeous." I whisper in her ear and feel the goosebumps on her leg. I'm spurred on by the reaction her body has to me.

"Let's go back to your place." Her lips lightly brush against mine.

She doesn't have to tell me twice. As she finishes her drink, I settle our bill. Her giggles are almost as thrilling for me as her surprised face. I am excited to see the look on her face when we're alone. I text Kat we're ready to go home.

We walk out to the car, and she stumbles a little. I put my arm around her waist to steady her.

"I've got you, gorgeous."

"I'm not used to heels this spikey," she explains. Another giggle escapes her lips. Damn. I accidentally got my girl tipsy.

Kat meets us at the curb and holds the door open for us. I help Harper in and go to the other side. I'm reconsidering my plans, but I won't take her back to Zac like this, so we're going to my place. I pull her into my side, and she snuggles in.

"You smell good." She puts her head on my shoulder, and I kiss her forehead.

It's like that action reminded her of my lips, and she leans in for a kiss, and I gladly oblige. It's not urgent like our first kiss, but softer, sweeter. She pulls away and giggles again.

"You taste like whiskey."

"And you didn't like whiskey?" Admittedly, their Old Fashioned was perfect. If she didn't like it there, she'll never be a convert.

"Not really. But it was missing a splash of Julian." I laugh, and she joins me in her own joke.

I brush her hair back from her face and give her a quick peck. She's crashing, the energy and fire leaving her body. "Settle in, and we'll be home shortly."

I love living in Manhattan. The food, the music, the people. It's the best city in the world. Except for times like now. I hate this fucking traffic. It's only about six miles to my place, but it'll take forty minutes or so, according to Kat's GPS on the dash. I put some soft music on and run my fingers through her hair. She's quietly humming the Ed Sheeran song, her hum vibrating over my shoulder. After a few minutes, the humming stops. I'm not sure if she doesn't know the next song, or she's asleep. Either way, a warmth fills my chest, and I'm content. I can't explain it, but her presence, her touch, is a balm to my soul.

Kat gets as close to the elevator as possible, parks the car, and opens my door. "You sure this is the right move?"

Kat's question makes me pause. "Probably not, but it's the only one I've got." I pray the elevator is empty until we get upstairs. "Do you mind helping me?"

"I'm not sure I want to be an accomplice," she teases.

"Some alibi you are." I chuckle.

I gently extricate myself from Harper and slide my hands under her to carry her upstairs. She stirs in my arms and burrows her cheek into my chest. Kat helps with the keycard in the elevator and follows me into the apartment. Now is the decision. If I put her in the guest bedroom, she'll wake up disoriented and alone. If I put her in my bed, she'll wake up disoriented but next to me. Which will cause her less distress?

I look at Kat for guidance. Wordlessly, she walks to my guest room and turns the covers down. "Trust me, you'll thank me in the morning."

I lay her down, and she doesn't move. Kat helps with her boots and sets them at the foot of the bed. The rest of her clothes? Kat barely shakes her head. She's probably right. Waking up in different clothes raises other questions I don't want her to worry about. I'd never take advantage of a woman. Always the gentleman.

I put a glass of water and a bottle of Tylenol on the nightstand, give her a little kiss on the head, and gently close the door. Kat's leaning against the kitchen counter, drinking an energy drink from my refrigerator.

"Be careful, Julian," she warns.

"I know."

Kat eyes me, reading me like a book. "She's got you going off script."

"I know."

She takes another sip of her drink and studies me. I let out a loud sigh and run my hand down my face.

"Go ahead. Say it." Kat and I have been together for years. As my driver and my friend, she's the keeper of all my secrets. Well, almost all of them. She's seen me with numerous women over the years and never commented. Not once. But now?

"You're falling for her."

I glance over my shoulder toward Harper's bedroom. "No,

you're wrong." I try to act nonchalant, but when I turn and look at Kat, and she's calling bullshit. Her arms crossed, head tilted, tells me she's not buying it. Time to come clean.

Apparently, I'm not a slow burn kinda guy. Because I'm not falling. That's ancient history. "How could I not? She's so fucking hard to resist." I bow my head in resignation. In real life, I'm an instalove man after all.

———

I wake up early the next morning, and she's gone.

CHAPTER
TWENTY-THREE

HARPER

―――――

I'm a disaster wrapped in a bad idea, sprinkled with regret. I swear I'm never drinking again. Ever. Twice now I've over indulged and fallen asleep on Julian. OMG. I'm dying inside. I'm writing Jay-Z a strongly worded letter about the dangers of his product. Will cause user to fall asleep, resulting in total mortification for which there is no recovery short of the witness protection program. New city, new identity. That's the only answer.

I woke up at three in the morning, fully dressed, in the guest bedroom of Julian's apartment, alone. Probably for the best, but still so embarrassing. I don't even remember coming up to his apartment, let alone crawling into bed. What did I say? What did I do? Ugh.

I'm grateful Ashleigh left clothes in there, and I want to thank her for the save, but then realize I'll have to confess why and think better of that. I stuffed my "fuck around and find out" clothes into a tote from the closet and snuck out.

Did I consider going down the hall to find Julian and join

him in his bed? Yes. Yes, I did. But in my champagne-addled mind, I decided that wasn't the best idea. While I doubt he'd be upset, there wasn't any amount of mind-blowing kisses and soft caresses that could get me to that sexy place again. Best to leave with what little dignity I had intact.

I grabbed an Uber, snuck home, and am currently holed up in bed. I heard Zac take Noodle for his morning walk. He probably doesn't even know I'm home. My door is cracked open, but I usually leave it that way, so Noodle has free reign of the place. I'm hit with another round of disappointment self-talk because taking care of Noodle is my job. The reason I live here rent free to write a book. With Julian. Who probably thinks I'm a drunk woman with multiple personalities. I scream into my pillow.

My phone vibrates again, for the I-don't-know-how-many-times. It's time to face the music. Multiple missed calls and text messages that have been steadily increasing in urgency fill my screen. I beat myself up again for making him go through this. I'm a horrible person.

> Hey gorgeous! Imagine my surprise when I found you missing. Just making sure you're okay. Let me know.

> Seriously, the city is a glorious but very scary place. Did you get home okay?

> My doorman said you got in a car in the middle of the night. I'm about to trace the license plate.

> Do I need to come over and check on you?

> Worried now. Please tell me you're okay.

> Sorry, I can't respond because I'm dying of embarrassment right now. 💀

> My heart just started again. You had me so worried.

Sorry. Not my best moment.

My phone goes off with a FaceTime request from Julian. This is the last thing I want to do, but I need to be an adult. It's also the least I can do. The man was genuinely concerned. I scrubbed my face when I got home, and my hair is in a messy bun. I'm a sight. But with irresponsibility comes consequences. Time to pay up.

"Hi," I squeak out as I plop down on my pillow.

His hair's a mess, like he's run his hands through it a thousand times. His stressed face relaxes a little, and that sexy grin graces his lips. Add regret to my overflowing cup of feelings. I can't help the grimace I make.

He visibly exhales. "There you are. I was about to file a missing person's report. How ya' feeling?"

"Okay," I answer honestly. "I don't even have a headache." Only dying a slow death of humiliation here.

"Seeing your head on that pillow is a woeful reminder of what I'm missing out on." He gives a little groan that makes my stomach flip. He's being way too kind. "I didn't even get to find out how you like your eggs in the morning," he teases.

"Scrambled, like my head," I mumble.

He goes off screen and I wonder if he's finally come to his senses about me. "Sorry about that. Had to do something." He focuses back on me and his face gets serious. "Why'd you run, Harper? Did I do something wrong?" His voice is low, rumbly. So sexy. Endearing.

What? How can he think he did anything wrong? I was the one teasing him, leading him on, and then I crashed. I can't keep seeing him. Besides, I need to finish this book. He needs to finish this book.

"What? Of course not. You were a perfect gentleman and have been kinder than I deserve."

"Then why did ya' run?" A trace of his Southern accent surfaces, and it makes him even more adorable.

Why did I run? Because I'm having feelings I've never had before. Because I don't know what I'm doing. Because he has a secret. And I have one too because I know his. Because I'm his muse.

I bite my lip, debating which answer he gets. "I was scared."

His eyes darken, and his normally cheerful face looks stern. "Of me?"

I've upset him. "Yes," I whisper. The hurt washes over him. I gave him the easy answer. "No, not like that. I don't think, I mean, you wouldn't."

"What's got you spooked, gorgeous? Am I coming on too strong? Because make no mistake, I want you, but I'll back off, if that's what you need."

Noodle pushes my door open, and Zac is trailing behind him. "Hey CJ, met the delivery guy downstairs with your breakfast." He sets the brown paper bag on my nightstand and plops down on the other side of the bed, while Noodle snuggles between us.

"I'll let you go," Julian says, a little clipped. "Glad you're okay." He disconnects the call.

"Oh shit, sorry. I didn't know you were on the phone." He doesn't look sorry. "I didn't even know you were here until I met the delivery guy."

"I didn't order…" I grab the bag and look inside to find a Styrofoam container filled with scrambled eggs, an everything bagel, and crispy bacon.

Shit. I'm the worst human on the planet right now. He sent me breakfast from the diner down the block. Now I feel sick at what he must think of me.

> Thanks for breakfast. I don't deserve it.

Or you. Lawson taught me to be a woman of worth. That I don't need a man to complete me. And I shouldn't settle. But what if Julian isn't settling? This breakfast? He's the poster child for if he wanted to, he would.

> I hate to break it to you, but you're wrong.
> Gorgeous, you deserve the world. 💯
>
> I don't feel like we parted well. Can I see you
> today?

Can I summon the courage to see him today? I need a day or two to clear my head. Think clearly. I respond with my head, not my heart.

> Not sure I can muster up enough dignity. I'll let
> you know when I'm ready.

> Whatever you need, but you've got nothing to
> be embarrassed about. But I'll give you space.
> You're worth the wait.

And that is why I need to figure out what to do. Because when he finds out I know his secret, it could all come crashing down.

CHAPTER
TWENTY-FOUR

JULIAN

———

Giving Harper space is hard, but it's the right thing to do. It's been three days. Each day I send her a text in the morning and before bed, checking in, letting her know she's on my mind. Constantly. Her replies include an emoji that I spend way too much time deciphering. I've made sure each day she gets dinner or the sweets she loves so much. I'm giving her what she wants and even what she doesn't know she needs.

And an unexpected bonus to this Harper separation is that I get to work with Priscilla more. We're making pretty good progress on the book, all things considered. We've spent some time getting acquainted too. I'm drawn to her and totally enjoying our chats. While she hasn't mentioned wanting to meet again, I've warmed to the idea. If we're going to meet these tight deadlines, we're going to have to work together. Eventually, I'm going to have to trust her to keep my secret.

JB: Do you have a boyfriend?

I'm not sure why I asked or why I even need to know. Yet, I impatiently wait for the green light that shows she's online. I've never been an anxious person, but lately, waiting for Priscilla and Harper to respond to me is making me a nervous Nellie.

PRISCILLA: I didn't think we shared personal information.

JB: I'm not asking for your socials or anything. Curious if you're in a relationship, that's all.

PRISCILLA: You looking for advice?

Am I? I'll admit, Harper keeps me guessing. I hate the uncertainty of where I stand. Where she stands. The combination of the demanding project, Harper's magnetic energy, and Priscilla's mystery has left me feeling completely off balance.

JB: I consider you a friend. Friends share.

Five minutes pass until she responds. I swear, it feels like five hours.

PRISCILLA: Do you think there's anything to the romance novels we write, or are they pure fantasy?

Well, that question came out of left field.

JB: I believe in romance and love.

I consider my quick response. I've watched my siblings and friends fall in love. If I don't believe in a happily ever after, then I question what it's all for.

JB: And hope.

PRISCILLA: Me too. Hope keeps me going.

Priscilla makes me think harder, go deeper, and I've done some genuine soul searching. She challenges me, and I find that very attractive. When you find someone that makes you a better version of yourself, it's someone you need to keep around. I've never met her, but I want more from her.

I'm not sure if it's feelings or curiosity. But if I'm developing feelings for her, what does that mean about the feelings I have for Harper? What I feel for Harper is real. I'm certain of it. But I can't deny this pull towards Priscilla. It's like that inexplicable pull Jacob had in *Twilight* but with no creepy vampire baby to explain it away.

JB: Do you want to meet? It could improve productivity.

She reads my message and logs off. Did I scare her? She was the first to suggest we meet. Where did she go?

———

Two days of no login or response. Two days for me to stew about her. And Harper. Both silent. Two days and I've got the worst case of writers block I've ever experienced.

When my laptop pings with a chat notice, I rush to open the message.

PRISCILLA: Let's meet at How You Brewin' in Tribeca tomorrow at 4pm.

I'm flooded with relief that she's back. I've grown attached and was worried something happened. If I don't agree to meet, will I lose her forever?

JB: How will I find you?

PRISCILLA: I'll have a book with a flower, of course.

JB: Very Meg Ryan of you.

PRISCILLA: Wondered if you'd catch the reference. Looking forward to seeing you tomorrow.

I snicker at the movie reference. We debated the best rom-coms for twenty minutes last week. She was insistent *You've Got Mail* was in the top five, with her favorite being *How to Lose a Guy in 10 Days*. That's a banger, no doubt, but I put *Notting Hill* higher on the list than her. After engaging in enthusiastic conversation and discussion, we ultimately concluded that I'm the bigger romantic. She leans into the absurd and comedic part of the movie. Regardless, we're both suckers for a good romance and a happy ending.

———

I arrive at the coffee shop twenty minutes early and pause across the street to gather myself. The large window gives the cafe light and allows me a clear view of most everyone in there. It's a happening spot. I scan the crowd inside and find a woman sitting at a small table in the center of the room, a book and flower prominent beside her laptop. She has her head down, typing away.

Priscilla is even earlier than me. I'm about to cross the street, excited to meet her, when she looks up and I stop. Fuck. It's Harper. I never suspected Priscilla was Harper. My Harper.

Why didn't she tell me about her writing project? She mentioned her class at NYU, but I didn't ask what kind of class. That's my fault. I'm usually better at asking those kinds of questions.

Honestly, while I'm surprised, I'm also relieved. That connection I feel to Priscilla makes more sense now. Of course I like my writing partner. I'm attracted to Harper in every way imagin-able, even when I didn't know it was her.

A cold wind whips down the street, and it chills me to the bone. From the wind or the decision I need to make, I can't be entirely sure. I look around on the busy street, hoping someone else walks in with a flower. Anyone else. Maybe it's a coinci-dence or my author's brain creating a scenario out of thin air. I pull out my phone and message Priscilla to verify.

JB: Going to have to reschedule. Family emergency. Sorry.

Harper looks at her laptop, scowls, and her fingers fly across the keyboard. Then she scans the coffee shop, disappointment on her face. A look that I caused. I feel terrible.

PRISCILLA: Another time then. Hope everyone is okay.

She closes her laptop and packs her things. She looks sad, and I need to fix that. What if I bump into her on the street? Then I can be with Harper while I figure out how to tell her.

I pop the collar on my coat and wrap my hand around the strap of my messenger bag. I put my head down and walk towards the coffee shop, strategically bumping into Harper.

"Oh, I'm sorry. Harper?" I put my acting chops to the test, the surprise feeling foreign to my tongue. This collision is a little reminiscent of our first New York meeting.

"Julian, what are you doing here?" Another surprised look, but this one is mixed with annoyance. I feel terrible for what I did to her.

I'm quick on my feet and tell her a bitter lie. "I finished a meeting with a client." I pat my laptop bag as evidence of my story. She looks a little bewildered.

"Of the millions of people in the city, what are the chances I randomly bump into you? Twice now." The playful twinkle in her eyes and her flirty touch tells me our unexpected encounter doesn't bother her at all. An amused smile plays on her lips. I release a sigh of relief, a wave of calm washing over me.

"Serendipity, to be sure. Can I buy you a coffee?" I nod toward the coffee shop she just left. I'm doing my best to think quickly and not act shady.

"I'm disappointed in you." She shakes her head.

"Why?" Panic creeps in. She knows. She must know.

"Did you forget I don't drink coffee?" She pokes her lip out in a pretend pout, and she's adorable. I need to get off this panic rollercoaster. It's making me crazy.

"I didn't forget, gorgeous." I lift my hand to her face, and the warmth of her cheek calms my nerves. "You've got me a little discombobulated at this moment. You overwhelm me, that's all. How about the best hot chocolate in New York?"

She bites her lip as she considers my suggestion. With a slight nod, my afternoon is turning around. I still have to figure out how to tell her I'm her writing partner, but for now, I'll enjoy our time together.

"Let's duck in here to keep you warm while I make arrangements. It will take a few minutes." It's a perfect mid-October day, but the wind off the river is a little brisk. We turn back to the café, and I pull out a chair for her while I go to the back and make a quick call to Kat.

When I get back to the table, she's scrolling on her phone, celebrity gossip posts filling the screen. Priscilla told me she uses social media for inspiration and to generate ideas for her characters. Now that I know Priscilla is Harper, the clues were obvious. I can't believe I didn't put it together sooner.

I lean over to get a better look at the picture of Madelyn Reynolds at the beach with her friends and the ridiculous headline speculating she has an eating disorder. "I really hate these sites. I've told you not to believe everything you read. That girl will eat more pizza than me and wash it down with a full-bodied beer. Eating disorder, my ass." Another surprised look from

Harper. "She's watching what she eats in public because of sites like this."

I take the chair in front of Harper, and she puts her phone in her bag. "Sorry, I was scrolling. I can't believe you know Madelyn Reynolds like that."

"Yeah, we went to college together. Promise me you ignore all the trash they write about me."

She cocks her eyebrow and fires back at me. "Even the article about you sponsoring the local baseball teams in the city?"

I laugh and slap my hand on the table. "I knew you googled me!"

She blushes and sits up taller in her chair. "I needed to know exactly who I'm dealing with." When she bites her bottom lip, my dick pays attention. She's right. She needs to know who she's dealing with, and I'll tell her. Soon. I just need to find the right time.

CHAPTER
TWENTY-FIVE

HARPER

―――――

Who I'm dealing with indeed. Maybe Julian bailed, or maybe he saw me and got scared. Either way, he's not ready to disclose his secret identity. That's fine with me. I'm okay with him doing this at his pace, but it doesn't mean I have to make it easy for him. I require trust in a relationship. Yes, it goes both ways. I'm ready to strip down our identities and our bodies. It's obvious Julian is used to being in charge, calling the shots. I'll let him have this one. For now.

Kat greets us and whisks us away to find the best hot chocolate in New York. Julian types away on his phone, supposedly making more arrangements for our afternoon. Kat and I chatter about the latest season of *The Bachelor*, both admitting it's our guilty pleasure. While Julian's attention is on his phone, mine is on him. His lips curve into a small smile and I can't resist the urge to kiss him. I lean over, and he quickly hides his phone. I'd normally call him on his red flag behavior, but his smile only grows.

"Quit being nosy. You'll spoil the surprise." He bops me on my nose. I sit back with a playful pout. He shakes his head and leans in for a sweet kiss, and I quickly take it up a notch. I remember where I am and pull away, not feeling comfortable getting hot and heavy while Kat pretends not to notice.

"What surprise? You said we're going for hot chocolate and…. what are we doing here?" Kat brings the car to a stop next to a heliport, where several large, sleek, black helicopters sit. A man in a pilot uniform opens my door.

"Good afternoon, Miss Cartwright, Mr. Decker. Everything is ready and on schedule." He extends his hand to help me out of the car, but I turn and look at Julian.

"I thought we were getting hot chocolate?"

His grin is bright enough to light up the night sky. "We are. I promised you the best hot chocolate in New York, and that's what you're going to get." He puts his finger below my chin and closes my mouth before giving me a light kiss. "I'll never tire of surprising you." He says that more to himself, but I shake my head. I can't believe this man.

We walk to the enormous helicopter, and I pause. The wind comes off the river and blows my hair everywhere, adding to the chaos and my growing fear. "I've never been in one of these, and it's a little terrifying."

"Wes has clocked thousands of hours flying. It's safe, I promise. Do you trust me?" That's the thing. I trust him. More than I probably should. But that trust doesn't stop my stomach fluttering with nerves.

"I thought the hot chocolate would be in Brooklyn or …."

"Something like that. Come on, this will be fun." His eyes dare me to take the risk. Truth or dare. Doesn't matter. I'll give in every time.

We get in the helicopter, and it's nice. The soft, buttery leather seats make it easier to relax. When the door slides shut, it's quieter than I expected. "Do we need headsets? I always see headsets." Through my aimless rambling, the tension in my voice becomes noticeable.

"Not unless you need them for the full experience." He puts his arm around me and pulls me in tight to his side. "Wes will give us a tour if you want."

"That would be fantastic. But, um, where are we going?"

"I promised you the best hot chocolate in New York, and that's where we're going. You'll be home in time to take Noodle for his evening walk. Promise."

Spending time with Julian is unpredictable and overwhelming. Julian is larger than life, and that's his normal setting. His current setting is off the charts. Happiness fills his face, and his excitement fills the cabin. All his contagious energy washes over me, and I let my nerves disappear and enjoy the moment. Enjoy Julian.

As we fly over the city, Wes points out landmarks while Julian adds his own commentary, which includes places he wants to take me and all of his favorite spots. I wish I had a recording of this because I'll never remember it all. I take a quick video, and Julian snatches my phone and takes several selfies of us and texts them to himself.

"For my eyes only. You choose what you want to post and when, if ever. I caution you about the attention, though. It can be a lot and spiral out of control. But you're in control of what you want to share." He gives me a quick kiss, and the phone clicks with another picture. "I can't help myself."

We fly along the coast and almost an hour later land in the backyard of a massive house on the waterfront. "Where are we, and whose house is this? Are we still in New York?"

"We're in Sag Harbor, and this house belongs to Devlin Mill-banks. Honestly, I probably spend more time here than he does. Now that I think about it, it's the best kind of beach house. Full access and someone else pays for it." His laugh fills the cabin, and I can't stop myself from joining him.

"Devlin Millbanks? Why do I know that name?"

"He owns the New York Liberties and a few other things. He's my dad's best friend and my mentor. I'll introduce you when we're back in the city."

"He's not here? Are you sure we won't get arrested for trespassing?"

"Well, the evening's young, so who knows." When he wiggles his eyebrows, that little mischievous glint in his eyes confirms he's joking. I think. "Wait here."

Julian enters a code into the garage door keypad and moments later, drives out in a cherry red vintage mustang. "Get in, gorgeous."

"I hope we're not adding grand theft auto to our crime spree tonight."

Julian responds with a laugh. He puts his arm across the back of the seat and squeezes my shoulder. "Trust me." Trust. It's such a powerful word. His earnest desire to make me happy makes it impossible not to trust this man.

He takes me to a small cafe and introduces me to the owner and his wife. We sit at a table overlooking the ocean and order our hot chocolates. "You won't need to change these at all, I promise. Pure heaven in a cup."

The thick, sweet chocolate has the perfect ratio of whipped cream and caramel. The toasted marshmallow on the side is the ultimate garnish. Julian's right. Heaven in a cup.

"This place is amazing. Thank you for sharing it with me." The warm, sweet chocolate has my taste buds celebrating this decision.

"Anytime, gorgeous. We'll take our dinner to-go. Noodle awaits." Julian gets several sandwiches bagged up, and we eat them on the flight back to the city. When we land, Kat is waiting for us.

This isn't how I thought my afternoon would go, but I'm not complaining. As promised, we're home in time before there's a Noodle problem. And now the awkward good night. While my body really wants to invite him up and jump his bones, my heart tells me to wait. We can't have secrets between us before I take that next step. What I feel for Julian is more than lust, although currently, that's pretty freaking strong. My vibrator and I will have quality time tonight, that's for sure.

"Can I see you tomorrow?" His eyes are drinking me in, signaling a yes is all it will take to make him happy.

Scuffing my feet on the sidewalk, I can't look him in the eye when I tell him no. "I'm sorry. I'm going to Zac's hockey game tomorrow."

When he perks up at my rejection, I'm surprised, which only enhances his grin. What's he up to? I'm clearly missing something here. "Got it. Well, goodnight gorgeous." He gives me a way too brief and unsatisfying kiss and goes back to the waiting car.

Yeah, I'm gonna need fresh batteries tonight.

CHAPTER
TWENTY-SIX

JULIAN

———

The teams are on the ice for warmups as I make my way to my seat. It only took three calls and the promise of a signed puck from Chance Fuller to get the location of her seat. One more call to get the ticket next to her. Totally worth it. I'm not shocked her seats are rink side against the glass and not with the other girlfriends. Harper is a hockey fan through and through.

There's a cluster of New York Havoc players huddled in front of my destination. And there she is, laughing at their antics, her ponytail swinging across her shoulders, giving me a clear view of the name across her back. Burns. Seriously? Not what I wanted to see, but then, with Harper, that's the point. She keeps me on my toes. And I like it.

"Is he really your favorite Havoc?" She snaps her head to me, and I'm awarded with another one of her surprised expressions.

"What are you doing here?" She looks like she got caught with her hand in the cookie jar. Her surprise turns into a cheery grin. "Do I have a stalker?"

"Not how most people react to a stalker."

She pretends to be stern when she leans in to tell me her answer. "Not all stalkers are Julian Decker. Are you going to hurt me?"

Although this is playful flirting, the weight of the words sits with me. *Are you going to hurt me?* "Not intentionally."

Confusion fills her face, and before I can clarify, Zac skates up and joins the other players. His scowl is anything but playful, but maybe that's his game face. He balances a puck on the toe of his stick and tosses it over the glass. I catch it before it hits me on the head. He wiggles his eyebrows and winks at Harper.

"Looks good on you, CJ," he says through the glass. "Come on, boys. Let's kick some ass." He skates away, the others fist bump the glass at Harper and follow him. The men behind us chatter with speculation, their eyes fixed on her, questioning her relationship with the players. I need them to ignore her, but that's nearly impossible to do.

Harper shakes her head at her friend's antics before she sits down. Before I sit next to her, I hand her the puck.

"I think this is yours." I lean in for a chaste kiss. As the blush fills her cheeks, I know I hit the mark.

"You seem to be the most popular girl here. Quite the fan club."

She's still laughing. "Apparently." She settles back in her seat while the Zamboni cleans the ice, and a staff member brings her a beverage and popcorn. Our seats are full service, and she's enjoying all the perks. "What are you doing here?"

"This is what I do."

"What? Hit on girls at hockey games?" She smirks at me.

"In case you forgot, I'm a sports agent. I'm working." I give her my best business face while I brush invisible lint from my sweater.

"So glad I've got a front-row seat to watch the playboy sports agent work then." She tosses a piece of popcorn into her delicious mouth, and her cheeks hollow out as she takes a sip of her drink. My thoughts go to a sexy place, and I'm momentarily speechless.

"Interesting choice of attire. How does Lawson feel about it?"

She shrugs. "He knows I'll always be his number one fan. I don't have one of his new jerseys and, honestly, this one is probably safer here." She scans the arena, and everyone is in Havoc teal and orange. She's probably right. A Renegades jersey would make her a target in this rowdy crowd. "Besides, he likes Zac. He's the one who set us up."

She's got me there. And when she says it that way, I need confirmation they are just friends without benefits. I need to get that clarified for the sake of my sanity. Maybe I should tell her about the princess to end the teasing and get a solid answer from her.

She continues to eat her popcorn and take in her surroundings. The arena is filling up, the place becoming a sea of teal and orange. A girl sits next to Harper with her "Wreak Havoc 22" sign, and it's covered in hearts. Props to her for shooting her shot.

"Burns, huh?" she asks Harper.

"Yep," Harper responds. She continues to snack on her popcorn.

The girl leans into Harper, lowering her voice. "I heard he's wild in bed."

Harper laugh-snorts at this information, and suddenly I'm invested. "Yeah, he has to rub his Noodle every night, or he can't sleep. Goalies are always a little freakish that way."

The girl's eyes go wide at that inside and kinda-strange information. And then I laugh. Harper smirks and goes on eating her popcorn, totally unfazed. We have the pregame ceremonies, and when they introduce the starting lineup, the girl holds up her sign and yells, "I love you, Henry!" I catch Harper roll her eyes when Henry Saxton skates to his place on the blue line, looks over at them, and blows a kiss. The fangirl assumes it's for her and jumps up and down like a crazy woman. And as annoying as it is, I realize I want Harper to jump up and down for me.

Harper leans into me. "Harvard is such a cutie, but an insufferable flirt. I should give her his number to teach him a lesson."

She has his number? I remind myself these guys are her friends, and she's not a puck bunny, so the brief wave of jealousy passes. I still don't have the full picture, but I know enough. She's not that girl.

We watch the game, but I enjoy watching Harper. She's a rabid, vocal fan, chirping the refs for terrible calls, and cheering for her friends. When Lawson smashes into the boards in front of us, she's surprised. She immediately goes feral, cheering him on, while beating on the glass. The Havoc and Renegades continue to fight it out on the ice. The score is tied with one minute left in the game. And with a last-minute goal, Lawson scores on Burns, giving the Renegades the win. In a show of good sportsmanship, he taps Zac with his stick. The fans don't like it, but from my vantage point, Zac calls Lawson an affectionate name, and they both chuckle.

"What are you doing after the game?" I ask her. I've been making plans in my head for the past few hours, and I hope she's up to them.

"What do you have in mind?" she asks skeptically.

"Anything you want?" And I mean it. All I want with her is more time.

After a thoughtful pause, she holds her hand out. "Come on, I'm gonna let you take me home where I will consult my friends Ben and Jerry and figure out what the hell I'm doing."

She might not be jumping into my bed, but I'm so desperate for her, I'm willing to take whatever she's willing to give.

CHAPTER
TWENTY-SEVEN

JULIAN

————

Kat drives us home, we walk Noodle, and return to her apartment. Zac's apartment? Still not sure. This is where we usually say goodnight, but this time feels different.

"Now what?" I ask. Hope fills my chest as I wait for her answer.

"I told you. I've got a date. You're welcome to tag along." She reaches out and takes my hand as she enters the building. The doorman holds the door as Noodle saunters through like he owns the place. I follow along like another obedient puppy.

We enter the apartment, and Noodle sits in the kitchen, waiting. She laughs and gives him a treat. "He's so spoiled," she says. "Make yourself at home. I'm going to change if that's okay with you. Ice cream is in the freezer. Grab a beer, whatever you want. I'll be right back."

She wanders down the hall, and I stand in the foyer, uncertain what to do next. This is unfamiliar territory for me. Is Burns going to be home soon? How will he react to me drinking his beer? Do I care? No, not really. I look in the freezer and find several pints of ice cream, all Ben and Jerry's Karamel Sutra Core. Of course she likes complex ice cream. It's two flavors of ice cream with caramel and toppings. No simple flavors for her. And the name makes me chuckle. I pull out a pint and a spoon. If she's anything like Ash, it's straight out of the carton for her. I grab a sparkling water and make a mental note of the contents of their refrigerator. Lots of clean food, probably Zac's, and enough junk food to let me know she's not a strict salad and water girl. I've been with enough of those to know they are hangry all the time.

"What are you looking at?" I ask Noodle. He's curled up in his bed, watching me like I'm the most interesting thing he's seen today. Maybe I am.

Harper joins me in the kitchen, and she's caught me off guard this time. Every transformation this girl makes fascinates and terrifies me at the same time. Right now, it's how fucking gorgeous she is in her home-for-the-evening-look. Her hair's piled up in a messy bun, which is the sexiest hairstyle because it's so carefree. She's wearing flannel pajama bottoms that are covered in pink dinosaurs, a black tank top, with a lace bralette peeking out from the straps. I've seen her dressed in leather, hockey jerseys, and jeans that hug her ass, but nothing has been as sexy as this look. She has a freshly washed face and is makeup-free. "Fuck, you look good."

"I thought you promised to be honest." She reaches around me, grabs the ice cream, and eats a big spoonful. "I figure if we're friends," she says with a mouthful of ice cream, "you need to see the real me. This is it." She waves her hand up and down her body. "This is my at home, TV binge watching, ice cream eating, typical look. I'll understand if you want to run."

If she thinks this scares me, she doesn't know me at all. I reach for her wrist and tug her to me. My hand cradles her makeup-free face as my arm wraps around her waist. "The only place I want to run is into your arms. You are so fucking sexy I can't stand it."

Her eyes flutter like she's glitching. Did I break her? I press my forehead to hers and inhale. "I'm so turned on right now, Harper." Her soft lips cut off my words as they come into contact with mine. This kiss is slow, lazy, and comfortable and tastes like sweet cream and caramel. I'm lost in her kiss, hoping it never ends. A kitchen kiss is intimate, and intimacy isn't usually my strong suit. Trust issues keep you from letting someone in. But this woman's burrowed her way into my heart and soul.

She takes a step back and snags her ice cream, acting like the kiss didn't faze her. "Come on, let me show you what a typical Friday night with me looks like."

I obediently follow her into the living room. She sits on the floor with her back to the couch and takes a bite of her ice cream. "Oh, this is the perfect consistency." Her eyes close, and she moans around the spoon. I've never wanted to be a spoon more in my life.

I sit on the floor next to her and watch, gobbling up every detail to make a memory I can pull when I need a definition of perfection.

She turns her attention to the table that has a partially completed puzzle. She bites her lip as she searches for a piece. "Do you like puzzles, Julian?"

"Um, sorry, what?"

"Puzzles? Do you like doing puzzles? Keep up, Decker." She looks at me like I've got two heads.

"I rarely slow down enough to enjoy one," I answer honestly. "But they remind me of rainy days at the beach. When I was younger, we had a beach house, and when the weather was bad, my mom would pull out a puzzle, and we'd all work together to finish it. Alexander would methodically finish a section and move on to another one. I spent most of my time finding pieces for Ash to place. She'd get so excited when she found one, and it made everyone laugh." The memory brings up feelings I thought I'd buried deep. "I haven't done a puzzle since."

She leans into me and lays her head on my arm. "That's sweet. I love how you take care of your sister."

"Yeah, it's funny. Xander and I competed a lot, fought like cats and dogs when we were young, but never with Ash. Not sure if it's the age difference or if she's so much like our mom, but we always knew she was to be treated with love and respect. Poor girl."

"Why do you say that?" She puts another puzzle piece down.

"We can be a little overbearing."

"Nooooo," she says sarcastically and giggles. "I've heard stories. Did you really punch Cole?"

"That wasn't me. It was Xander, and yeah, it's true. I'm more of a lover than a fighter." I wiggle my eyebrows at her. My reward for a touching story is a punch in the arm. To gain sympathy, I rub my arm to soothe the nonexistent pain. She's not phased.

She takes another bite of her ice cream and moves to her knees to reach for another piece. "Found it!" She gives herself a silent clap and bounces on her knees. "That one's been driving me crazy."

We stay like this for hours: telling stories and working on the puzzle together. She lets me put in the last piece, and I'm rewarded with another kiss. I'll never be able to separate the taste of caramel and vanilla from her.

Harper tries to hide her yawn, but it's no use. She can't hide anything from me. "It's getting late, and you should get some rest." I help her up from the floor and pull her into my arms. I need to tell her I'm her writing partner. She gave me so many opportunities, but I'm a coward.

I give Noodle a quick scratch behind his floppy ears and give her a quick, chaste kiss before I leave. Soon. I'll tell her soon.

CHAPTER
TWENTY-EIGHT

JULIAN

————

The Renegades have a rare day off in New York. They play New Jersey tomorrow, so a quick morning practice and then the city is theirs. I'm spending the day with Chance, and Harper is spending the day with Lawson. We're all having dinner later this evening. Resisting her will be a near impossible feat for me tonight, but I'll show restraint in front of her brother. She gets to control the narrative about us, and that includes telling him.

I know the second Chance arrives because my apartment immediately fills with chaos and love. It follows him wherever he goes. He's the most lovable guy you'll ever meet unless it's on the ice. Then all bets are off. But on solid ground, a total cinnamon roll kinda guy. He's a contradiction, like Harper. He's soft and gooey on the inside, but a bearded, gruff six-foot-three, broad-shoul-dered man on the outside. Maybe I'm a contradiction magnet?

"Hola, hombre!"

I turn to find my best friend behind me. He puts his long

arms around me and picks me up, squeezing so hard my back cracks. I laugh at his greeting because that's the only correct response when Chance enters the room. His belief and trust in me launched my business. His friendship makes me a better man. I miss my best friend, and after my emotional roller coaster last night, I'm grateful he's here.

"Still not bilingual." He puts me down, and I grip his bicep. "It's good to see you, buddy."

We settle in with junk food and catch up on life. Next thing we know, it's time to head to the restaurant.

"I can't wait to see Harps," Chance says. "It's been awhile. She's a really great girl."

"Uh, yeah. I know." I wince a little, ready for Chance to bust my balls. There's no way I can hide my attraction to her from him. He knows me better than anyone on this planet.

"Yeah, I guess you do. Hey, I meant to tell you Lawsy invited Burns tonight since he and Harper live together now. Have you met him?" Chance is chatting away as we walk down the sidewalk to the restaurant. It's faster to walk during this time of day, and it's only a few blocks away.

"We've met." Fuck. I still don't know what's going on with him, but the way she kissed me gives me hope she's into me and not him. She said she was a traditional-relationship girl, so I'm clinging to that. Well, Priscilla said that. Same thing, right? "What's the deal with them?" I try to sound casual, but Chance stops and looks at me. I school my face to look unaffected regardless of his answer.

He gives me his suspicious eye, shrugs, and continues walking. "You know Burns played with Lawson in Atlanta. Hell, Harper practically grew up with the team since Lawsy was both her guardian and team captain. I'm sure the lines blurred a lot, but he did the best he could. Harper's known Burnsy for years, so with the trade and all, it made sense."

Still not giving the answer I'm looking for, but her

upbringing around a hockey team reinforces her comfort with the Havoc players.

We make it to the restaurant, and the rest of our party is already here. They're tucked away in a large, round booth, giving us a little privacy. Harper is absolutely stunning, sitting between Zac and Lawson.

I shake hands with Lawson and sit next to him, leaving Chance by Zac. I have Harper directly in my line of vision. Exactly how I want it. The waiter is there to take our drink orders. "I'll have an Old Fashioned. Harper. Champagne?"

She nervously laughs, her cheeks flush as she glares at me. "No, thank you. Water is fine tonight." I enjoy teasing her. Zac puts his arm around the back of the booth, but I notice he's not touching her. He's fucking with me, too. The three of us are playing games, and Lawson and Chance are unwitting observers.

We order dinner and I'm disappointed Harper sticks to the menu. The conversation focuses on hockey and the game last night. Even though they play for opposing teams, they're still friends.

"Be honest. Who were you cheering for last night?" I enjoy watching her squirm.

All eyes shift to Harper, and she considers my question. "Well, I'm always team Cartwright, no matter what. But I'd hate to lose Noodle, so I'm a big Havoc fan now."

"CJ, I can't believe you like Noodle more than me." Zac pouts.

"I like Noodle more than most people, so don't take it personally," she quips.

Chance laughs, and for once, it irritates me.

"Is that anyway to treat your roommate?" Lawson chides. Roommate? Yes! Roommates. Dog walker. Not boyfriend.

"He's tough. He can take it," she says playfully. I reminisce about our kisses last night, and my jealousy eases. She's comfortable with him. He was Lawson's teammate. It's an unspoken rule you don't mess with a teammate's sister. Until you do. Zac Burns is more like a brother to her. But her teasing has kept me on my toes. I've enjoyed the chase, but I'm ready to catch her now.

"How's the NYU writing program going?" Chance asks.

I look at him in disbelief. How does he know about my writing? Oh, he's asking Harper. Everyone knows about her writing, except me. She hasn't really shared it with me, but that's one stone I can't throw since I haven't shared it with her either.

"I'm working under a deadline, so that's additional pressure, but it's good," Harper replies. "Almost fun." My head snaps to meet her gaze. She drops her eyes and studies the dessert menu.

"I think it's badass," Zac adds. "I can't believe she's writing a book about me." She elbows him in the ribs. "Hey, that hurt."

"It's not about you," she mumbles.

"It's about a handsome hockey player who's great in bed. Of course it's about me," he laughs. At this comment, Chance throws an elbow his way. "Hey, that really hurt."

"Goalies are only untouchable on the ice," Chance says. This time, Lawson laughs.

"Have you met your writing partner yet?" Lawson asks.

She digs in her purse, this conversation clearly making her uncomfortable. "Not exactly." She hides behind the menu, avoiding eye contact with me. She bites her bottom lip, and I want her teeth on me. This dinner, pretending like we are mere acquaintances, is killing me. I'm grateful Zac hasn't outed me, but I'm sure he has his reasons.

"I'm not a romance reader," Zac says. "But I'm looking forward to the love story of Gavin Snow. I mean, he's going to marry a girl he didn't knock up, and I want to know why. CJ says romance novels are practically instruction manuals for what women want, so I'll check it out." He laughs at his own joke.

"That's fascinating," I say, working to keep my face neutral while my heart is beating like I finished the New York Marathon.

"I hear that program is quite elite. You must be an amazing writer to be in it."

"She's gifted," Lawson chimes in, bragging about his sister. "Her first novel is brilliant. I've encouraged her to self-publish, but she insists it's not ready."

"You've written a novel?" That's another secret she's kept. Of course, I have no room to judge given the secret I'm holding on to.

She nods her head, still not looking at me.

"I'd love to read it." I mean it. Reading her book would give me insight into her creativity and her voice. I want to know everything about Harper Cartwright.

"Yeah, Julian's a big reader, and he loves romance books," Chance says. "He'd be a good person to give feedback."

"Maybe," she shrugs.

"Tell me about the book you're working on now," Chance continues, always the inquisitive one. "What's the main female character like?"

Her dark eyes are soft, so fucking gorgeous. She finally looks up, and our gazes lock. "She's just like me."

Fuck me. She knows.

"Check, please."

CHAPTER
TWENTY-NINE

HARPER

————

Well, it's out there. I knew the minute it clicked with him I know he's my anonymous writing partner. He tried to hide his reaction, and I'm sure no one else noticed. But I was looking for it. And for a brief second, I saw it. There was a panicked glimmer in his eye, but he hid it well.

After dinner, we said our goodbyes and went our separate ways. My hug with Lawson was too short and too tight. We had a great time today, but missing him is my new normal. The team is flying out after their game tomorrow. I might see him for a few minutes after the game, then I'm not sure when I'll see him again. The thought makes me a little sad.

Zac and I take a cab home, and once settled, he puts his arm around me and pulls me in. I'm confused until he says, "I know you miss Lawson. I'm not your big brother, but I'll do my best to be there for you like he would."

Everything hits me at once. Being with Lawson. Revealing my secret to Julian. I can't help but worry about his reaction and how it will affect our dynamic, both in our writing and personal lives. Zac has been incredibly sweet. All my emotions bubble to the surface, and I cry into his shoulder. He pulls me tight, kisses my head, and strokes my back.

"I've got you, Harper. I've got you." When he calls me Harper, it hits different. It's deeper. After a few minutes, I cry it all out. I'm sure I'm not the first crier this cab driver has seen today, but I feel better. And foolish. I wipe my eyes and pull away.

"Thanks, Zac. I appreciate everything you've done for me. I couldn't ask for a better friend in New York." A grin fills his face and his eyes light up.

"You and Decker going to the Renegades game tomorrow? Honestly, I'm a little surprised Decker hasn't been blowing up your phone now. Maybe he hasn't recovered from dinner." And that light feeling leaves in a rush. What is Zac talking about?

"Recovered from what?"

"CJ, I've never seen anyone use so much restraint to keep his eyes off of you. I'm telling you, he was working hard to stay casual. That guy's smitten."

I shake my head gently, trying to sort it all out. Now that our secret is out, how is this going to impact him? Is he still interested in me? I've done my part. The ball's in his proverbial court. I played my hand. Cards are all on the table. Well, most of them, anyway. I'll wait to hear from him. I check my phone in case. Nothing other than a new coupon for Bath & Body Works.

"Why didn't you out him? Tonight would be the perfect time to call him out in front of Lawson." Admittedly, I was worried he would, given their history.

"I told you. You're an adult, and I'm not reporting to Lawson. Am I still worried? Abso-fucking-lutely. But short of your bodily harm, I'm not telling him anything. I respect the hell out of that man, but he's not my captain anymore."

When he mentions Lawson not being his captain, it's another thing that chips away at my delicate emotional state. I hate that Lawson's lost his leadership role and his new jersey doesn't have his captain's C. At least he got to keep his number 96.

I've come to appreciate Zac so much more. He's a good guy, even if he is a fuck boy. He hasn't met that "different" girl yet. But he will. And I vow to walk beside him when he does because it's going to turn his world upside down.

The cab pulls up to our building, and I get out, followed by Zac. I hug him, and he pulls back and tucks my hair behind my ear. Worry crosses his face as he tries to manage my emotional roller coaster.

"Thanks, Zac. Your friendship means more than you know." I give him a playful shove. I'll always cheer for my brother, but I may have become a full-blown Havoc fan.

He laughs and throws his arm around me as we enter the building.

"CJ, you sure do like playing with fire, and I'm here for it. Just don't get burned."

"Well, let's hope I don't need to call New York's bravest, or that will be a whole new book I'd have to write." We both laugh as we go upstairs to get Noodle for his nighttime walk.

CHAPTER
THIRTY

JULIAN

———

I watch Zac and Harper embrace when they get out of the cab. Should I have gone home after dinner and planned how to approach this? Absolutely. Did I? Fuck no. We need to talk. I couldn't offer to take her home, or Chance and Lawson would know something's up. My confidence waivers as I watch this scene unfold on the sidewalk.

"Does it look like she's been crying? She looks like she's been crying." Kat, tilting her head, looks at me through the rear-view mirror, her expression unreadable.

"Are you asking me or talking out loud like a crazy person?"

Shit. I said it out loud. I've stalked her home, and now I'm sitting in my car watching her. Like a fucking crazy person. "What am I doing, Kat?" I exhale. I put my head in my hands and try to get a grip.

"What happened at dinner that would make her cry?" Kat asks. So she has been crying. Fuck.

"I don't know. There was lots of laughter, joking. Pretty lighthearted. Maybe it was hard for her to say goodbye to Lawson, but she'll see him tomorrow. I don't know what would make her cry. You don't think Zac did something, do you?" I swear if he hurt her, I'll kill him and throw his body in the East River.

"Doubtful. He's consoling her. What did you do?" She raises her eyebrow and glares at me.

She knows I haven't told her everything. Looking back at our conversations, she gave me the opportunity to tell her, but I didn't. I wonder how long she's known. Granted, I withheld the details, but I've never lied to her. But maybe this is good. We aren't hiding anymore. I can be vulnerable with her. Vulnerability is intimate. Sexy. Yeah. A spark of hope ignites.

"I didn't do anything. At least not intentionally." My voice fades as they come out of the building with Noodle. I'm glad to see Zac walks with her in the evenings when he's home. Or is it because she's upset? Or they're more? I'm questioning everything.

"Go home, Kat. I'm flying without a net here, and you don't need to see the carnage." I open the door to get out and meet the couple on the sidewalk.

Zac puts his arm out and pushes Harper behind him while Noodle licks my shoes. Two opposite reactions to my unexpected appearance. Harper's surprised look is a little more apprehensive than happy, and I feel responsible.

"Jesus, Decker, you scared the hell out of me," Zac says when he realizes it's me. I guess men jumping out of cars after dark in New York is suspect. Whoops.

I can't help but stare past him, my eyes fixated on Harper. She's hiding behind him, but I can see the corners of her mouth turn up.

Shifting my focus back on him, I put my hand on his shoulder. "Sorry, man. Thanks for watching out for her." I want to thank him for the way he protected her from a potential threat, but the look he's giving me says he knows.

With a desperate plea in my eyes, I look back at her, hoping she will hear me out. Forgive me. "Harper, can we talk?"

Zac and I wait for her answer. Whatever she says, we'll obey. This girl owns us both.

She bites her bottom lip while she's thinking and finally nods to herself. Decision made. "Sure, let's take Noodle for his walk."

Zac looks back and forth between us, doing his own assessment. "Yeah, I'll head back upstairs. Got your phone?" He's still in protection mode and, while I appreciate it, he doesn't have to protect her from me. Ever. She pulls it out of her back pocket as proof. He turns around, glances at Kat watching us from the car, and gives her a fuck-boy head nod. That's all it takes for her to drive off, and I'm officially on my own.

I take Noodle's leash from Zac, hold out my hand to her, and she accepts it. Her fingers intertwine in mine, her small hand fitting perfectly, despite the size difference. Okay, so far, so good. We walk to the park in silence. I'm taking this time to map out a plan, to decide where to even begin this difficult confession. Which I should have done before ambushing her on the sidewalk.

We walk around the circle of the small park in silence, allowing Noodle to do his business and sniff a spot every few feet or so. She must be growing impatient with me because she leads us over to a bench and sits. Noodle and I dutifully follow her. I put his leash between us, and she releases my hand to pick up the dog. He snuggles into her lap like it's his spot. She absently rubs his ears and waits for me to talk.

Taking a deep breath to steady my nerves, I start with a question. "So why Pricilla Jenkins?" I might as well acknowledge the proverbial elephant in the room.

"It's my mom's name. I wanted a way to keep her alive." Her gaze is sweet, wistful. The tender, sentimental pen name touches me deeply. It speaks volumes about her character. And I'm not surprised one bit. Family is everything to her.

I reach over and stroke her cheek, turning her head to look at me. Our eyes connect, and I think we'll be okay. I hope we'll be okay. "That's beautiful." With a gentle stroke of my thumb against her cheek, I watch as a blush slowly spreads, and she shyly lowers her eyes again. "You're beautiful." My desire to kiss her overwhelms me, but we need to talk first.

"How long have you known?" How much grace has she given me? How long did I think I was being stealthy when she already knew?

"I suspected pretty early on. Charlotte seemed, um, familiar." She looks down shyly and shrugs. While she has every right to be smug or angry, she's actually quite demure.

How many times did she ask me what she was to me? Fuck. A muse. In retrospect, I can't help but chuckle at that conversation. Her feisty response was a leather skirt and a hot first kiss.

"Are you mad at me for not telling you?"

She gently shakes her head no. "It seemed important for you to stay anonymous. I was hopeful you would tell me eventually." Her usual confident voice is timid, pensive, and my heart hurts hearing her this way. I can't stand my sassy girl sounding down.

"I'm sorry I didn't. It's not that I don't trust you. I do. Implicitly. And I would have. Told you, I mean. I, just." I pause to allow my resolve to settle as I let her in. "I needed to sort my head out about my reasons for keeping this secret buried deep. I'm very protective of my business and my reputation. They're intertwined in a way that's making me rethink a lot of things in my life."

"I get it." Sadness surrounds her. And I caused this. It's time to come totally clean. For us and for our book.

First, I need to know if she's sparing my feelings or deep down, she's angry, hurt even. Or disappointed. I give her a peck on her lips, and she doesn't slap my face. Doing good so far, Julian. It's time to keep going.

I sit up, shoulders back, ready to own this. "I'm glad you know. You're the third person on this planet holding the secret intel that I'm JB Moore." She knows how much this means to me, but I also want to stress I'm really serious about keeping my anonymity.

"Let me guess, Chance and Ashleigh?"

I chuckle at her logical choices. "Absolutely not. Chance can't keep a secret to save his life, and I couldn't take Ashleigh's ribbing. No, my editor, Casey Samuels, and Professor Daniels, although I'm still stumped at how they got that information." I'm awarded with another one of those surprised looks I crave. "And now you. It's a pretty elite group. Are you prepared to take this secret to your grave?" I'm teasing, kind of.

"Why the national-security-level secret? Are you ashamed or embarrassed?"

"What? No. Well, not ashamed." I put my face in my hands. Why is it so important that I keep this secret? "I don't know. I enjoy having a secret identity. Maybe? People think they know me, but they don't, not really. I'm an introvert going through life pretending to be an extrovert. And a closeted romance writer. But I'm my business, my brand. My agency is built on a perception, a reputation. Most of my athletes like the charming playboy image, so that's what I give them." I look at her to gauge her reaction. And she's smiling. She reaches out and runs her fingers through my hair, her touch slowing my racing heart. No wonder Noodle likes it so much.

"I won't tell a soul. I swear." She bites her bottom lip and asks, "Truth or dare?"

"Truth." I've revealed my darkest secret. I can't imagine what else I can share at this point. I'm belly up, all my weak spots exposed.

"Are you really a playboy, Julian Decker?"

A wicked smile fills my face. "Depends how you define playboy. Not everything is how it appears." I turn on my charm and hope it works.

"I don't know. It appears like you want to kiss me." Her

mood has improved dramatically, and a sparkle has returned to her eyes.

"And then again, some things are exactly how they appear."

I take her face in my hands and pull her to me, kissing her with everything I have. My mouth, my heart, my soul. My secret. It's all hers.

CHAPTER
THIRTY-ONE

HARPER

———

That kiss, electrifying and passionate, was the most amazing of my life; fireworks exploding behind my eyelids. It's all downhill from here because nothing, and I mean nothing, will ever top the way he caressed my face, teased my mouth with his tongue, and did things that made my heart flutter. Literally flutter. What kind of physical reaction is that? A holy fuck, this man is magical, I'll never be able to write a book boyfriend half this sexy, incredible man is what that is.

We pull apart, and he rests his forehead on mine.

"So, where do we go from here?" I ask.

"My place?" he asks hopefully. Leaning in, his lips brush mine with a feather-light touch, a warmth spreading through me that sends shivers down my spine. Tempting. Oh, so tempting.

Noodle squirms off my lap and I stand up. Our connection breaks, and my head clears a little. I want to continue this, whatever it is, with Julian, but how will it work with our project?

Does it complicate things? Or maybe we work closer, deeper, and it makes us better?

"Sorry, can't." I nod towards Noodle. "I mean, where do we go from here as writing partners?"

He shrugs. "We work together, but closer, in person, and maybe naked?" His ability to go from seduction to teasing is fascinating. I can't help but wonder how that translates into other areas.

I punch him in the arm as we walk back towards my place. "Do you have a one-track mind?"

His laughter fills the air as he throws his head back, unable to contain his amusement. "Absolutely. I'm daydreaming about Harper Cartwright every waking moment. And come to think of it, she's in my nighttime dreams too. So yeah, one hundred percent one track mind, gorgeous." He puts his arm around my waist and pulls me into him. He kisses my temple as we walk.

When we get to my building, he steps back, holding me at arm's length. I already miss the warmth of his embrace. I've obviously lost my mind because I should say yes instead of goodbye right now.

"You should save those lines for the book. But it'll be a short novella because the girl will be all in by chapter three."

"These aren't lines, Harper. It's like you opened my eyes to a whole new world, and I want it all." He looks at me with so much depth and sincerity, I can't help but believe him.

"I don't know what to do," I confess.

He pulls me into a hug. "Follow your heart." His breath tickles my ear and sends shivers down my spine. That's so Julian. He leads with his whole heart while I lead with my head. It's pretty funny how he brings out my romantic side, since I'm typically more practical and realistic. But he makes it easy for me to see the dreams, the possibilities.

He steps back, his tone all business. "I have a few meetings, and we have the game tomorrow night. I'll pick you up at five.

But then Saturday. You. Me. Charlotte. Gavin. All in one room. Hammering it out."

I quirk my eyebrow at him and try to look scandalized, but it doesn't work. Damn, I'm going to need fresh batteries again tonight.

"On laptops, silly," he chides. "It's time to move the story along, don't you think?"

He gives me a quick kiss and turns away before I can react. He walks down the street with his shoulders back, hands in his pockets, and I swear he's whistling.

Noodle pulls on the leash, trying to follow Julian, but I hold him back. As he looks up at me with sad eyes, I totally get how he feels.

"I know, buddy. Me too."

Upstairs, Zac's scrolling on his phone, SportsCenter the constant background noise in the apartment. I unclip Noodle's harness, and he scurries to his spot by his treat jar. This dog is spoiled, and I'm not discouraging his behavior.

I'm not discouraging Julian either. I can't help it. For some inexplicable reason, it makes me happy when he's happy. And seemingly, I make him happy. But my logical side is still skeptical. How do I follow my heart when logic tells me to be careful?

I'm lost in thought when Zac asks, "Everything alright with Decker?"

"Hm, yeah, fine." Still distracted, I head to my room. I wash my face, put on my pajamas, and wonder if Julian's home yet.

Truth or dare?

Which do you want?

Truth.

Truth it is. Shoot.

Why am I your muse?

I wait for a response, and it doesn't come. My mind races with different scenarios of why he's not answering. Why he wouldn't want to answer. I finish getting ready for bed and snuggle under the thick comforter. When I turn off my lamp, my phone lights up the room.

> Now I remember another reason I hate the subway. Bad cell service.

I appreciate the sacrifice he made to have this conversation with me tonight. Julian on the subway? He really must care about me.

> Truth? I was still reeling from bumping into you at NYU. You captured my attention, and I wanted to know more. You're gorgeous. Sexy. Smart. Witty. Kind. All the things a heroine should be. You got my writer brain going. I'm desperate to know more. Everything. But if the lines get blurred, tell me, and it's out. I care more about Harper than Charlotte.

Wow. I wasn't expecting that. I close my eyes and reflect on everything he's said about me. To hear how he sees me is flattering and, well, I need to sit in that for a minute.

> Hey, you still there?

Yeah.

> Did I scare you?

A little.

> Listen to your heart, gorgeous.
>
> It's time for you to be the main character in this story.

CHAPTER
THIRTY-TWO

JULIAN

———

My last call of the day went longer than it needed to, and now I'm late for my date with Harper. Running on Julian time is nothing new, but I want to be punctual tonight. It's important. She's important.

As I walk out of my office, Violet hands me a black bag from the NHL store. "Thanks Violet. I appreciate your help in making this happen. You're doing great. Enjoy your weekend." I appreciate the extra tissue paper and bow she added to make the gift more special. Maybe Violet will work out after all.

When we pull up to Harper's building, she's waiting outside. She looks amazing in figure-fitting jeans and a simple button-down shirt and sweater. There seem to be two camps when it comes to female hockey fashion. They either dress to impress or they dress to cheer. Harper is the fan type, and I like that about her. What I don't like is her waiting on the New York sidewalk.

"What are you doing out here?" When she narrows her eyes at me, I realize I sound harsher than I intended. I do my best to recover from my mistake. "I don't want you getting cold." Holding her by her shoulders, I press my lips against her forehead. It's a greeting, far too tame for my liking, but we're short on time.

"You said you were running late, and I didn't want you to have to wait on me." She offers a slight shrug, her eyes kind, and I feel the warmth of her forgiveness wash over me.

I pinch her chin between my fingers and make her look at me. It takes everything I have not to get lost in her dark eyes. "Gorgeous, I'd wait a lifetime for you."

She rolls her eyes at me and groans. "Save the words for the page."

"But did they make you swoon?"

She shoves at my shoulder. "Absolutely not."

Forget being late. That needs to be fixed immediately. I lean down to give her a simple, sweet kiss, but one taste of her lips, and my mouth has a different idea. She tastes like peppermint and happiness. I lose myself in her for a moment when a short honk gets my attention. I glance at Kat, and she taps her watch. Shit. Right. We're late.

"Not even a little?" I tease.

"Maybe a little."

I laugh as the lie leaves her lips. A little, my ass. I lead her to the car, and we settle in for the short ride to Penn Station.

"How was your day? Any good drama?" She's always hungry for the latest celebrity news.

"Not really. Mostly boring contract negotiations. Nothing as exciting as seeing you tonight." I tuck a strand of hair behind her ear. "My god, you're amazing."

"Please, stop." She's not convincing me.

My warm breath ghosts over her skin as I lean in, whispering secrets into her ear, the scent of her perfume filling my senses. "I will never stop telling you how incredible you are, Harper." A blush creeps onto her cheeks, a rosy hue spreading as she reacts to my words, her eyes lowering with shyness. I fucking love it.

I reach behind us and grab the bag. "I got you a little something for tonight."

Her eyes light with excitement, and I'm gifted with one of her surprised looks. "Is this?"

I shrug. "Open it."

She pulls out the Lawson Cartwright Renegades jersey, and her high-pitched squeal frightens Kat. I laugh at both their reactions. Harper lovingly runs her fingers over the name on the back and then tightly hugs the jersey to her chest. "Thank you, thank you, thank you." She kisses my cheek several times. "You have no idea how much this means to me."

"I'm getting an idea." She bounces with joy at my quiet chuckle.

"Look away," she orders as she tosses her cardigan and unbuttons her shirt. Always the gentleman, I comply. Thankfully, the heavily tinted windows prevent anyone from seeing Harper without a shirt on. Although I try to look away, I see her reflection in the window, and I can't help but lick my lips at the tease of her perky breasts in a lacy pink bra. She tosses her shirt over the seat and covers up in the red jersey.

Her arms wrap around my waist, and she presses her cheek against my shoulder. "You make my heart flutter." Her whispered confession wraps around my heart.

"Same, gorgeous. Same."

"We're here," Kat announces. Harper looks around, confused.

"That didn't take long. I thought we were going to New Jersey?" Her face is a mask of confusion as she tries to figure out our location.

"We are. Traffic is a bitch, and Kat has a date, so we're taking the train." Introducing her to different parts of New York is one of my favorite things to do. Today, it's Penn Station and a quick train ride across the river.

"I thought you hated the subway?"

"Yep, not a fan. But this is different. Come on." She lets me take her hand, and we make our way to the track as they announce boarding. Several people are wearing hockey jerseys, but Harper's Renegade jersey stands out. She's entering enemy territory, but I'll be by her side the entire evening.

We're rink side again, and when Chance and Lawson come out on the ice for warmups, Harper jumps up and cheers for them. There's no swarm of Havoc players vying for her attention. Tonight, she's all about her brother. She values family, and that's another thing that makes us compatible. Family means everything to me.

Our popcorn is sitting on the ledge in front of us while Harper snaps pictures on her phone. Chance slams against the glass, popcorn flies into my lap, and her laugh fills the arena. Lawson slams into him, and she laughs harder. Seeing her happy is becoming my new kink.

"Glad you could make it," Chance shouts at me through the glass. "Why aren't you wearing my jersey?" He pokes his lip out in a pout.

"You don't pay me enough for that!" He kisses the glass in front of me, and his lip prints are in my line of sight. Great, I'll have to look at them the entire game. What a loveable asshole.

Harper loops her arm around mine, and Chance arches his eyebrow. I shrug, pretending I don't know what's going on.

The Renegades dominate tonight, and New Jersey isn't happy about being down four goals on their home ice. They're pounding on Chance and Lawson pretty hard, but it only increases their chirping and smack talk. When Jack Houston checks Chance into the glass right in front of us, I wince at the hit. That had to hurt. But at least the lip prints are finally gone. My best friend's face is pressed firmly against the glass, and Harper smacks the glass and yells at them. I swear I see them smile as they skate away.

"He's so hot," Harper says when she sits back in her seat.

"Who? Chance?" I may have to rethink my friendship with the loveable and handsome hockey player.

"No silly, Jack. He's the king of the hockey thirst traps." Jack

Huston is media gold and I'm not surprised Harper follows him. He's got a new viral video every week, ranging from his snappy media clips to his shenanigans with his brother.

I roll my eyes and pretend to ignore her. That lasts until she puts her hand on my thigh. Nope. Not ignoring her anymore. I lace my fingers with hers and give her hand a squeeze. She wants thirst traps? I'll send her some of me. There's no denying I want all of her attention directed at me.

Lawson is cooling off in the penalty box, and Harper watches him with an eagle eye, not missing a thing. "I was worried Lawson would miss his team in Atlanta, but he's having a good time."

"Appears that way." The clock ticks down, and the game ends in a Renegades victory. Lawson is awarded the number one star of the game.

"Come on, want to see him before they leave?"

"I didn't get credentials." She looks sad and I need to turn that frown upside down.

"I got you, gorgeous. Let's go."

I give her a tap on the nose. When Frankie told her I was the one to get sports tickets, she didn't fully understand the implication. I can get her access and tickets to any team, anywhere. Being the number one sports agent in the country isn't usually that big of a flex, but I'm about to use it.

CHAPTER
THIRTY-THREE

HARPER

He takes me by the hand and walks us through checkpoints and doors like he owns the place, not a lanyard, credential, or ID shown.

"How do you do it?" I shouldn't be amazed or shocked anymore, but I am. Doors are literally opened for him. This guy is connected. Sports. Hollywood. It's like I'm hanging out with the quarterback and prom king. It's an unfamiliar feeling because I wasn't that girl back in the day. My high school days were full of new surroundings, grief, and trying to hide from the world. I talked to my therapist more than anyone and, well, that didn't make me the popular girl.

"Do what? Because I'd prefer to show you rather than tell you." His breath tickles my ear and goosebumps cover my arms at his innuendo. I feel the heat fill my face and I'm sure I'm blushing.

I slap his arm in fake admonishment. We approach a door that says *Credentials only* where two burly guys block the access.

"Hey guys, sorry about the loss tonight," Julian says as he approaches.

The taller of the two responds. "Happens." He half shrugs. "At least it wasn't the Kings. Those assholes destroy a locker room when they win."

Julian chuckles. "Sounds about right. Hey, this is Cartwright's little sister, Harper. She wants to see him before he leaves."

The other guard gives a skeptical appraisal as he looks me up and down, his eyes focusing on my jersey. "He kicked our ass." He crosses his arms, blocking our entrance. His kind eyes soften his tough-guy act.

"Sorry, kinda." I smile sweetly, batting my eyelashes.

Julian chides me. "No, you aren't."

"He's still doing media, but you know the way," the shorter guard tells Julian as he opens the door. His heavy New Jersey accent makes me giggle.

We walk down a back hallway past several doors that go to training rooms and offices. As we walk past the Demons' dressing room, I'm surprised to hear music and laughter. They lost a game, but spirits seem to be high. Is that Jack singing some country song about breaking hearts? That guy is adorable. I can't wait to check my social media feeds to see if I'm right.

"Rather go in there?" Julian asks, quirking his eyebrow at me and bumping shoulders.

I smile and take his arm. "I've got more than I can handle right here."

We take another turn and are outside the visiting Renegades dressing room. The beats are pumping when Julian cracks the door open. With that smack down of a win, I'm not surprised.

"Wait here. I'll let Lawson know where to find you. You okay for a minute?" He looks up and down the hall, but we're alone.

"Yeah, fine, thanks." I've spent more hours than I can count waiting in arena hallways like this. Does Julian think this is new for me, or is he being polite?

My phone vibrates in my bag, and I pull it out to find a text from Zac.

> Going out with the boys. You're invited when you get back to the city.

> I'm tired, but enjoy yourself and I'll take care of Noodle.

> Is the girl you gave Harvard's number to psycho?

> I don't think so.

> Too bad. HAHAHA

"At least you're dressed appropriately tonight." Lawson picks me up and swings me around. He's still in his sweaty gear, and between his skates and pads, he's a giant.

"Eww, you stink" I squirm out of his arms. He kisses me on my head and gives me a Lawson look of approval.

"Hey, I'm glad I could see you tonight before we head out. I miss you, Harps. But you seem okay. You're okay, right?" He gives me his caring-brother stare, and I ignore the sweat and smell for another hug. He spent half the day yesterday asking me the same thing.

"I'm good. Really. You seem to be bonding with your new team."

"Yeah, it's a change, but they're good guys. They haven't hazed me or anything." Lawson is one of the most respected guys in hockey. I'm sure the younger guys are excited to play with him and learn from one of the greats. "I'm glad you weren't alone tonight. You and Decker seem more friendly since last night." He's questioning me, and rightfully so. Thank goodness he's letting me talk instead of his usual overprotective inquisition.

I look down and consider how I want to answer that when the devil himself steps out of the dressing room. "Hey gorgeous,

I see you found him. Great game, man. You were on fire." Julian is all calm and relaxed as I'm twisted up trying to decide how to answer Lawson's question.

Julian reaches for my hand, and I glance at Lawson's face. He's watching every move.

"Um, thanks. What's going on here?" Lawson isn't upset. I'd describe it as confused, with a sprinkle of uncertainty thrown in for good measure.

"Yeah, well." I stumble over my racing thoughts. I'm not sure what to say. What is going on with us?

"Well, we've been hanging out a little, and honestly, I'd like it to be more," Julian says matter-of-factly. Has he lost his mind? My brother is still hyped on adrenaline and carrying a hockey stick. He could kill him. Julian looks at me for approval and I'm stunned. He squeezes my hand, signaling he's not done. "We're friends for now. But Harper calls the shots. She knows where I stand." Julian leans in, and Lawson mirrors the movement. "She's amazing."

Lawson looks between the two of us, processing what he said. "You like him?"

That's a loaded question. My gaze falls on Julian, and the familiar warmth of affection blooms into an uncontrollable smile. I look at Lawson and give him a playful half shrug. "He's alright." Both men laugh at my horrible attempt at lying.

"Well, good luck," he says to Julian. "She is amazing." He looks at me and says, "And you know what to do." I'm a little shocked and slightly disappointed there's no macho bullshit threat of *you hurt my sister, I'll kill you*. I know what to do. Do I? Is that the *call me, and I'll kill him* message? Is it the follow your head, not your heart advice? Is he telling me to be careful? What do I know to do? I want to ask him what that means when he's called into the dressing room.

"I gotta run." He leans down and gives me a hug and a kiss on the cheek. "I love you, Harps. I'll call you tomorrow." My first question tomorrow will be clarity on what the hell *I know what to do* means.

I hold on a little longer, ignoring the sweat and smell. "Love you too."

He holds his hand out to Julian. "Good seeing you, Decker. Treat her well."

Julian shakes his hand. "I intend to. Stay safe." Lawson nods and goes into the locker room, where he's greeted with a hero's welcome.

I turn to Julian and slap him on the chest. "What the hell was that?!?!" I'm not sure if I'm angry, confused, or scared, but whatever I'm feeling, it's all Julian.

He takes my hand and holds it against his heart. "What? Am I a dirty little secret you wanted to keep hidden? Are you ashamed of me? Was I supposed to ask permission to date you? What was I supposed to do?" His teasing makes me question what I wanted him to say or do. I get lost looking into his mischievous blue eyes.

I give up. "Come on, I'm gonna let you take me home." I go to walk back the way we came, and he stays in place. "What?"

"I meant everything I said. I want to be your friend. I mean, we're already friends, but I want more than that, but it's your call. You set the pace here. But I'm ready to move our story along. I'm not much of a slow-burn guy." Obviously.

Open communication and maturity from a guy isn't something I'm used to. Most of the guys I've dated leave me dissecting every sentence, weeding out the subtle gaslighting, and psychoanalyzing their intent. Then I agonize over what I could have done differently, leaving me emotionally drained. This straight shooting is refreshing. And off putting. I'm unsteady as I navigate these unfamiliar waters, but I'm excited about where this is heading.

CHAPTER
THIRTY-FOUR

HARPER

_____

It's hot in here, and I kick at the comforter and only to find myself twisted in the sheets, Noodle snuggled into my side. My foggy morning brain processes last night. I must have tossed and turned more than usual to be in this tangled mess.

Julian told Lawson we're friends. And last night proved that. On the way home, we talked about everything from dream vacations to the best television series endings. I said it was *The Good Place*, and I stand by it. Julian insisted it was *Breaking Bad*. Our lively debate ended in a compromise. We'll both watch the shows and revisit our decisions at a later date. But I know he'll come around to my side.

I enjoyed last night because it was real. A regular date, of sorts. Or at least I'm calling it a date. Life isn't always fancy restaurants and chauffeured cars. At least mine isn't. Sometimes it's hotdogs and hockey games.

I complete my morning routine, my mind racing with anticipation for the weekend. We agreed to work on our book today, but didn't make any firm plans. Dressing in yoga pants and an oversized sweatshirt, I look up a yoga class to clear my head. I need to have my wits about me if I'm spending time with Julian today. One look into his baby blues and I'm a goner. For us to work on our project, I need to stay focused and resist his charms.

Julian said he's ready to move the story along. I wasn't sure if he was talking about us or the book, but after some very vivid dreams, I'm ready to give Julian more of me. Maybe all of me.

When I leave my bedroom, I'm surprised to find Zac and Julian in the kitchen. I check my watch because there's no way they are both here looking like *GQ* models before nine o'clock.

"Look who I found waiting in the lobby," Zac says in way of a greeting. Lobby? Is he just getting home?

"Good morning to you too," I say.

Noodle trails behind me, smells both guys, and makes his way back to me.

"I can't believe you stole my dog," he mumbles.

"Do you blame him?" Julian says.

"Fuck no," Zac replies.

"What are you doing here?" I ask Julian.

"I came to kidnap you and Noodle today," he says casually. Whether it was the word kidnap or Noodle, Zac scowls at him.

I'm not sure how to reply when Zac pipes in. "I'm leaving for a three-game road trip this afternoon." He lowers his voice when he asks, "Are you going to be okay?" He's left me alone before, so I'm not sure why he's asking. Except that was before Julian showed up to kidnap me.

I give him my best morning smile and take his hand. "I'll be fine. I promise."

"I'll take good care of them," Julian says from behind Zac.

Zac scoffs and turns his attention back to me. "By the way, thanks for keeping my reputation alive." He puts me in a head-lock and rubs my scalp with his knuckles. I'm laughing too hard to push away, but I see movement out of the corner of my eye.

"What reputation is that?" I laugh as I try to wiggle out of his grip.

He releases me and I notice Julian's hand is on Zac's shoulder. A gentle warning. He drops his hand when I'm free.

"You told that puck bunny I rubbed my noodle every night," he says with a glimmer in his eye. "I told her how much you love my noodle, and her friend left me without a satisfying end." At that statement, I punch him in the stomach, hard. I pull my hand away and shake it out. It's like hitting a brick wall. His laughter fills the kitchen. "CJ, I thought you learned the last time." He pulls me in again, kisses my head, and walks past me, headed to the bedrooms.

Noodle circles around my feet, signaling he's ready to go out. I reach for his leash, and Julian puts a cup in my hand instead.

"Here, I got this for you. I remember you don't drink coffee and felt hot chocolate was a little too much in the morning, so I gambled on tea."

"Thank you." I inhale the comforting aroma of Earl Grey tea and sigh. There's a hint of lavender and milk. How did he guess a London Fog is my favorite morning drink?

Julian gathers Noodle's leash and clips it to his collar. "I'll take him out while you pack up. Get everything you need to write, Noodle's food and necessities, and an overnight bag if you want." He wiggles his eyebrows suggestively, and I laugh. "We'll be back in a few minutes. Come on, Noodle. You're gonna love Central Park." He gives me a quick kiss on the cheek, and he and Noodle are out the door while I stand processing my unexpected morning.

I go to my room and grab my laptop, notebook, my favorite pens, and throw them in a large tote. I don't need much for overnight if it goes that way, but I grab a change of clothes and my travel toiletries just in case. Packing up Noodle takes a little more thought, but I'm done before they return.

"I was a little surprised to see him downstairs when I got home this morning," Zac plops on the couch.

"Yeah, I bet."

"Would have thought he'd be in your bed."

I turn on my heel and give him an are-you-judging-me-look.

"Don't look at me like that," he chuckles. "I didn't give him enough credit. He's good."

"What the hell does that mean?" I glance at the half-opened front door. He'll be back any minute, but I'm curious what Zac means by that comment.

"He's playing the long game. Admirable but risky."

"What are you talking about? He's not playing a game."

"Sure he is, CJ. I told you, he's crazy. Hell, he's even willing to pick up dog shit for you." He turns the TV on and flips to the sports channel.

"He's a nice guy, Zac. Maybe you should try it sometime." I say it with more bite than I mean, but I don't need him planting doubts in my head. I have enough confusion as it is.

"Hey, I'm a nice guy." I've hit a soft spot and feel a little guilty.

"I don't think you're qualified to give relationship advice. I mean, what was her name last night?"

"Henry."

"What?" I'm confused. I thought for sure he was with another random woman. Not that I'm judging. Well, not exactly.

"We were out at The Great One. Henry met up with that bunny you gave his number to. I was chatting it up with her friend, and Shelley walked in wearing some guy like a second skin."

"Who's Shelley?"

"My ex," he mumbles under his breath as hurt fills his face. My irritation dissipates, and I join him on the couch.

"The dog walker? The one who moved to Brooklyn?" I take his hand in mine and give it a little squeeze.

"Yeah. Maybe I'm not totally over her." He exhales and looks at me with the saddest expression I've ever seen. "I'm not sure if she saw me, but I saw her. I went back to Henry's and crashed there." He sighs. "I thought you would have company." He looks at the completed puzzle on the coffee table from the other night and laughs. "Yeah, he's good." I disregard his assessment of Julian. He doesn't get it.

I lay my head on his shoulder. "We're friends," I tell him as Julian knocks and opens the door all the way, Noodle running toward us. "There's my best buddy," I say as Noodle runs up his ramp to get on the couch and jumps on me, his leash trailing behind.

CHAPTER
THIRTY-FIVE

JULIAN

————

Her head is on his shoulder. "We're friends," she says as I open the door. The cozy scene I walked into makes me uneasy, but I need to keep my cool. I trust her with my secret. I can trust her with whatever this is, right? "There's my best buddy," she says to Noodle. Well, at least she's talking about the dog and not me. Being her best buddy is not at the top of my list.

"He chased a squirrel, but it didn't end well." I try to assess what's going on between them. In the kitchen, they behaved like siblings, but this is a little more intimate.

She jumps away like a kid getting caught with their hand in the candy jar. I stay poker-faced so she doesn't freak out about my lack of trust in her. I trust her. I do. But I'd prefer her to tell me where I stand with her.

"Did you chase a squirrel?" She takes his face and rubs her nose against his. "You silly boy."

"I can't believe you stole my dog," Zac says to himself.

"This conversation isn't over," she says to Zac. Apparently, I interrupted them. "Are you okay if Noodle and I go on an outing today?"

"Sure, I'm headed to the rink shortly. Back late Tuesday night." He gives his dog a scratch near his tail, and his entire body wiggles.

"I have a bag each for me and Noodle," she says to me. "Is that okay?"

"Sure, bring anything you need. Kat's waiting downstairs."

"Oh, I'll hurry." She hops up and rushes down the hallway.

"No rush," I yell after her.

Zac turns to me and stares me down like he would during a penalty shot. "Hey man, when you break her heart, can you try to time it when I'm home? It might be above Noodle's paygrade." I glance down the hall where she disappeared. Is that what they were talking about?

"Breaking her heart is not on my to do list." Why does he assume I'll hurt her? Is that what he's worried about? If anything, I'm the one at risk of being destroyed.

She appears at the top of the hall with a heavy bag draped over her shoulder. "Here, let me take that." I reach for her bag, and when I look down, I see her laptop and a hint of black lace tucked in the pocket. I stifle a grin, because it seems I'm not alone in my desire to move forward. My imagination runs wild with possibilities.

"Noodle's bag is in the kitchen." I grab it and have both arms filled with everything to have a sleepover. And if we don't have what we need, I'll buy it.

Harper takes Noodle's leash and opens the door. "Stay safe. Let me know if you need anything," she calls out to Zac.

"I will."

We head to the elevator, Noodle leading the way.

"He seems excited," I comment.

"Um, yeah."

"You seem distracted. Everything okay?"

"Fine, I just," she lowers her eyes and focuses on Noodle.

"Look, if you don't want to do this, say so. You don't have to..."

"No, no." She fervently shakes her head. "God no. I'm fine. I've had more human interaction before nine o'clock than usual." She sighs, and I relax because she still wants to do this. I worry I'm coming on too strong.

"Got it. Not a morning person. Need more caffeine?"

"Maybe." She bites her lip, and I can practically see the wheels turning as she processes her next thought. "I'm slow to get moving in the morning. I don't understand those hop-out-of-bed-to-conquer-the-day-types. So, are you one of those?" Her shy smile tugs at my heartstrings and ties them in knots. I find her blend of bashfulness and boldness endearing. She's complex and completely unpredictable and I love how she keeps me on my toes.

"Only where you're involved. I showed restraint this morning, or I would have been here much earlier. So not a morning-orgasm girl. Got it." I'm not sure if her head shake is in disbelief or disapproval. Either way, she's adorable as her blush colors her cheeks. I can't contain my pleasure that I can do that to her.

Downstairs, Kat takes the bags and puts them in the back. Noodle looks up at the SUV with skepticism. Given that he needs a ramp to access the couch, even Noodle knows it's not possible for him to attempt jumping into the car. With complete resignation, he plops down on the sidewalk. Unlike me, he concedes to an impossibility when he sees one.

Harper leans down to pick him up, and they get in the car. Noodle settles comfortably on her lap, and she absently pets his head. Is her hesitation really that she's not a morning person or she uncertain about me? Us?

I lean over and give her a quick kiss to test the waters after my orgasm comment.

"I apologize. I haven't given you a proper good-morning greeting." The kiss is sweet, gentle, innocent.

An evil grin slowly fills her face. "You call that proper?" She reaches out and puts her arm around my neck and pulls me in, giving me a kiss that is anything but sweet. This kiss feels like a promise of what's to come. Maybe she's a morning girl after all.

Noodle's bark brings a giggle to her lips, and I reluctantly let her go. I meant it when I said I wanted to work on the book. It's important to me she understands I want more than to get her in my bed. Although, to be fair, I definitely want her in my bed.

We get to my place where Noodle acts like the king of the city, making friends with everyone he meets. Well, almost everyone. You know who doesn't like Noodle? Digsby. We meet Mrs. Dilworth in the lobby, and she is practically salivating to meet Harper. The introductions are short-lived when Digsby smells Noodle's noodle. Damn, even dogs deserve consent. After a quick apology, we rush upstairs and double over, laughing when we enter the apartment.

I give Harper time to get settled and comfortable. She puts Noodle's food and water in the kitchen and feeds him several treats. He's snoring in his bed before I can even comment.

"He's had a big day."

"Apparently," I chuckle. "How about you, gorgeous? What can I do for you?" I pull her into my arms, liking the way she feels tucked into me. Being with her is as natural as breathing.

With her cheek on my chest, I just stare, she looks so content. Wrapping her arms around my waist, she leans in, shutting her eyes as if savoring the moment. I could stay like this all day.

I give her a quick kiss on the top of her head. "Let's get some writing done. Then maybe we can go to the park this afternoon." If I kiss her on the lips, we'll never get any writing done.

She releases me and looks around. "Where do you usually work? Dining room table? Couch? Counter? Office?"

"All of the above. What's going to work for you?"

"Normally, I'm a kitchen-counter girl, but I can't put my back to this gorgeous view." She walks over to the French doors and opens them to the balcony. The cool fall breeze blows in, giving me chills. Not sure if it's the cool air or Harper that has my body humming.

While she's enjoying the view, I move the bar stools to the other side of the counter so she can look outside. Win-win. I slip into my office and grab my laptop, and when I come back to join her, she's already typing away.

Our morning continues like that. Both of us typing, collaborating, reading, laughing. I make more progress in a few hours than I have in weeks. Harper is a talented writer, and her words flow with ease and elegance. At some point, she migrated to the reading chair and set up a cocoon of pillows and blankets. She's made it her writing place. We complete several chapters and at this pace, we'll finish well ahead of the deadline.

"It's time for the s-e-x chapter," Harper announces. Her hair is down from the clip, and she's hiding her gorgeous face behind her curtain of hair.

I kneel next to her and tuck her hair behind her ear. "Are you blushing?" My thumb brushes along her cheek and the pink rises.

"No, I mean, I don't know." She shakes her head, her eyes looking anywhere but at me.

"Harper, look at me." I put my fingers below her chin and lift her eyes to mine. Her doe-eyed shyness is adorable. I like this almost as much as her surprised look. "If at any point I make you uncomfortable, promise you'll tell me." She gives me a little nod. "Now here's what I suggest. Let's both write this chapter, and we'll read them and decide which point of view we want to use. How does that sound?"

She bites her bottom lip while she considers my words, and it's taking every bit of willpower I have not to kiss her, take her to my bedroom, and work out the sex scene in real life. But Harper still isn't ready for that, and I mean every word I say to her. I want her to always feel comfortable with me.

"Okay."

Good girl. "Okay. Are you ready to do that now, or do you

want to take a break? We can grab some lunch and take Noodle for a walk." At the mention of his name, he wanders over to us and jumps up, trying to get to Harper.

My phone vibrates, and when I pull it from my pocket, Harper glances at the name. By the look on her face, I imagine she's picturing me with other women. "I'm going to take this call while you decide what you want to do." I answer the call on speaker because I want to be transparent. I want her to see me for who I really am, not some playboy.

"Maddie, how are you?"

I'm greeted with a dramatic sigh. "Jet lagged. This press junket is exhausting. I just flew back from London, and man, are my arms tired." Her laughter gets Harper's attention.

I roll my eyes. Even though she can't see me, Harper can. "Your jokes never get better. Hey, while I'm thinking about it, thanks for the restaurant recommendation in SoHo. We loved it."

Harper looks up at me with that surprised look again. Maddie is Madelyn Reynolds, Hollywood It-Girl. She's also an old college friend. We dated for a few months before graduation, but we were better friends than lovers and besides, I didn't want to move to California. We've stayed friends all these years, and she's currently engaged to a reality-TV producer.

"Isn't it simply divine? I knew you'd love the Old Fashioned. The food was amah-zing."

Shaking my head at the way she knows my drink of choice and weakness. "I wasn't aware you ate food anymore. I read you had an eating disorder or something."

"Gotta watch this girlish figure." Her teasing lilt fills the room.

"Hell, I thought vampires only drank the blood of virgins." That gets me another laugh.

"Like I could find one of those in LA. I'd starve."

Now I laugh. "How's fiancé Frank?"

"It's Fredrick, and stop acting like you don't know his name," she scolds. "He wants me to ask you to reconsider *The Bachelor*.

He'll meet all your demands, and you can screen the girls before production."

"No can do, Mads. Tell Frank I'm flattered, but no with a capital N-fucking-O."

She sighs. "Fine, I want you to find a nice girl. Chance isn't a substitute, you know."

"Don't worry about me. He's not my type." I glance at Harper and catch her watching. She quickly looks down and types franticly. I'm dying to see what she's writing.

"Fine. Listen, I need four basketball tickets for tonight. Freddie is trying to land some rapper for a new series, and his sources struck out. I told him I might know a guy." Her giggle makes me shake my head at her lack of subtlety.

"Courtside?"

"You're the best! Love you J. Come see me soon, K? Bye." Conversation ended.

It takes one text, and minutes later, I've secured four courtside tickets. I send the link to Maddie and get a screen full of kiss emojis.

I stand behind Harper and put my hands on her shoulders, peeking at her mostly blank screen. She still has a search tab open for Madelyn Reynolds, and I can't help but feel satisfied that she's jealous. That's a good sign.

She snaps her laptop closed. "Let's take a break. I'm starving."

CHAPTER
THIRTY-SIX

HARPER

———

"How do you know Madelyn Reynolds?" Balancing Noodle's leash in one hand and holding Julian's hand in the other, we make our way to the lunch spot. These two guys keep my nervous fidgeting at bay. I don't want to sound jealous, but call me curious.

"She's an old college friend." That conversation sounded more than casual acquaintance.

"Did she date Chance?" She mentioned him, so she maybe that's how they met.

"No, we dated for a few months senior year, but she was made for Hollywood. She's a sweet girl. A serial romantic. This is her fifth or sixth engagement, but she's never married. I give her shit and never bother to learn their names."

I'm amused and concerned at the same time. Julian, no J, dated Madelyn Reynolds. Mads. He's had the most desirable women in America on his arm. I can't figure out what he wants with me. I try to drop his hand, and he tightens his grip.

"Have I told you how adorable you are when you're jealous?"

"What?" I sputter. "Why would I be jealous?"

"That's what I want to know. Because gorgeous," he says as he stops in the middle of the sidewalk and steps in front of me. "You have nothing to be jealous of. You shine brighter than the biggest star in Hollywood. Baby, you have me wrapped around your finger." He cups my cheek and gives me the sweetest kiss. Can this guy be for real?

"Come on, I need to see what you do with this menu." He tugs me down the sidewalk, and we enter a casual neighborhood cafe. They've got outdoor seating with heaters, so we sit on the patio with Noodle.

My phone vibrates when Lawson calls, and I'm transported back to our conversation at the rink last night. I decline the call and send him a text, letting him know I'll call him later. Another errant thought I want an answer to pops into my head. "Why did you tell Lawson about us yesterday?"

"I'm not going to ask permission to court you like it's the nineteenth century, but he deserves to know I'm interested. It's not right if he finds out about us from someone else. I'm sorry if you wanted to tell him." Would I have told him? Eventually. Maybe. Probably. I appreciate Julian isn't hiding me, but it feels a little soon.

"I can imagine you in turn-of-the-century garb. You'd make a hot Bridgerton brother." I put my hand to my chest and pretend to swoon.

"For your information, I happen to like regency romance. Not the part where women are married off like property, but the formality and tension. It's hot." He says that without breaking eye contact. He's dead serious.

I look around to see if they can turn the heaters down because it's a bit warm out here. His genuine laughter only encourages my blush.

After amusing him throughout lunch with my menu adaptations, we take Noodle for a walk through Central Park. His little legs work double time to keep up with us, and he tires quickly. You want to know what actually makes me swoon? It's when Julian picks him up and carries him home. It's incredibly sexy how he cares for others, even Noodle. Being with Julian makes my stress melt away and I'm relaxed. He's got me completely spellbound.

We arrive back at the apartment, and Noodle collapses beside his bowl with a dramatic flourish. Although typically midafternoon is prime writing time for me, I'm not in the mood for it. My creative juices are flowing, but the keyboard is the last thing I want to put my fingers on. I'm in the mood for Julian.

"What do you want to do?" I ask innocently. I hope he's on the same page.

He looks at me, swallowing hard, and I celebrate that he's thinking what I'm thinking. Yes!

"Let's do a writing sprint. Thirty minutes. We'll both write the next chapter and then swap." I'm astonished at his suggestion, and not in a good way. That's what the practical me would have said if I wasn't trying to follow my heart. A writing sprint?

Sure, writing sprints are fun. You let the stream-of-consciousness flow. No worrying about the right word, punctuation. The focus is getting the words on the page. As a perfectionist, I've never let anyone read a sprint, so I'm a little hesitant.

"Nervous?" he asks.

"No, why would I be nervous?" I put on an air of fake confidence. I'm always self-conscious when someone reads my writing. That's one reason I haven't published yet.

He chuckles. "I'm setting the timer for thirty-five minutes. I'll give you a few minutes to get settled. And go!"

I dash to the comfortable reading chair I've claimed as my writing spot. I have a lap desk and lots of pillows. I snuggle in and wake my laptop up. I reread where I left off and gasp. Shit. Julian's laugh fills the apartment.

"Tick-tock, gorgeous," he teases. I close my eyes and take a deep breath. I forgot we're at the sex scene. Gavin and Charlotte have fallen in love through notes they leave on his counter when he's away. It's a twist on the pen-pal trope. They've been on a few dates now, and when she comes over to walk the dog, she's surprised to find him at home because he got benched. They can't deny their attraction any longer, and it's time for their first sexy scene.

Okay, I can do this. Write a sex scene from a male point of view. Easy. A little boob play, maybe a fingering, a few tugs and then wham-bam-thank you-ma'am.

I write, my fingers flying over the keyboard. The strokes. The growly words. His commanding touch. It's carnal. Hard, rushed. He's not at all hesitant, and his tongue does things I've never experienced, but I'm open to it. He's so turned on he takes her against the wall, their clothes a tangled mess around their feet. It's quick, hard, necessary.

Of course, the entire time, I'm imagining Julian. His kisses are possessive and claiming. I imagine his lips on mine and squirm. Is it hot in here? Did he turn up the heat? I take my sweatshirt off, leaving me in a t-shirt and leggings. I glance up and find Julian staring at me, a smirk on his face. It's like he knows exactly what's running through my mind.

"What? It's hot in here." He shakes his head and focuses back on his laptop. A few minutes later, his alarm goes off, and he brings his laptop over, eager for the exchange. I shut mine and hug it to my chest, protecting it from his eyes.

"I never do this." The disclaimer just rolls off my tongue. His critique of my writing matters to me. So does how well we work together as partners. Both on the page and off.

Apparently, I amuse him as he laughs at me. "What? Write? Because we've been doing it for a few weeks now." His teasing sends my nerves into overdrive.

"I mean this. Writing without obsessing over every word, nuance. I'm nervous."

His blue eyes darken, any hint of humor removed in response to my distress. "Harper, you're always safe with me." He's on his knees in front of the chair, pleading with me like a desperate man. His words drip with sincerity and I have to trust him.

"I know," I sigh. I reluctantly open it and hand it to him.

As he reads, I shrink down into the chair and pull a blanket over my head. After a minute of tortured silence, he laughs. A full out chortle. My worst nightmare is happening before my eyes. He's laughing at my writing. Worse yet, he's laughing at my sex scene. Every ounce of insecurity floods my veins, and I want to give up this writing folly. I'll make dog walking a full-time gig.

A few minutes later, he peeks under the blanket, a concerned look on his face. "Harper, what's wrong?"

A tear escapes and I quickly wipe it away. "I didn't write a comedy," I say weakly.

He puts a finger under my chin and turns my face to his, forcing me to look into his caring eyes. "No, you didn't. It's good. Hot. But I'm confused because I don't know if it's what you want or what you think a guy wants. But from my point of view, I can assure you, their first time won't be a quickie against the wall. He cares about her."

His hand palms my cheek, and he wipes my tear away. "She's not some puck bunny he'll forget. He's going to savor every single inch of her." His look is so serious, it makes me forget he was even laughing. Every word he says is slow. Sensual.

"He's going to memorize what his touch does to her." His eyes drink me in, moving slowly down my body, taking me in inch by inch. His finger slowly traces down my arm, my body sparking to life at his light touch. "Pay so much attention to every detail of her body that he can recall it when he's desperate for her and she's not there. He's going to take her to his bed and worship her."

I can't help but wonder if he knows how wet I'm getting, how turned on I am. "He's going to lap at her pussy until she comes on his face and is ready for the ecstasy of coming on his cock." Our eyes meet, and his tongue licks his lips. Oh, he knows all right.

Holy fuck! I'm lost in his words. My insecurity melts away, replaced by a surge of confidence and eager anticipation, a thrill that tingles throughout my body.

But a tortured look fills his eyes. Is he talking about the book or us? If it's about us, I'm hesitant because his intensity is over-powering. I have no words, yet he seems to have plenty of them. And they have a profound effect on me. It's as if they can melt my heart and leave me forever changed. Goosebumps prickle my arms as I fight the urge to pull him close, desperate to feel his touch everywhere. It's not the first time my body's reacted to his words like this. If he worships me like he describes, I'm going to spontaneously combust. I'm ready to cash in on the promise he's making.

He's stunned me into silence. I breathe deeply and fill my lungs with air, attempting to slow my rapid pulse. My brain tells me I should acknowledge his words, say anything, but I can't. I'm ruined. Digging deep, I give him what few words I can muster.

"Oh. Okay."

Well, that's just brilliant.

CHAPTER
THIRTY-SEVEN

JULIAN

———

After reading her scene, it takes every ounce of restraint I have not to give it to her exactly as she wrote it. My god, I'm getting hard just imagining banging her rough and wild. I get it. The carnal need. The pent-up sexual tension. The feeling that if we don't physically connect, the world may end. Her words are descriptive. Raw. Intense. And so fucking sexy. Is that what she wants? To be fucked against a wall? I'm more than willing to oblige. The second or third time, maybe. But our first time? No. It won't be some animalistic urge. It will be about her. For her. I want to prove to her sex is more than a fuck against the wall.

And it's the first time I've ever had these thoughts about a woman. Sure, I've fucked like an animal. I've had sex with different women in different ways, but I've never felt the need to slow down time, enjoy the person, not just the act. She's absolutely worth the wait.

And I tell her that. I search her eyes for a response. "Oh, okay," she mutters. And now I'm the one that's at a loss.

Her hesitant tone knocks down my usual confidence a notch. "Can I read yours?" She's quiet and I'm dying to know what she's thinking.

"Of course. Turnabout is fair play." Handing her my laptop, I get up and walk to the kitchen, glancing at Noodle curled up in the afternoon sun. I mentally recite baseball stats to get my dick under control while I pour myself a drink. I sneak a peek at her as she reads, and she has my favorite surprised expression on her face. Her mouth making a perfect O induces impure thoughts again. That's enough to undo the baseball stats. My dick is ready, but I'm not sure she is. Taking a big gulp of my bourbon, I head down the hall towards my bedroom. I need to give her space and I need to think about baseball.

I'm gazing out the window, taking in the sight of people enjoying Central Park on this beautiful autumn afternoon, trying to keep my dick down. It's nearly impossible not to think about the gorgeous woman in the other room and all the things I want to do with her. I'm lost in my thoughts when I'm startled by arms hugging me from behind. Her head is on my back, and I can feel her exhale.

"That was beautiful," she says.

Her enjoyment of my words and feelings fills me with a sense of satisfaction. But she must know by now. She's my muse. Everything I wrote between Charlotte and Gavin is what I want for her. With her. When I picture Harper, words pour out of me like Niagara Falls, and I have to sift through them to find the right ones. Beautiful words? Not really. Needy words. Absolutely.

"Tell me what you liked about it." While I am interested in her writing critique, my focus is wholly on her.

"I'd rather show you." Her hand snakes down my hip and moves toward my cock. I intertwine my fingers with hers and slow her advance. I'm not opposed, but I need to make sure she's ready for this next step. Once we become friends with benefits, there will be no turning back.

She tenses, and I turn around to face her. Her beautiful lips have a slight pout. Placing my finger under her chin, I gently tilt her face towards mine, captivated by its radiance. As I bring my mouth to hers, I whisper the only words I can manage to utter, my lips barely able to form them. All logic is gone, and I'm officially awarding primary decision making with my head below the waist. But this is too important to leave unsaid.

"Harper, are you sure? Because make no mistake, I want you more than the air I breathe. But you need to be ready because this is going to change us. I believe for the better, but just know, we will change. Are you ready for the new us?"

"Yes." Her consent given against my lips is the hottest thing I've ever experienced. With each tender touch of our lips, I inhale her words, their meaning washing over me like a sweet caress. I've never felt so amped up and relaxed at the same time. Another contradiction. Like her softness to my hardness.

My hands cradle her head, my fingers wrapped in the soft strands of hair at her nape. To deepen our kiss, I gently guide her head back. Her mouth and tongue taste sweet and decadent. I need more. My voice is gravelly and lower when I growl, "I want to taste all of you." I'm rewarded with another one of her surprised expressions. "I meant it when I said I want you to come on my face and then on my cock."

"I thought that was for the book."

"Oh, we'll put a version in the book, but I need to test it all out on my muse, make sure it's perfect," I tease. I walk her to the bed, and when the back of her legs hit the side, she falls back. Exactly where I want her. I'm not taking any chances, so I hit the remote to drop the privacy shades. She's for my eyes only, and I don't share. "Do you trust me?"

Her grin, full of eager expectation, stretches across her face as she nods.

As I take the hem of her shirt and gently lift it, her arms shoot straight up, readily helping me along. I appreciate her willingness to assist. Her skin is cool and smooth beneath my fingertips.

I'm rewarded with ample breasts held captive by a pale blue lace bra. It's sweet but in my way. With her breast in one hand, I reach for the clasp with the other. I'm normally a fan of lingerie, but Harper doesn't need scraps of lace to get me excited.

My tongue starts the exploration of her body. I kiss down her jaw to her ear, neck, and collarbone, savoring the way she responds to my touch. She tilts her head back to give me better access, and I file that information away. She likes it there.

"I'm one lucky man because, gorgeous, you are exquisite." As I lap at her nipples, I feel them responding to my touch. I playfully lick and blow a soft breath, spreading a tingling sensation over her skin. I'm rewarded with an arch of her back and pleasure filling her face.

With that encouraging look, my life's mission shifts to making her feel good a hundred different ways. Make it five hundred. A thousand. Infinity.

My fingertips skim down her side, following the contour of her waist and hips, her hourglass figure pure feminine perfection. I let my fingers breach her waistband, slowing, relishing her soft skin. I glance at her to make sure this is still what she wants. Her hands answer as she helps pull down her leggings. It's obvious she's desperate, and I'm driving her crazy with my slow pace. Too bad, gorgeous. I'm enjoying the delicious torture. I take her leggings off with care and see a set of lace panties that fit her curves perfectly. My mouth continues down her body, and I kiss her hip as I work my way to the apex of her thighs.

I'm worked up from this foreplay, and I'm reconsidering the wild passion she mentioned in her writing. I could easily make that fantasy come true, and I will. Now, I remind myself, is the time for slow, sensual, meaningful pleasure. She needs to know this is more than a casual fuck for me.

Her hands reach for her panties to slide them down and I playfully pop them. "No you don't, gorgeous. Trust me." Her arm goes up and covers her eyes as she gives an irritated groan. I can't help myself when I chuckle at her frustration.

I slip my fingers around her panties and work them off. She lifts her ass to help, her eagerness getting the best of her. Missing her tender kisses, my lips search for hers as I explore the heat between her legs with my fingers. When I find her clit, the kiss goes from sweet to fuck me in point two seconds. I fucking love how she responds to my touch.

Our kiss breaks when my finger slides into her wetness while my thumb massages her clit. A little gasp escapes her lips. "You like that, gorgeous?"

"Mmmhum," she purrs.

"Fuck Harper, you're drenched. Are you turned on for me?" I know what I want, but I need her to tell me what she wants.

"Yes," she murmurs. "Your words had me, and now this is almost too much." Her hands are all over me, gripping my hair tightly. She's pulled my shirt out of my pants, and her hands on my skin are a blessing I don't deserve.

"Why don't you lie back and give me room to play, gorgeous?" I nudge her knees apart and settle in, kissing the inside of her thighs before my tongue laps at her pussy. She's so responsive it's like I have my own cheering section, and I'm encouraged to keep going. I suck her clit and fill her with my fingers. I find that spot, her breath hitches, and she clenches around my hand.

"OhmygodJulian," she mutters. "There." Her words fade into a moan that becomes my life's theme song. A surge of pride, powerful and exhilarating, fills me as I relish in her pleasure. Sure, I've satisfied women in bed, but this feels different. It's more.

"Ride it out, Harper. I'll give you another, I promise," I say before my tongue goes back to work. Quitting my day job is a serious consideration because I want every moment of my time devoted to making her feel good. Honestly, I've never experienced such deep job satisfaction before.

CHAPTER
THIRTY-EIGHT

HARPER

———

Julian's head is between my legs, and as much as I miss his kisses, this is so much better. I wrap my hand around his blonde curls while my other hand plays with my overly sensitive nipple. Actually, everything is sensitive. "Ride it out, Harper. I'll give you another, I promise."

My orgasm hits me with such intensity that my back arches and my thighs clamp together, but Julian doesn't stop. He continues to flick my clit with his tongue until I can't stand another second. He chuckles when I try to push him away. I'm still coming down. Every inch of my body is sensitive and on high alert. I need a minute.

But he's not stopping. His kisses come up my belly, and he gives each of my breasts attention, and I almost come again. His pride in his orgasmic accomplishment is pretty clear when he kisses me. I reach between his legs, and he's hard as stone.

"My turn?" As he said, turnabout is fair play.

"Oh baby, I'm not done with you. I made a promise, and I

always keep my promises." His grin is playful, sexy, and mischievous. The thought of multiple orgasms feels both thrilling and terrifying. I'm not super experienced. Honestly, I'm lucky if I have an orgasm without taking care of it myself afterward. I'm worried Julian may kill me, but oh, what a way to go.

Julian is always thoughtful and attentive, and apparently that transfers to the bedroom. He's giving me a new perspective on writing sex scenes, that's for sure. I was way off, but I'll have to decide how much of him I'm willing to share on the page.

"It's not fair I'm naked and you're not," I whine. In a flash, he pulls his shirt off and tosses it on the floor. OMG. His chest is like a work of art, all hard abs with ridges that are begging to be touched. I assure you, those pictures on the internet were absolutely not airbrushed. His abs and V line are a sinful combination, and my fingers can't resist tracing his happy trail. I pop the button of his jeans as he nibbles on my earlobe.

"You undressing me is so sexy. I want to bury myself in your sweet pussy and make you come so hard you beg for it again." His words are raw and needy, sending shivers down my body. My brain glitches, and my fingers momentarily stop. His chuckle lets me know he's fully aware of what he's doing to me. When we shed his pants and briefs, I sputter.

"Where were you hiding that? Were you wearing Spanx?" Leave it to me to make a sexy moment awkward.

He erupts into a deep, hearty laugh, causing his stomach to ripple, and his sizable erection to bounce against it. I can't take my eyes off it. Feeling it underneath his pants was one thing, but seeing it in the wild is beautiful and a little terrifying. With a sexy, fuck-me grin, he stands motionless as I cautiously reach out and wrap my hands around his cock. His girth and length would give my vibrator an inferiority complex. I'm doing the mental gymnastics, trying to figure out if it'll even fit.

Without giving me time to overthink, he gently places me on the bed and kisses me once more, washing away the awkwardness. He pulls me on top of him, and while he kisses my neck and that spot right behind my ear, I grind on him.

"That's it, baby. Use me to feel good." His encouragement is all I need to come again, but this time, I'm energized. I want him. All of him.

He reaches into the nightstand for a condom, and I quirk an eyebrow at him. He said he doesn't bring women home, so why does he have condoms here?

It's like he knows my unasked question. "I was hopeful you'd be in my bed," he answers as he sheaths himself. I hope he can't read all my thoughts.

He rolls us until he's over me, his hands sweeping my hair away from my face. I long for his lips. No, I demand his lips, and I kiss him fervently with all my might. I feel his gentle touch at my entrance. He enters me slowly, inch by glorious inch, and I stretch to accommodate him all the way. He fits. We work. I'm grateful my yoga is paying off. My brain is doing another happy dance.

"You okay?" His thumb brushes my cheek and his eyes fill with lust. All I can do is bite my lip and nod. I'm more than okay. I'm filled with ecstasy and Julian's dick. And possibly love. Probably love. That feeling might be the sex talking, and I will myself not to say it.

He thrusts slowly, his hips rolling in ways that let me know he's a great dancer because this man can move. His mouth and hands are everywhere on me at once, and when I lock my ankles behind his ass, I'm rewarded with a groan that will play on repeat in my brain forever.

My body must like it just as much because another orgasm crashes through me, and I cling to him like he's my life ring in the middle of the ocean. When he comes, he cries out my name and praises me, making me feel this was something special for him, too.

He rolls to the side, keeping us connected, and pulls me

tightly in his arms. I return his tender kiss, and we let ourselves enjoy the moment a little longer.

This bliss is unlike anything I've ever known. I'm sated and wrung out, never experiencing multiple orgasms before. And maybe I have a little side of nerves too. The higher the mountain, the harder the fall. A random thought and reminder to be cautious.

He gently brushes my hair away from my face and kisses me on the forehead. "You are the most incredible, beautiful, sexy woman in the entire world." His blue eyes darken. My writer brain kicks in, and I wonder if this is the exact image of smoldering that I've always envisioned. I could get lost in his expressive eyes.

"You're in post-orgasmic bliss." I dismiss his rambling. He's probably used to this kind of sex. Not me. I've apparently been playing in the minors and now I've been called up to the big leagues. And holy hell, do I mean big leagues.

"I mean every word I say." His genuine tone leaves little doubt he means it.

Julian gets up to attend to the condom, and I roll over with a feeling of serenity that won't fade. I'll close my eyes for a minute.

CHAPTER
THIRTY-NINE

JULIAN

————

When I return from the bathroom, an angel is sleeping peacefully in my bed. What we did was more than sex. It was a celestial experience. She made my body come alive in ways it hasn't in my thirty-one years on this earth.

I've always been a sensitive, tuned-in guy. I probably process more feelings than most men, and it's what helps me connect with people. A faint smile graces her angelic face, filling my chest with pride. I debate joining her so I can hold her in my arms, but I have things to do while she recharges. She needs to rest so we can do more of that together again.

I put on my pants and grab my phone. A Decker Connection group text has been popping off about Ashleigh's wedding next month, and since it's a small, intimate affair in Charlotte, she needs a final headcount.

> Put me down for a plus one.

TREVOR

Figures. Will she still be around next month?

Hope so.

ASH

Got it. Will she also have security I need to account for?

She's in business mode here, and I chuckle at my mild bridezilla sister. Not that she could be that bad. She's stressed, that's all.

Nope.

DANI

Great. A supermodel to make me feel like a cow.

EMMA

You are not a cow! You're beautiful, glowing, and growing a human inside you.

Comment loved by Alexander, Ashleigh, Trevor, and Darcy. Dani is seven months pregnant and looks amazing. I heart Emma's comment too.

EMMA

Should I include her in the bachelorette party?

She'd probably love that, but I haven't talked to her about it yet. Will keep you posted.

I send a separate text to Chance.

Keep it on the DL about my date. I want to surprise everyone.

The chat continues to blow up, but I have other calls to make and things to do. I'll catch up with them later.

They're in for a surprise when they see Harper. I'd go stag before bringing a high-profile date to Ashleigh's wedding. But Harper? I want her by my side. I need her there. The fact she's friends with Ashleigh and Darcy is a bonus. If I have it my way, she'll be a part of the Decker Connection from here on out.

Ashleigh and Cole's guest list is small: family and their closest friends. They're having a second reception right before spring training that will include his teammates, all her friends and clients, and anyone who wants to party and celebrate with them. It will be quite the bash. I hope Harper will join me for both, but that's a decision she has to make. I'll never pressure her to do anything.

I make a quick call to a friend to make dinner plans and then check on Harper. Somehow, Noodle has miraculously climbed onto the bed and is nestled in Harper's arms. Lucky dog.

I crawl into bed and make myself the big spoon. She stirs and wiggles her ass in my crotch, waking up my dick. That is not why I snuggled with her, but damn if I don't like it. Unfortunately, I've made plans, and against my dick's demands, I have to tell him no.

Holding her like this, feeling the steady beat of her heart against my chest, evokes a sense of belonging I've never experienced. I'm usually not a cuddler, but I could get used to this. "Hey gorgeous, did I wear you out?"

She turns her head toward me, a lazy smile on her face. "Hey. What time is it?" She rubs the sleep from her eyes and finds dusk setting in, creating a soft dim glow in the room.

"Time for dinner. Come on, I've made reservations." Her smile vanishes and is replaced with panic.

"What? Reservations? I didn't bring anything nice to wear."

I keep my hands above the sheets and trace her body with my fingertips. I can't start anything now. That's for dessert.

I groan a little to myself. "While I enjoy you dressed up, I really like you naked." This is killing me, and I'm reconsidering my grand plan. Seeing her stretch as she wakes is making it extremely tempting to stay in bed with her. But knowing how excited she'll be gives me the willpower to get up. "Our dinner guests will be fine with what you wore today. Come on, it'll be worth it. I promise."

She stands beside the bed, totally naked. I close my eyes and exhale. Sometimes I hate my brilliant ideas. *You can do this*, I tell myself as I step into my walk-in closet. I get dressed in my most casual clothes and put on a Liberties baseball hat to complete the look. I don't want her to be self-conscious at all. She's a ten no matter what she wears. When I enter the bedroom, she's pulling on her leggings.

"Here, put this on under your sweatshirt." I hand her one of my long sleeve thermals. "It might get chilly when the sun goes down."

The sight of her in my clothes makes me possessive in a way I can't quite explain, but I like it. More than I probably should.

"We need to take Noodle out before we leave," she says.

"Already taken care of. We're going to take him down with us, and Frankie will walk him and bring him back."

"Your doorman walks dogs?"

"Baby, this is New York. People will do anything for the right amount of incentive." I take Noodle's leash and hold out my hand to her. We meet Frankie in the lobby, and he assures her Noodle will be well taken care of, and they head into Central Park.

"Are you up for a short walk to dinner?"

"Sure." She heads down the sidewalk, and I pull her to a stop.

"Nope. This way." I point to Central Park across the street. "We're having a picnic." There's one of her surprised but joyful expressions I crave.

We walk through the park, swinging our clasped hands like a

couple of lovebirds. We're enjoying the leisurely pace until we reach our destination. The Central Park Zoo.

"Oh, it looks like it's closed." She sounds disappointed, and as hard as I try to keep a straight face, I can't stop my grin.

"What did I tell you? This is New York. Anything is possible." I walk toward the employees-only gate and am met by Becca, one of the zookeepers.

"Hey Becca, this is Harper, our guest of honor." Harper looks at Becca and back at me, then back to Becca.

"It's nice to meet you, Harper. If you're ready, follow me. Your dinner guests are waiting for you."

We walk through the zoo, and Harper oohs and aahs over different habitats. Becca points out the ones that have overnight indoor and outdoor access and suggests we look for them when we leave. We're walking hand in hand, and I knock shoulders with her, making her laugh. "I bought you a season pass, and you can come as often as you like." This brings her to a hard stop.

"You did what?"

I panic and second guess myself. I thought she'd like the zoo because she loves animals.

"Um, you have a season pass? I have one too, and I thought since it's so close to my place..." I'm interrupted by Harper throwing her arms around me and peppering my face with kisses.

"That's the sweetest thing anyone has ever done for me. Thank you, thank you, thank you."

"You're welcome. But um, that's not all." Her eyes light up with excitement. I take her hand, and we catch up with Becca. As we round the corner, the next exhibit comes into view. On the sidewalk, there's a table for two with dinner, complete with fake candles.

"Here you go," Becca says. "The night watchman will take care of everything when you're ready to leave." She looks at

Harper's astonished face and nods, knowing what's to come. "Enjoy your evening."

It dawns on Harper where we are, her mouth open in surprise as she spins in a slow circle, gazing at everything around her. She's stunned. Speechless. I pull out my phone and snap a picture, capturing the moment for posterity.

"Want to feed them? They left the gate unlocked that will get us closer, but we can't go into the actual enclosure without a zookeeper. Maybe next time." I shrug.

"I can feed them?" Her voice is at least two octaves higher than normal. I may have broken my girl in the best way.

"Of course you can. You're the official patron of the Central Park otters. It'll take a few weeks for the brass plaque, but..." And I'm interrupted by another round of kisses.

"This is too much, Julian. Way too much. I mean, I just, wow. Wow! How?"

"An angel was sleeping in my bed, and I wanted to give her something special." I actually reached out earlier in the week about the patronage, but dinner was more of a spontaneous idea.

Fearful she's glitching again, in her excitement, she spouts off facts about otters. "Did you know sea otters, not these otters, these are river otters, but sea otters hold hands when they sleep? It's adorable. Wait, I can really feed them?" Her excited ramblings amuse me, and her excitement is off the charts.

"You can really feed them. And visit them anytime you want." I put my arm around her and kiss her temple. Is this what my siblings feel when they found the one? Because right now, this feels really fucking good.

CHAPTER
FORTY

HARPER

————

I've died and gone to heaven. First, Julian gave me so many orgasms my body had to sleep and recharge. Now, this incredible man has given me the gift of a lifetime. I get to feed otters. I want to squeal, but I hold it back, so I don't scare the adorable creatures.

Putting on the gloves, I grab a metal bucket and open the gate to the enclosure. As I open the gate, it lets out a high-pitched squeak. The noise startles me and I look at the equally startled otters. I step slowly toward the low fence separating us from our new friends. I'm close enough that I'm able to grab a small fish and some grapes from the bucket and toss them into the water. I watch the adorable creatures swim after their dinner and they take their food out of the water. I'm fascinated to watch them use their hands while they eat, their sharp teeth tearing at the fish. The contrast between their sweet faces and high-pitched squeals adds to their undeniable cuteness. This scene reminds me of why I love otters.

Julian takes the bucket from me and holds it, so I have both hands free, allowing me to have my moment. I'm so excited I continue rambling. "There were otters near my house in Minnesota growing up. As a kid, I was obsessed with them. My mom would make up bedtime stories about the otter family." I haven't thought about those stories in years, and my heart clenches when I think about my parents. After we finish this project, maybe I'll write those stories down. I might write a children's book.

Julian's voice brings me back to the present. When I glance at him, his eyes twinkle with joy, but I doubt it's because of the otters. He's barely paid them any attention. His focus is wholly on me. "I confess, I don't know much about otters, but they kinda remind me of Noodle."

His observation snaps me out of my melancholy thoughts. "Maybe that's why I love him so much. Otters are water puppies!" He laughs with me, while I enjoy this experience with childlike wonder.

One by one, I feed them all, giving each one a name that suits their personality. When the bucket's empty, I turn my attention back to Julian. This gesture is generous. Outrageous. But more than that, it's thoughtful. He remembered my comment about otters and turned it into a magical moment.

Is this what dating Julian will be like? Because he's definitely all consuming. Intense even. I've discovered Julian is overly attentive and perceptive. He picks up on nuances and details made in casual conversation. Case in point, we're having dinner with otters.

Julian is the definition of *if he wanted to, he would*. And is that so bad? When Zac said he was afraid of Julian's level of crazy, is this what he meant? Because this is crazy.

Our dinner is a simple affair, an upscale picnic with delectable offerings of baked brie, succulent fruit, an assortment of cured meats, and croissants so buttery and delicate they practically melt in my mouth. The food is enjoyable, but the company is extraordinary. I even stop gushing over the otters, although honestly, they still have a fraction of my attention. Julian clears his throat, obviously nervous.

He's always so sure of himself that his hesitation freaks me out a little. "Um, hey, I know it's a few weeks away, but would you like to go to Ashleigh and Cole's wedding with me? It's in Charlotte, and we'd have to make arrangements for Noodle, but I'd like you to be my date."

I'm curious why he's nervous about this. "Oh, wow."

"Oh, wow? Is that oh, wow, I'd rather set my entire book collection on fire? Or more like, oh wow, I think this is the best thing that's ever happened to me?" He cocks his head to the side and challenges me to give him an honest answer.

I shake my head at his silly question. Because his two extremes are exactly that. "First, I can't imagine anything that would ever make me burn a book. Ever. And the best thing that ever happened to me was when you asked for my number. So, I'd say it's somewhere in between."

"So why the oh?"

"Well, it's a small wedding, right? I don't want to intrude." Ashleigh and I spent a weekend in New York once because we helped our mutual friend Darcy. She invited me to their spring reception, which surprised me, considering I'm not one of her closest friends. I'd never expect to be invited to her wedding.

"You wouldn't be intruding. At all. You'd be my tissue holding, won't laugh when I'm crying at my baby sister, support date. I'll need you. Besides, the girls would love to have one more for their girls' night before the wedding. It'll be fun." He's really selling it and I have no doubt it would be fun. But I don't want to be a distraction for him, pulling him away from precious moments with his family. I want what's best for Julian.

"But I understand if it's more of a commitment than you want to make right now, seeing as this is all new and every-thing." His voice trails off, his usual confidence and swagger gone. Does he really think I'm hesitant because I'm unwilling to make a commitment to him?

"Don't be daft. It has nothing to do with us being new. I just don't want to be a distraction for you at this special family event. I'm okay to duck out or blend into the wallpaper when you need me to."

He leans over and kisses me. It's sweet, cozy, adoring. "Gorgeous, you're the very best kind of distraction. And besides, you could never blend into the wallpaper." He claps his hands and the otters look his way. "Then it's settled. We'll have fun. But let's not tell anyone until we get there. I want it to be a pleasant surprise. Hey, do you have a passport?"

"I need a passport to go to Charlotte?" His train of thought isn't always linear, his brain constantly multitasking. I'm not sure where this question came from or where he's going with it.

"No, but maybe we could sneak away for an extra day or so. We should be close to finishing up the book, and a celebration will be in order. What do you say?" He pops an olive in his mouth and quirks his eyebrow, waiting for my answer.

Certainly, he's figured out I can't say no to him.

"Okay, but ONLY if we have the first draft done. I can't relax with a deadline looming." And that's the reality. I'm task driven, and if this isn't done, I won't be able to enjoy myself.

"Great!" He stands and goes to the fence overlooking the otters. "Did you hear that fellas? She said 'yes.'" He turns and leans against the fence, his face hidden in the shadow of his hat. I can't help but laugh at his ridiculousness. I join him at the fence, put my arms around his neck, and kiss him. It's sweet, but it's evolving into private bedroom-level kissing. My mind races along with my pulse.

"Come on, lover boy, take me home. I need to say thank you properly."

Apparently, he doesn't need to be told twice. He takes my hand and practically drags me out of the zoo. We reach his place in half the time it took us to get there. Frankie greets us, assuring us that Noodle is happy and settled in the apartment. Julian gives a quick thank you and pulls me to the elevator, not stopping to talk.

Actually, there was very little talking for the rest of the evening, and I'm not mad about it. Sometimes, words are overrated.

CHAPTER
FORTY-ONE

JULIAN

———

I reluctantly took Harper and Noodle back to Zac's after our amazing weekend. We spent our time collaborating. A little writing. A little Netflix and chill. A lot of sex. Yep. Collaboration all around. It was fantastic. I want to keep collaborating with Harper all the time.

Unfortunately, work requires me to be in Chicago for the day, but I should be home this evening. I'm probably annoying Harper with my frequent texting, but I don't care. I can't get enough of her. As I'm waiting for my return flight, I get a surprise text from my girl.

> Want to come over for dinner? The guys are home and I'm cooking for them. 7:30?

I picture her surrounded by hockey players, only this time there's no glass between them, and I'm immediately jealous. But I don't want to interfere with her friendship dynamic either. She doesn't mention other friends often. Specifically, girlfriends. I wonder what Harper's version of girl time is?

Ashleigh taught me the importance of girl time, and I encourage her to do it often. Hell, sometimes I even host Ashleigh's girls' nights. I'm excited for Harper to hang out with the women in my family at the wedding. I know they'll welcome her to their tight-knit group.

> I don't want to cause any trouble. Zac doesn't like me.

He doesn't know you. But I understand if you're tired.

> Do YOU want me there?

Of course, but seriously, no expectations. You had a life before me, with other people and tons of stuff going on.

My life before Harper feels like a distant memory. Between sports, networking, and socializing, my calendar was overflowing, and I was in constant demand. Everyone always wanted a piece of me. But my time with Harper is different. She wants nothing, yet I want to give her everything. It's been almost twenty-four hours since I've seen her, and I feel incomplete. I need to see her. But she had a life before me too, and I don't want to complicate that.

> I did. And it was empty and filled with busyness. You've wrecked me, Harper, and I'm not sure what to do with myself now. I'll be there as soon as I can.

Wanting to maximize my time. I catch up with Patrick before boarding the plane. No major issues to deal with, and I'm grateful. I spend the flight writing, so I have more time with Harper.

The book is coming together, and the check ins with Professor Daniels are encouraging.

When I arrive at their building, Zac is returning from walking Noodle. "You know, for someone who has a live-in dog walker, you sure walk your dog a lot," I say in greeting.

He laughs as the doorman holds the door for us. "I miss the little guy when I'm gone. I wish I could take him with me on the road. You think I can work that into my contract?"

"If you had a good agent, you could," I clap back.

"Not sure I can afford that kind of agent." That's a fallacy the other agencies like to spread. That we take a higher percentage for the services we offer. We don't. The percentage is based on the athlete. Higher maintenance, ill-mannered athletes pay more, if we agree to represent them at all. We have standards.

"I'm available whenever you want to chat. Just be sure to tell Waters you approached me."

"How do you know John Waters is my agent?"

Shit. Busted. "Small world, man. I get paid to know things."

When he opens the door to his apartment, we're greeted with laughter and delicious aromas.

"Look who followed Noodle home," Zac says as we enter. The laughter stops, and Harper practically cross checks two hockey players to get to me.

"You're here." She jumps into my arms. With one swift movement, I swing her around and our lips connect in a kiss that washes away the weight of the entire day.

"Hey, gorgeous. You look domestic." I nibble on her ear. "And edible."

A blush fills her cheeks, and she playfully slaps my chest. "Stop." She turns and looks at the hockey players, all with various looks of disbelief on their faces. "Let me make introductions. This is Marc-Andre Clarmont aka Mac, Henry Saxton, but they call him Harvard," she giggles. "And Jetsy. I mean, Connor Jetson. Boys, this is Julian Decker." Of course I know these guys, but it's sweet she introduces me like I'm not versed in their backgrounds, stats, and draft history. And I'm positive they know me, or at least my agency and reputation.

She stands beside me, and I wrap my arm around her like a stage-five clinger. I'm aware they're just friends, but in this testosterone-filled room, I want to make it clear to everyone that Harper's my girl.

Harvard leans over to Jetsy and forgets to use his quiet voice. "He really is a pretty boy, isn't he?"

Zac laughs and offers me a beer. He and I sit at the counter and watch the entertainment in the kitchen. Harper resumes her role as drill Sargent, and I can't help but admire how she puts these guys in their place. Each person has a specific role, and Harper's is to control the chaos. She oversees the three burley hockey players, and they obediently obey her instructions.

"I feel like I'm watching an episode of Hell's Kitchen," I comment to Zac as we watch them all bump into each other.

"Yeah, except she's scarier than Gordon Ramsey," Harvard says under his breath.

"I'm giving cooking lessons, although Mac is pretty decent already," Harper says with pride.

"I learned the French ways from my French-Canadian mother," he replies, his accent thick.

"Hey, I chopped up the veggies," Jetsy whines. She pats him on the cheek to placate him. It's a sisterly gesture, but I still try to keep myself from going caveman.

"What are we having?" I ask the chefs.

"Chicken pot pie," Harvard says proudly.

"She's tired of pasta," Zac says, playfully rolling his eyes.

They finish up the cooking, and Harper sends everyone to the table. "Hey, you don't need to wait on us. I've got it," I say to her. I'm all for turning traditional roles on their ear.

"Not the way she likes it," Zac says. I'm not sure if he meant the double entendre, but I bristle anyway.

Harvard laughs at me. "She makes a big deal out of the

presentation, but once she sits down, she's done. The rest is up to us. We do what she says." He motions with his head to sit down.

"It's like she's trying to domesticate us," Mac adds, and they all laugh.

"I heard that," she sing-songs from the kitchen.

She brings the food to the table, and it looks delicious. She serves each of us and then takes a seat next to me. "Dig in, boys."

They gobble it down like they haven't eaten in days and, in reality, it's only been a few hours at best. Athletes eat often, and the food consumption still amazes me after all these years.

Harper's amused. This. Helping friends. I'm witnessing her in one of her happy places. She's not a party girl. She's the girl that stays home, takes care of her people. I see how loyal and kind she is, and it makes me know I can't lose her.

She leans over and says behind her hand, "I promise it's safe to eat. I supervised."

"Hey, we're getting better. Jetsy made a frozen pizza the other day and remembered to take the plastic off," Harvard says. They all laugh while I visibly cringe.

"You live in New York City and had frozen pizza? That's sacrilege," I say. Jetsy shrugs it off.

Everyone's having a good laugh and getting along. After second and third helpings, the guys slow down, their calorie consumption met. They clear the table, and I take Harper's dish to the kitchen.

"Hey, let me clean up. Ya'll cooked." They look at me suspiciously.

"Trying to impress CJ," Harvard comments. "Smart. We get treats when we do stuff like that." What kind of treats do they get? My mind immediately jumps to the type of treat I'd like, but we're in mixed company.

While I'm cleaning up the kitchen, arms wrap around my waist, and I savor this blissful moment. "This is nice," I tell her. "I love seeing you happy."

"Have you seen me unhappy?" Come to think of it, I haven't. She has different levels of happiness, but I haven't seen her sad or angry. Not that I want it, but I'm looking forward to it. I love learning how she handles her emotions, each with unique expressions. I need to know everything about this woman. I'm beyond infatuated.

"No. Tell me, what does that look like? Is it ice cream and rom-coms?" I turn to face her, and there's a gleam in her eye. That look tells me I've messed up and I'm about to hear about it.

"Do you really think I'm that basic? I'm a little offended." She's giving me a hard time, and if we were alone, I'd spank her for it.

"Gorgeous, you are anything but basic." She gives me a little kiss and walks away. My eyes are glued to her as she sways her hips, reminding me she's far from basic.

She drops onto the couch and throws a pillow at Zac. "Hey, Zac, what's my go to karaoke song?"

"Is that what we're doing tonight because I can't do that sober," he says, deadpan.

"No, but can we do that soon? I miss our karaoke parties."

A slight pang of jealousy hits at the mention of their shared history. I move past it and channel that feeling into learning more about her. I've noticed she's always listening to music, but now I'm learning she likes to sing too.

"Zac's done karaoke? But not with us?" Jetsy acts genuinely hurt by this slight.

"When I was in Atlanta, CJ wanted to go out with us, but she wasn't twenty-one yet, and Lawson wouldn't let her get a fake ID. The only place we could take her out was this shady karaoke bar." I'm not sure if Zac is telling this story for the benefit of his teammates or me. Yeah, they go way back, but I'm drinking up every detail he's sharing.

"You make it sound like you're so much older. Eight months, Zac. Eight months!" She playfully hits him with a pillow, and Noodle moves out of her line of fire. This sibling type behavior seems to be a normal form of communication between them.

He swats the pillow away, laughing at her. Yep. Sibling is the best way to describe their relationship. She was his Captain's little sister. She grew up with a literal hockey team and twenty or more bonus brothers.

"We'd go to this hole in the wall karaoke place, and she'd make us sing." I try to picture a hockey team singing karaoke, and I cringe. It couldn't have been good.

"I didn't *make* you sing," she interrupts and rolls her eyes.

I've finished in the kitchen and sit next to her, pulling her into my side. "I didn't," she whines to me, like I have to be convinced. I'd bet she didn't make them do anything. They were under her spell and did anything she asked. Like karaoke. Hell, I saw her wield that magic in the kitchen tonight.

I kiss her on the temple. "I'm sure it was their idea," I chuckle.

"Anyway, this girl has some pipes." She does? Now I'm curious.

"And her go-to song?" I ask.

"I'd advise you not to piss her off," he warns. "Because she can channel Carrie Underwood pretty fuckin' good."

I wrack my brain to decipher what song he's talking about, and she plays "Before He Cheats" on the Bluetooth speakers. The warning song fills the room, and Harvard stands up and sings off-key into his pretend microphone. Harper cackles at his antics. Well, okay then.

CHAPTER
FORTY-TWO

HARPER

———

We're making great progress on our book. I'm excited about our final meeting with Professor Daniels in a few weeks. I really like what we've created and think readers will enjoy it. As we submit each chapter, it's edited and reviewed, eliminating the need for the typical editing and revision process at the end. We've got immediate publication rights when it's completed. It's hard to imagine I'll be a published author by the end of the year.

I'm going to Julian's office today to work on the book with him for a few hours between his meetings. Since there won't be a bed in sight, we'll likely get more writing done, anyway. We keep getting carried away when we're writing the steamy scenes. I'm wearing his favorite red lip stain today because I have a special surprise for him. We've done a lot of things, but me going down on him isn't one of them. Yet.

I insisted on taking the subway, but Julian wouldn't hear of it. When Kat drops me off at the glass high-rise that is home to The Decker Agency, I have my working-woman-in-New-York-

City moment. I'm surrounded by men in suits and women in professional dress moving quickly, getting to their next high-powered meeting. The atmosphere feels very corporate and unfamiliar, but I can imagine Julian here, closing multimillion-dollar deals.

When I step off the elevator and enter The Decker Agency, I'm a little taken aback. The office has a low-key vibe, with its open layout and casually dressed employees. Various groups of people are chatting and laughing with each other. A quiet hum of conversation fills the air. An enormous wall is covered with large screen TVs, each displaying a different sporting event. A far cry from the corporate feel downstairs.

I'm greeted warmly by the sweet receptionist. "Miss Cartwright, I was told to expect you. Mr. Decker's meeting is running long, but let me call Violet, and she'll escort you to his office, where you can wait for him."

"Oh, I don't want to be a bother. I can wait here." As I glance at the large waiting room filled with comfortable seating, I'm approached by a tall, distinguished looking man dressed in dark jeans and a sweater. He's casual, but professional. He looks more like a finance bro at the club than a sports agent. Although admittedly, I've only seen Julian out of work, and I've never been to Lawson's agency, so maybe they're all this way.

"You must be the mystery woman who has charmed our Julian into a permanent goofy smile." I shake my head and scoff at his assessment. "I've got her, Brit," he says to the receptionist. He turns his attention back to me. "I'm Patrick McCoy, Julian's business partner." He extends his hand, and I take it.

"Harper Cartwright. It's nice to meet you. Julian's told me about you." Julian respects Patrick and has the highest regard for him. He says Patrick is the brains behind the business, but he doesn't give himself enough credit.

"And yet he's told me so little about you." He scans me from head to toe. I'm wearing a pencil skirt, heels, and a conservative blouse. My hair is pulled up into a high pony for a polished and professional look. I wasn't sure what to expect in his office, and I didn't want to embarrass him in front of his colleagues. After scanning the room, I've clearly overdressed.

"Come on, you can wait in his office." Patrick holds his arm out, showing me the way. Patrick introduces me to Violet, and they leave me in the office to wait.

His office is inviting, personal, and totally Julian. It feels like an extension of his apartment. Relaxed, livable.

His simple, modern desk is off to the side of the room, giving me the impression he doesn't do much work there. It's uncluttered. The only thing on it is his closed laptop next to a large monitor. There's a sitting area with a red sofa and a few leather chairs set around a large coffee table. I bet this is his primary working area because Julian is about people, connection, not computers and emails.

He has several bookshelves filled with pictures, sports memorabilia, and one case full of lewd snow globes that have piqued my curiosity. I can't wait to ask him about those. Chance Fuller's blue and gold college jersey is framed and hung prominently next to Julian's diplomas from Michigan and Wharton. It's not surprising that Chance's non-NHL jersey carries more value to Julian. I recall the way he talked about his best friend saving him and giving him the idea of becoming an agent. His sentimentality is touching.

I drop my tote bag with my laptop and notebooks in a chair and continue my perusal of his office. He has a collector's wet dream of signed baseballs, hockey sticks, and footballs. Most include personal notes to Julian. Similarly, the pictures are candid and personal. This isn't a trophy case; it's his life, his people. It makes him more endearing in my eyes.

Julian walks in, makes a beeline for me, and greets me with a casual but workplace appropriate kiss. I can't stop my giggles.

"I missed you," he whispers. How is that possible when it's been less than twenty-four hours? He left last night around ten o'clock, and it's not even lunchtime. He looks around the office and seems disappointed. "I thought you might bring Noodle."

"Zac's home and keeps grumbling about me stealing his dog. Said something about you getting him a Noodle-inclusive contract. You might win him over yet." I playfully push him away.

There's a light knock on the door and Violet nervously interrupts. "Mr. Decker, I've ordered your lunch. Is there anything else you need?"

"No, thank you, Violet. I'll let you know when we're ready to eat. Thank you." She nods and closes the door behind her.

"Hiding your secret?" I tease.

"You." Kiss. "Are not." Kiss. "A secret." Kiss. "I want to announce us to the world when you're ready. But I'm okay with a soft launch at the wedding this weekend." He kisses me before I can respond. It's hot, needy, and turning me on. His hand slides under my skirt and up my thigh. While this is not what I planned, Julian is more the spontaneous type, and who am I to argue? I'm glad Violet closed the door, but the back wall is floor to ceiling glass.

"You look like a hot-as-fuck librarian. Like the day I saw you at NYU." He trails kisses down my neck. "Is that what you had in mind? Remind me of the first time I wanted to make you mine? Fuck Harper, you're driving me crazy right now."

"Well, not exactly," I hedge.

He pulls back and looks at me. His ocean blue eyes swirl with lust, and I'm encouraged to act out a fantasy I've had since I saw the first office sex scene in *Scandal*. "Why don't you go sit at your desk, and I'll show you what I was thinking."

His smirk goes to his eyes, and he looks intrigued. He obeys and sits in his office chair, spins toward me, and gives me the *now what* look. I've never done anything like this, but his grin gives me the confidence to proceed. He must be able to read my mind because he leans back further and puts his hands behind his head.

I saunter over and stop in front of him and go down on my knees. His eyes light up with anticipation as I reach for his belt and unbuckle it. I work the button on his pants, and he gets hard before my eyes. I pull his pants and briefs down to his knees, and he's where I want him. I've never felt so powerful and desired in my life.

"Babe, you don't have to," he starts, but I shut him up by licking him, taking him in my mouth, tightening my lips around the head of his cock. He's girthy and long, and while I worry about taking him all in, I relax into the moment. I grip him at the base and get to work with my mouth. His hooded eyes are locked on me, his hands gripping the arms of his chair. I moan, and he must like that because he's reciting a poem of praise for me.

"This image will be a forever memory, babe. My god, you're an angel with a demon mouth. You're so fucking amazing. You're mine, Harper. Gorgeous. Fuck babe, you've got me. I'm yours whether or not you want me. Your mouth is sinful and beautiful. Those red lips will kill me, but I'm gonna die happy." Julian is always chatty and talks during sex, telling me what feels good, asking what I like. But this? It's pure praise.

I up my game, taking as much as I can without gagging and hollow out my cheeks. He must really like that as his hand caresses my face with so much affection, I might die right here. Making him feel good is my only desire. Maybe I have a secret praise kink? Or maybe it's all Julian.

"Babe, I'm about to come down your throat if you don't stop," he warns, and I go harder, signaling that's exactly what I want. The thrill of doing this to him spurs me on. I'm loving this feeling of empowerment. Adoration.

He comes hard. I can see the intensity in his eyes, but he restrains himself from shouting. We're in his office, after all. I'm so damn proud of myself, and this fantasy was everything I wanted. When I stand and lick my lips, his eyes go wild, and I realize I may have made a mistake. Oh no. I can't stop my panic because I think I've unlocked another level of Julian's crazy.

CHAPTER
FORTY-THREE

JULIAN

———

"Babe, I'm about to come down your throat if you don't stop." I don't want her to stop. Ever. The things this woman does to me has me twisted every which way. Harper on her knees is a fantasy come true. I've imagined those red lips around my cock more times than I care to admit. Combine that with her prideful grin and I'm done for. She knows exactly what she's doing to me. Her mouth is ruthless, and I'm addicted. She takes my warning as encouragement, and holy hell, I want to yell her name, but I have an office full of people outside my door, and instead, I bit my lip.

When she licks her lips, it's like any restraint I had is exhausted. I can't help but pull her onto my lap and kiss her passionately. I want this mouth on me 24/7. Probably not reasonable or practical, but she scrambles my brain so hard that I want to live impractically.

"Gorgeous, you are my reward and punishment." I stand her up and kiss the top of her head and make my way to my bathroom to clean up. I glance out the glass wall and say a little prayer that no one from another building saw us. I mean it when I say I don't share.

When I rejoin Harper, she's sitting at my desk, laptop out, and typing away. "What are you doing?" I put my head on her shoulder to get a peek at what she's writing.

"Getting a few thoughts down while they're fresh." Her eyes never leave the screen. I'm amazed that she sucked me off and now acts like it never happened. How does she flip that switch?

I lean over her shoulder to remind her I'm still here and read what she's writing. I can't help but chuckle at her intense focus as she recounts our recent playtime. Her eyes sparkle with excitement. "You really think Gavin Snow can string that many words together? Babe, he's a hockey player. Words are not his strong suit. He's better with his stick."

Spinning in her chair, she glares at me in disapproval. "You're saying your best friend, my brother, my roommate, can't woo a woman with words?"

"Zac? Absolutely not." I'm laughing as I open the door. "Thank you, Violet." I take the delivery bag from her and close the door. "Come on, let's eat and then work. I'm spent." At that, she scoffs and rolls her eyes at me. And this is what I love about her. She doesn't bat her eyes and kiss my ass. She gives it back to me.

Today, we're writing the last few chapters of our book, and we don't agree. Again. I'm glad she argues with me. She's pushing me, us, to be better.

"Charlotte wouldn't hide and lick her wounds," she says. "She'd stand tall and kick him where it hurts."

I swallow and almost choke on my sandwich. I gulp down my water and compose myself. Harper is unphased by my almost near-death experience and takes another bite of her salad. I give myself an internal high five that she didn't change it or pick anything off. I pride myself on being a quick learner, but every time I think I've cracked her code, she throws me a curveball.

Case in point, this discussion about Charlotte. Harper's my muse, so any character trait for Charlotte she corrects is often a piece of my Harper puzzle I'm working to complete. Once I can breathe again, I look at her for signs of teasing. There aren't any, and I'm on high alert because I'm about to unlock a new insight into Harper. "What does that mean, exactly?"

She shrugs. "She's a woman who knows what she brings to the table. That's not conceit, but she's not riddled with self-confidence issues. It also means she's not afraid to fight. She's not rolling over." She pulls out her phone, searches for a song, hits play, and goes back to her salad.

Another fun Harper trait I admire is her connection to music. She has a song for almost every occasion or feeling at the ready. Some people communicate in movie quotes, Harper uses songs. I swear, her secondary communication style is lyrics. She's created a running playlist for our book that evokes the feelings or mood for each scene, chapter, or overall story. I tease her she's creating a Broadway jukebox musical to accompany our book. I glance at her phone and see this song is called "Revenge." This Pink song makes me want to protect the jewels.

I listen for a minute, trying not to get distracted by her humming along. The song is fun and poppy until you listen to the words. I guess I'm grateful it's not "Goodbye Earl."

"What are you saying?" I can't picture my sweet, champagne drinking, giggly girl fueled by revenge. It's a contradiction. Again.

"I'm saying she's going to go scorched earth for them. If it means she has to get loud to make him pay attention, well, then she'll do it." This woman excites me and terrifies me at the same time.

We work through the last few chapters, continuing to disagree about the ending. We're both passionate and argue for what we want. I'm loving the give and take. Life isn't perfect, although this feels pretty amazing right now. We'll argue and fight in the future. That's real life. But the growth happens when you work through it. And there I go, focusing on the future. Because when I look at Harper, that's what I see.

We can't settle on the ending. Harper wants a happy-for-now ending, and I want a solid happily ever after. No questions about whether they'll be together in the future. Their story should be forever. I'm willing to wait her out, to see it my way. After all, I've got that forever perspective.

"I'll tell you what. Why don't we both write the last chapter, and we'll let Professor Daniels decide?"

She bites her bottom lip and considers my proposal. "Maybe. Let's swap first. Your words can be pretty persuasive. If we don't agree, we'll let an outside party decide."

A knock on the door interrupts our discussion. "Mr. Decker, it's time for your appointment with Logan Swindell."

"Thank you, Violet. Will you have him wait in the conference room for me? I'll be right there. Patrick can keep him company." After nodding, she walks away, leaving the door open. She's improving, but she's still jumpy and always looks scared. I want to ask who hurt her, but I'm afraid that will freak her out.

"Well, Mr. Decker," Harper mocks. "Looks like my work here is done. I have some writing to do before our flight tomorrow." She packs up her laptop, and this parting feels very formal.

"Come here." I tug her toward me.

"Your office. People can see," she mumbles.

"Good, I want them to see how fucking happy you make me."

CHAPTER
FORTY-FOUR

HARPER

———

Julian picks me up bright and early for our flight to Charlotte. I'm excited about this getaway, but it's our public debut as a couple, and the butterflies are fluttering. Well, public to the people that mean the most to him, anyway.

We submitted our final draft of the book last night, and my emotions are all over the map. I'm excited we finished the project with a great story. After reading my last chapter, he agreed mine was the better ending, so we submitted it. If we weren't under a tight deadline, there may have been more collaboration and compromise. His approach to their love story was all in. Mine was a little more cautious. Gavin leads with his heart, Charlotte with her head. Life imitating art, perhaps?

We get to the airport with no time to spare thanks to New York gridlock, and once we board, I can exhale. I hate being late and want time to relax for a few minutes once I get to the airport. Julian slides in with seconds to spare. He took a few years off my life when we ran through the airport.

He still won't tell me where we're going next week after the wedding. My only clue was to pack warm clothes, and if I don't have what I need, he'll buy it for me. That rules out a tropical island. His spontaneity is exciting but also nerve-racking for a planner like me.

"Juice or coffee?" the flight attendant asks Julian as we take our seats. The last passengers walk past, going further into the plane. I'll never tire of flying first class.

"Coffee for me, cream and sugar," Julian says. "A mimosa for my girlfriend, please."

At the use of the title, I turn and look at him and quirk my eyebrow. We haven't put labels on anything, even though I assume we're exclusive.

He leans over and nibbles on my earlobe. "Have I told you how much I enjoy your surprised looks? They're my reason for living."

"Is that what I am?" I can't hide my pleasure at the title.

"No, Harper, you're so much more."

Our conversation never lags on the two-hour flight, and my bottomless mimosas keep me giggling. When we arrive and get our luggage, the nerves hit with the reality of our soft launch, as he calls it.

"If you don't mind, I'm going to use the restroom before we leave." I'm not sure how far we have to drive and if we need to wait for an Uber. I need a minute to compose myself because of my nerves. Or maybe it's the champagne?

A little pep talk in the mirror, some fresh lipstick, and I'm good to go. That is until I see our Uber driver chatting with Julian.

"The groom is on airport duty?" I interrupt their conversation. Cole holds his hand out to shake mine and introduce himself when he does a double take.

"Harper?" His eyebrows shoot up, and he's genuinely surprised.

Julian holds his hand out and pulls me to his side.

"Harper's my date for this little soirée you're throwing, and she has promised to keep me from yelling 'I object' to save my sister from a lifetime of baseball and smelly socks," Julian teases.

"Well, in that case, she's my favorite guest here!" Cole laughs. "Because I won't let anyone stand in my way of marrying Leigh, and I'd hate to hurt her brother on such a joyous occasion." I adore that Cole still calls her Leigh, the name she went by when he fell in love with her.

"I promise to do my best." These goofballs make me laugh.

"The girls will be thrilled to see you. And no one wins the pool on who your date is, so that means it goes to the honeymoon fund." Cole takes my bags, and we go to the pickup area, where Matt, his best man, is waiting by the idling car.

"Do I want to know the guesses?" I ask.

"Probably not," Cole says.

"Definitely not," Julian laughs. "But I'm the winner, however you cut it."

"Are my eyes playing tricks on me, or is this Harper Cartwright? Fucking Awesome," Matt says when I get to the car. His excited greeting makes me optimistic about our debut as a couple. He hugs me, picks me up, and my feet dangle off the ground.

"The one and only." All this fuss from these guys is so embarrassing.

"Darcy is going to be stoked to see you." He puts me down, and Julian puts his arm around me, giving me balance again.

"Your brother isn't coming, is he?" Matt asks as he looks around for Lawson. The jovial atmosphere is settling my anxiety.

On the drive home, the guys are chatting and catching up, and I'm getting a glimpse of another side of Julian. Friend and mentor. These two young baseball players are part of the exclusive client list that he personally manages.

Cole Davidson, his future brother-in-law, plays for the New York Liberties organization on their AAA team in Nashville. During his offseason, he's excelling as a breakout songwriter in the music industry. He met Ashleigh two years ago when she was an intern for the Savannah Pajamas, and she had assumed another identity, not wanting anyone to know she was Ashleigh Decker, daughter of the MLB team owner.

Matt Hartman is Cole's best friend and dating Cole's sister, Darcy. Matt plays for the Carolina Reapers, and they live in Charlotte now. Darcy and I became friends when she was working things out with Matt. I'd like to take some credit in their happily ever after, but Julian says his Team True Love made it happen. Whatever.

"When can we expect wedding bells for you and Darcy?" I ask.

Matt turns red and cuts his eyes at Cole.

"Um, we're happy where we are right now. We're good. Darcy is busy with remodeling our house, her design business is thriving, and I just wrapped up my first professional baseball season. We don't need another big thing right now." Matt and Darcy's story is a happily for now, and it doesn't sound so bad.

"That's smart," Julian adds. "But make sure she knows what she means to you and keep telling her. She's a special girl."

"That she is," Cole adds.

"Am I witnessing a Team True Love meeting?" I ask. Julian and Chance consider themselves love gurus and pull a team together when someone needs some love guidance. They call their group Team True Love and, from what I've been told, they have a one-hundred percent success rate.

They all laugh at the ridiculous assumption. "Gorgeous, I do the best I can with these guys, but I'm focusing all my energies on you." He puts his arm around my shoulders and kisses me on the temple. Excuse me, is it getting hot in here?

Matt and Cole deliver us to the apartment Julian keeps in Charlotte. It's more glass and high-rise than his New York home, but when I notice it's next door to Reaper Stadium, I understand.

Julian insists I relax while he gets us settled. I'm looking out over the city when his arms wrap around me, and I lean into his embrace. "Welcome to my family's business. It's peaceful in the offseason."

"It's nice to be back in the South." I take another sip of my Chick-fil-a tea. We stopped for a quick bite of nuggets and tea to hold us over until dinner.

"Are you ready for our debut tonight?"

"I'm a little nervous. I don't want to take one second of attention off Ashleigh. This is her weekend."

"Don't worry about that at all. This weekend is a celebration of love, and baby, I haven't said those words yet, but you need to know, I love you." He leans over my shoulder and kisses my cheek. "And I scored another one of your surprised looks. I'm on a roll." He chuckles at his own comment and gives himself a fist pump in the air.

He loves me. He said those sacred, three little words. He loves me. I'm slightly shocked, but I need to pause and remind myself that I shouldn't be. Is this new information? Not really. His actions scream love while his words whisper deep into my soul.

What do I say to that? I love you too. Seems too reflexive, reactive. No, I want to tell him in my way, in my time. But make no mistake. I love this man with every fiber of my being. I love his kind heart, caring spirit, and fun-loving outlook on life. And I absolutely adore his body. But it's the inside of Julian that makes him so damn irresistible. He's a good man, through and through.

"I need to take a shower and get ready." His smile falters, revealing his disappointment. Probably because he's waiting for a response. Oh, he'll get one. Just not what he's prepared for. "Joining me?"

His smile returns. "You don't have to ask me twice. I'm feeling very dirty. Yep, definitely need a shower." He takes me by the hand and tugs me toward the bedroom. Now I can check shower sex off my bucket list.

CHAPTER
FORTY-FIVE

JULIAN

———

I always get excited when my loved ones gather, and this celebration of Ashleigh and Cole might be the happiest I've ever been in my life. Ashleigh's happiness fuels mine. Then, add Harper and BOOM, explosion of joy. I'm serious. She'll have to keep me grounded because I'm too excited to control myself. Case in point, I told Harper that I love her. I do. And it's important she knows that.

Then she didn't say it back. Not that she has to. It's not a requirement. Maybe she doesn't feel as strongly as I do. Maybe she's scared. Maybe, well, no. She'll get there. I'm confident she will. Our story isn't one of unrequited love. We're a fucking happily ever after if I've ever seen one.

Harper and I enter the venue, and it's like we walked into a floral explosion. There are garlands of white and blue flowers wrapped in white fairy lights everywhere. Almost reminds me of the wedding scene from *Twilight* that Ashleigh and I watched together when she was younger. It's beautiful and romantic.

When I cry over these flowers, Harper's going to think I'm a total loser.

"This is incredible," Harper says under her breath. Her phone vibrates in her bag, and her face fills with concern as she looks at the screen. "Sorry, do you mind if I step out and take this? It's Zac, and he shouldn't be calling me right now. I hope Noodle's okay."

"Sure, I'll be right here." I kiss her quickly as she puts the phone to her ear and walks back out the door.

I'm taking in the room's beauty, scanning the occupants, and ticking off the guest list for tonight's dinner. It's a small group tonight. We'll only have a few extra guests tomorrow, primarily family and close friends. But this time together is about our tight-knit group. The Decker Connection.

"Darcy can add wedding planning to her list of talents." I hug Cole in greeting. His sister is an exceptional designer who brings beauty and a touch of uniqueness to any space.

"Can't breathe." Cole wiggles out of my embrace.

"I don't tell you enough, but I love you. I love you not only for who you are as a man, but especially for who you are to my sister. Thank you. I will always be there for you. Better or worse," I ramble.

"Aren't those supposed to be my words?" Ashleigh asks as she rescues her future husband.

I wrap her in my arms and hold her tight. She's glowing in her off-white sweater dress. An absolute vision. "Love you," I say as I kiss her temple, my eyes watering. It must be dusty in here.

"Can I have her back, please?" Cole pulls Ashleigh to him. "Hug on your own girl."

"Oh, that's right, your date." Ashleigh rubs her hands together and looks around the room, seeking her out. "Where is she? Ditch you already?"

I scowl at Cole, my glare accusing him of spoiling my surprise.

Cole holds up his hands as he laughs. "I didn't say a word, promise."

"He didn't. He only said no one won the bet and I'm getting extra treats on the honeymoon. Honestly, he's been quite smug." She pokes him in the ribs, and he flinches, laughing.

Now everyone is making their way to greet me.

"Hombre, did she wise up and leave you already?" Chance asks. He gets a whack upside the head for that. He laughs if off because that's nothing compared to his usual hits on the ice. The Renegades played last night at home and are off tomorrow. Coordinating with his schedule is why Ashleigh picked this weekend for their wedding.

"Nice shiner. Will look great in the pictures," I tease. He had quite the fight yesterday. Even though Chance's face is a little damaged, you should see the other guy.

"He can stand in the back with me to hide my belly," my sister-in-law Dani says.

"You will never hide in the back, Sunshine," my brother Alexander says.

I hug her and her seven-month pregnant belly. "You are absolutely stunning." I take both hands and extend my arms, taking her all in. "And I mean it. You're stunning on a normal day, but pregnant? Radiant as the sun."

"I tell her that every day, but she doesn't believe me," Alexander scowls. His adoring eyes drink his wife up. She rolls her eyes at him.

She's turned the grump into a softie, and I'm here for it. "I brought an early birthday present for Tyler. I'll swing by the house tomorrow and give it to him." I give Dani a playful wink and am rewarded with a classic Xander scowl. Tyler is their six-year-old son and my favorite addition to our family.

"It better not breathe, make noise, or cause a mess," Alexander warns.

"Now where's the fun in that?" I tease. I live to be the fun uncle.

Tripp, superstar pitcher for the Reapers, and Trevor are having an intense discussion with Emma in the corner while Darcy appears to give instructions to the caterers. Matt is standing behind her, giving her a shoulder massage. Yep, everyone's here.

"So, she's not an actress?" Ashleigh asks.

"Nope."

"Or a model?" Dani asks.

"Nope."

"Or a rock star, TV personality, or celebrity?" Emma asks as she hugs me and joins our circle of curious girls.

"Oh, I know!" Darcy chimes in. "A princess!"

I can't help but laugh at that one. The Swedish princess problem.

"Nope on all accounts."

"Tell us one thing," Ashleigh begs.

What do I want to share? You know her is too easy, even though I doubt they'd guess. "She's the patron of the otters at the Central Park Zoo."

"What kind of clue is that?" Dani asks.

"You didn't?" Chance shakes his head in disbelief.

"Oh, but he did," Harper says as she joins the group. "And it was the sweetest, most romantic thing anyone could ever do." She wraps her arm around mine, pushes up on her tiptoes, and gives me a kiss on the cheek.

I'm not sure what happens next because I'm pushed aside. High-pitched squealing that could explode lightbulbs ensues, and the glammed-up bride, maid of honor, and sister of the groom jump up and down and attack my girlfriend. It's pure pandemonium of the happiest kind.

"I take it they know her?" Dani asks me, safely away from the excitement zone.

"Yep. And apparently, they like her best. At least I've got their blessing." Harper is being peppered with hugs and questions. I can't wipe the grin off my face watching this scene.

Harper is getting all the things a girl needs from her squad. A wave of love washes over me, a powerful emotion that leaves me breathless. My girl is the perfect fit as the Decker Connection's newest member.

When the girls catch their breath, I introduce Harper to Dani, Tripp, and Trevor, and we all settle down for a delightful meal celebrating the special couple. Toasts all around make me laugh and cry. Sure, I was emotional at Alexander's wedding in February. But this wedding? It hits different. Maybe it's because Ashleigh is my sister, my fellow lover of romance books, and an amazing human being. Or maybe it's because I know the feeling of being in love.

I picture a similar scene, but this time it's Harper in white. My chest tightens, and butterflies dance in my belly. I need her to say those three words back to me, and we'll be on our way.

CHAPTER
FORTY-SIX

JULIAN

————

Last night was the tamest, but most enjoyable, bachelor party I've ever attended. We started the evening at TopGolf, a two-story driving range, hitting golf balls and mocking each other's swing. We continued our evening at a dimly lit bourbon bar, sharing life updates and offering Cole our best wishes for his marriage to Ashleigh. No strippers. No women at all. Just seven guys enjoying the evening, and several of us missing our significant others. We called it a night before the clock struck midnight and went home. For me, that meant an empty bed in an apartment that isn't much more personal than a hotel room. Harper joined the girls for a bachelorette party sleepover at Alexander's penthouse.

It was hard to fall asleep, knowing Harper was so close, only separated by three stories of steel and glass. There's no denying my addiction to this girl. I wanted to sneak up there and steal her away, but I behaved myself. Look at me being all mature.

I wake to the scent of bacon, and the excitement of seeing Harper soon brightens my mood. Wait? Bacon.

I hop out of bed, throw on pants, and find my girl in the kitchen wearing a pair of pink silk pajamas. It's the hottest thing I've ever seen.

"Well, this is unexpected." I wrap my arms around her waist, pulling her back into my chest. My hand palms her stomach, teasing the waistband of her tiny silk shorts.

"We had so much food, I thought I'd share," she giggles as I nibble on her ear.

"I'd rather have you for breakfast," I mumble.

"Are you always like this in the morning?" She reaches behind her, finding my erection ready and willing.

"Only when you're around." She turns around in my arms and kisses me, making me totally forget about the bacon.

I lift her up and set her on the counter, the perfect height to feast on her. I run my hand down the lapel of her pajama top, the buttons shouting at me to release them, and I obey, until her top hangs open, her breasts offering themselves to me for a taste. I kiss down her neck, to her collarbone, and give her breasts the attention they deserve.

"Did you have fun last night?" I ask between kisses. I'm taking my time enjoying her. Kissing her favorite places, I coax a quiet moan from her. My fingers dip below the waistband of her tiny shorts and my hand finds the promised land. I skim and tease her soaked slit.

"Um, hum," she responds.

"Did you take the elevator in this?" Another wordless response that I take as a yes. "I hope no one saw you looking this delicious." I've never been the jealous type, but Harper, well, she's for my eyes only.

Her giggle flips my switch, and I go from slow and lazy to insatiable in less than a second. "I know you aren't much of a morning person, but I'm going to change that."

I pull her to the edge of the counter, and she leans back, her hands holding her up, giving me better access. I fill her with one finger, then two, while my thumb massages her clit, finger banging her like my life's happiness depends on it. By the look on her face and the sounds she's making, she's happy too. When she comes, she throws her head back and moans my name in a way that I want to remember for the rest of my life.

With a smug smile, I lick my fingers clean, and I'm rewarded with a new surprised look. This one is seductive, sexy, and curious. I crave to see this one again and again.

"So much better than bacon," I tease. My lips find hers, and I'm lost in Harper again. I lift her from the counter, her legs wrap around my waist, and I carry her back to the bed where I enjoy a full Harper breakfast buffet.

As she lays with her head on my chest, her fingers idly glide over my abs. We both got a full workout this morning, and we haven't left the apartment. I can get used to this kind of cardio.

"What's the plan for today?" she asks.

"Well, we need calories if we're going to continue to function. Then I'll give you options. Tyler has a ball game this morning. Xander, Matt, and Tripp coach the team, and it's pretty fucking adorable. Or we can explore Charlotte if you want. I can show you where I had my first kiss." I wiggle my eyebrows, and she laughs.

"Who was the lucky girl?"

"Paige Fulton. Sixth grade. We were in Freedom Park. Her brother threw a pinecone and hit my ear, cutting our make-out session short. It lasted about ten seconds." That was a lifetime ago.

"I wonder where Paige is now."

"Married to an IT guy with two kids and living in Wilmington."

She sits up and throws me another one of those surprised looks. "Seriously? You keep up with your first kiss?" Her insecurity is showing a little. I think she's still skeptical about my declaration of love. From her perspective, my public dating history doesn't bode well, and I'm aware of that. I'm determined to show her I'm not the man she reads about on the internet.

"First of all, she was my first heartbreak too. She broke up with me the next day. Shredded me for a solid week. But yeah. Her twin brother is Maddox Fulton, a pitcher for the LA Stars. That pinecone was extremely accurate and painful. Maddox and I stayed friends throughout school, and he signed with the Decker Agency a few years ago."

"Of course," she laughs. "Six degrees of Julian Decker strikes again." She gets up and makes her way to the bathroom. "I'm open to anything. I want you to enjoy this weekend with your family. Thanks for sharing it with me."

Her thoughtfulness, putting my family first this weekend, makes me love her even more.

———

I've been a blubbering mess all day. I'm an emotional disaster, and once the floodgates opened, the tears haven't stopped. My day has been a roller coaster of highs and more highs. My tears first appeared while watching my brother coach his son's little league game. The way Xander loves on his wife and son is the most wholesome thing I've ever seen. He's still a hard ass most of the time, except around them. And now my sister is standing in front of us, pledging her love to Cole, and it's fucking poetry.

"Here," Harper says under her breath as she hands me a tissue. I stopped apologizing for my crying after losing it when I saw Ashleigh in her wedding dress. Tears of pure, unrestrained happiness cascade down my face, a joyous overflow that I can't contain. Harper hasn't laughed or run away, so bonus points there.

I probably should have warned her I'm a crier. Most men get choked up one time or another. We're raised to hold it down, keep the tears at bay. And I do most of the time. But a super-sentimental movie or commercial gets me every time. And my siblings living their best lives with their soulmates is the most sentimental thing I can imagine. Having Harper here is the icing on the cake. Because all I can see is our future. Our wedding. Our kids.

"Thanks." I dab at my eyes.

She leans across me, hands a tissue to Chance, and I chuckle. At least I'm not alone. Harper takes my hand and squeezes. I'm so grateful she's here to support me and share this moment with my family.

After the wedding, we take more pictures than necessary, and then we head to the reception for a gourmet dinner. With dinner and toasts concluded, Cole rises, takes the microphone, and presents Ashleigh with an unforgettable grand gesture that belongs in a romance novel. Ashleigh is stunned when Cole welcomes her favorite band, Pineapple Sunset, to the party. While the hottest boy band on the planet is used to performing in large stadiums, they jumped at the chance to play this small, personal event for Cole. They became friends after he wrote a few songs for them.

They congratulate the happy couple and open their set with a brand new song. As a wedding gift for Ashleigh, Cole wrote this love song, and Pineapple Sunset will release it as their next single. Since everyone at the wedding is close family or friends, there's little chance this performance will go viral online.

Harper and the girls are on the dance floor, taking turns dancing with Tyler, the only child in attendance. I'm hanging in the back of the room at the bar. I can't resist snapping a picture to capture the moment, watching Harper's joyful and carefree expression light up the room.

My dad orders a whiskey and takes in the scene with me. "I don't think I've ever seen you like this."

"Like what?"

"Content. You're always moving, searching. Work. Family. You keep reaching for more, like it's never enough." I'm sure that's what it looks like from the outside.

I turn and look at my father. My same blue eyes look back at me. His usually stern face is less harsh now. The lines around his eyes are softer. It's been an emotional day for him, for all of us. He didn't hide his tears when he danced with Ashleigh, no doubt missing my mother. We always miss mom, but this momentous occasion hits harder, probably for my dad more than anyone. He's never dated since Mom died fourteen years ago. I wonder if he ever will. They had the love story I write books about. That one true love. The happily ever after.

His comment hits me to the core. I've accomplished more than most in my thirty-one years. I've worked hard to build my highly lucrative business. I'm blessed with loving friends and family, more money and notoriety than I need. I'm living the good life. I'm happy.

"I'm not sure I know what you mean, Dad. I'm grateful for my life and all that I have. I don't take it for granted." Sure, I stay busy. But I'm aware of how fortunate I am. I work hard and play hard.

"I know. You have your mother's humility." His face is full of pride when he glances at me before turning his attention back to the dance floor. "Son, it's wonderful to see you finally at peace, like you've realized you have all you need. I hope you'll slow down and enjoy it all, especially your happily ever after. While you have it." He smiles, a forlorn expression softening his features further, as he watches the women dancing.

"You're right. She's my missing piece."

Harper's laugh carries back to me, and I can't look away. She's captured my attention and I'm singularly focused.

"What about you, Dad? What's it going to take for you to be content? Are you open to love again?" I've always admired his devotion to my mom, but today, it makes me sad for him. Wouldn't it be amazing if he found love and joy again?

"I'm open, but unless she shows up at my door, I doubt I'll go down that road again. I don't want to be with a woman who merely wants me for my money." This I understand completely.

Being a billionaire can make it hard to find a woman not looking for a sugar daddy.

"Well, you never know," I tease. "Call me if you need Team True Love to run a background check or something."

His chuckle is music to my ears. I don't hear that from him enough.

"Love looks good on you, Jules." He cups my cheek, gives me a rare smile, takes his drink, and joins his friend Devin Millbanks. The two old friends sit back and watch the party from the sidelines.

I'm thinking about what my dad said when Chance escorts Harper to me at the bar. "I'm wiped. It's like I'm playing in a double-overtime game." He loosens his tie and guzzles a glass of water.

"You hockey players need more yoga and cardio. Ask Zac. He's feeling the difference," she teases him.

She settles into my side and fits perfectly. Yep, she's my missing puzzle piece. Or missing peace? Maybe my dad is right. I'm content with Harper by my side. Content. I let that word sit with me. This peaceful, slower pace is definitely something I could get used to.

"The newlyweds are leaving soon, and then we need to head out too," I tell Harper. "We've got a flight to catch tomorrow."

"Headed back to New York?" Chance asks.

"No. Italy. We've got a cooking class to attend." Cole isn't the only one who can pull off a grand gesture.

"What?" And there it is. Her surprised expression that I'll continue to chase, no matter how content I am.

CHAPTER
FORTY-SEVEN

HARPER

———

After a whirlwind week of amazing people, places, and things, I'm back in New York with nothing but my imagination to keep me company. Zac's games are on the west coast for the next few days, and Julian is in California on a work trip. I considered going to Raleigh to see Lawson, but the Renegades are doing the Canada sweep. Everyone is away from home.

So it's just me and Noodle. My laundry is done. The apartment is clean. My Christmas shopping is underway. I've practiced several meals we prepared in Italy, ready to serve them at our next hockey dinner. I've even binged the latest season of *Bridgerton*. Now what?

I had my last meeting with Professor Daniels today, and because of Julian's work travel, he had to reschedule his check-in. The meeting was encouraging, although his feedback was critical and fair. I've taken it and grown as an author. He thought the ending could be reworked, but the editor thought it was appropriate for Charlotte and Gavin. The book is getting a final proofreading and then a rush to print by the new year, maybe even before Christmas.

Forget the tight deadlines and brutal feedback. Falling in love took my storytelling to the next level. Julian's love has changed me personally and professionally. And I still haven't told him how much I love him.

I considered saying it while we were in Italy. Everything about that trip was amazing. We stayed in a charming villa overlooking the ocean, and every day we got a cooking lesson from a private chef. And in between meals, we biked through vineyards, wandered through museums or shopped in the local market. Four days was not enough time, but we had to get back to reality and obligations. He promised me a return trip soon. Without me telling him I love him.

Why didn't I tell him? I don't want it to be reactive. I want it to be just because. When we're spending a Tuesday at home watching TV and eating popcorn. Normal life. That's what I want him to know. I love him in the boring and mundane parts of life. But the problem is nothing with Julian is boring and he doesn't know how to have an uneventful Tuesday. I don't want him to think I love him because of his incredibly romantic gestures. I love him because of who he is as a man. At the next opportunity of mundane, I'll tell him.

We haven't talked much these past few days. The time difference makes it difficult, and he's dealing with some crisis with a basketball player in LA. He sends the sweetest texts that I see when I wake up.

Noodle and I are settling in for the evening with a new puzzle and a pint of Ben and Jerry's when I get an unexpected call.

"Hey gorgeous, what are you up to?"

"Just telling Noodle how much I miss you."

"Miss you too. Are you home right now? Kat is dropping off your dinner. Should be downstairs in a few minutes."

"You really don't have to do that. I bet she enjoys her downtime when you're gone." Apparently, he pays her a generous salary to be at his beck and call, and she doesn't seem to mind, but I hate to be a burden.

"She was out anyway," he says casually. "Hey, Ashleigh's calling. Let me see what she needs. I'll call you later. Enjoy dinner. Love you."

And like that, he's gone. Downstairs I discover a Chick-Fil-A bag, a bouquet of peonies, and a newly released book by one of my favorite authors. It's not fancy or expensive. No, Julian's romantic gestures cover the entire spectrum from outrageous to simple and thoughtful. I don't know if Julian knows how to do boring and mundane.

He told me to listen to my heart. And my heart shouts we belong together. I hug the flowers to my chest to calm my butterflies. Yeah, next time I see him, I'll tell him, no matter what.

CHAPTER
FORTY-EIGHT

JULIAN

———

Hearing Harper's voice raises my spirits and makes my shit day bearable.

"Hey Ash, what's up?"

"Jules, Cole's in trouble!"

Fuck.

CHAPTER
FORTY-NINE

HARPER

————

It's been two days since I've talked to Julian. I've texted him a few times to say hi, and he sends short, quick replies. Today, no response. I have a bad feeling about this. I called him a few hours ago, and he didn't answer. Sure, he could be at some business lunch, but he usually texts. A lot. I don't want to be that needy girl, but I want to make sure he's okay. Active imagination and idle time are not a good combination.

I call Lawson, and after our usual catch up, I try to act casual when I ask if Chance is around.

"Yeah, why?" His voice carries a hint of suspicion.

"I wanted to ask a quick question, that's all. He's Julian's best friend, and I figured he could help me with Christmas present ideas." He grunts acceptance and yells for Chance across the dressing room. They're getting ready for a game in Colorado.

I hate lying to Lawson, but I don't want him to worry. Although he pretends to be fine with Julian, he's carefully observing to make sure I'm treated well. Despite his pretense of not being overprotective, he does it from a distance. Doesn't mean he's not monitoring everything.

"Hey Harps, how are you?" Chance's jovial voice puts me on high alert. If something was wrong with Julian, he wouldn't be so chipper.

"I'm um, I'm okay. I know it's silly, but I was wondering if you've heard from Julian today."

"Yeah, a little bit ago. He was getting his hair cut for some red-carpet thing that Maddie roped him into and didn't have time to talk. You know I don't keep up with his circle. Whenever he's in LA, he always gets wrapped up and forgets us little people." I bristle at Chance's joke. Julian talked to Chance. He's fine. He's just not talking to me. And he's with Madelyn Reynolds. Okay then.

"Well, we're a bunch of missed connections," I chuckle, a hint of sadness in my voice. "And I'm glad to know he's okay." I plaster a fake smile across my face, a thin mask over the upset that's churning inside. "Hey, get a goal tonight. Or two."

"When I score, I'll dedicate it to you, Harps. See you soon." He disconnects our call, and I let the tears fall while I google red-carpet events happening in Los Angeles tonight.

One event is live-streaming and I get it ready to watch. I'm curled up on the couch with Noodle while beautiful people walk this red carpet, the women in glamorous dresses, the men in designer suits. It's the premiere of a music video with a charity concert afterward. I don't understand why Julian would be there, but I'm watching intently. Maybe Chance was wrong. This is the only red carpet I could find in LA tonight, so I wait nervously to see if my boyfriend is in attendance.

The paparazzi go crazy, yelling at the A-list movie star, Madelyn Reynolds, and my heart sinks. Maddie. In her form-fitting sequined cocktail dress, she's absolutely stunning, a vision of elegance beside a man I assume is her fiancé. She glances down the carpet, her eyes falling on Julian, who has a stunning blonde draped alluringly over his arm.

The camera focuses on Madelyn as she stops in front of a reporter, their conversation drowning out the shouts of her name by the adoring crowd and reporters. She explains she's there to support her fiancé, Fredrick, her voice soft but firm with quiet pride.

"Fredrick, we're all anxiously awaiting the announcement of the next bachelor. Any hints?" The reporter puts the microphone in his face, and the camera zooms in, hoping for the scoop.

"Why don't you talk to Julian Decker and see what he has to say?" Fredrick winks at the camera and steps away. The reporter calls Julian over. The blonde looks familiar, but I'm too fixated on Julian. His easy smile. His perfectly tailored suit. His arm around the blonde.

"Julian, care to comment on the rumor you're going to be the next bachelor?"

He chuckles before he responds. "I'm in a relationship, so no, not interested." The blonde snuggles in closer to Julian. Is he implying he's in a relationship with her?

The reporter shifts her attention to the mystery girl with Julian.

"Kelsey, what's it like opening for country-music royalty?" Kelsey? I rack my brain to place her. Is she the girl who won *America's Next Country Star*? Maybe. I only saw clips on TikTok, so I can't be sure.

She leans in and gives Julian a kiss on the cheek, a touch of lipstick remaining as a reminder. I'm pretty sure she was going for the lips, but he seemed to turn his head, so she missed. Given Julian's composure and acceptance of the circumstances, it's impossible to say for sure what's going on.

"Amazing. Everything is amazing right now," she coos. Julian smiles at the camera, holds his hand out, and guides her down the red carpet.

Anger radiates through my body as my call goes straight to his voicemail. I'm confused. Pissed. I don't control my tone when leaving a message.

"What the fuck did I just watch, Julian? You know what? Don't bother answering."

CHAPTER
FIFTY

JULIAN

———

I fucking hate life right now. I especially hate this mediocre singer draped on my arm wearing too much perfume that doesn't cover the stench of alcohol on her breath. But here I am.

When I got Ashleigh's call, my heart stopped. When my family needs me, I'll do anything for them. And that includes walking this red carpet as part of a so-called negotiation to protect them. It feels more like blackmail, but I had limited options.

Cole's working with a record label and Kelsey, an up-and-coming singer. When he and Ashleigh helped get her drunk ass back to her hotel safely, incriminating pictures were taken. Cole had his arm around Kelsey to hold her up while Ash went to the desk to get her room number. It wasn't on Kelsey's room key. While they waited in the hotel lobby, Kelsey tried to kiss Cole, exactly like she did with me tonight. Ashleigh was right there, but of course she's not in the pictures.

Unfortunately, a picture is worth a thousand words and ten

times as many dollars. The photographer knew the potential of his picture and reached out to Ashleigh on social media before publishing it. Only he didn't want money. When he directed her to Fredrick Hamilton, I was on high alert.

A story like this could tank Cole's baseball career, even if it's untrue. The Liberties have a strict morality clause in their contracts. While this scandal could impact his image, more importantly, it could jeopardize his potential call up to the Liberties this season. Not to mention my sister's reputation being questioned. Unfortunately, on the internet, appearances hold the weight of truth.

I contacted Fredrick, Maddie's fiancé, to kill the story, and that bastard blackmailed me. I didn't have time to rally my lawyers, so I had to work with what I had. In order for Fredrick to step in and kill the smear story, he wanted me to agree to consider his tv offer, which I won't do. His other ultimatum was to help elevate Kelsey's image with a few pictures. I agreed to that, although now I'm wondering if I can even elevate her to ground level. She's so fucking low.

I had a heart-to-heart with Maddie and spilled the details. She was furious and wanted to call it off with her fiancé immediately, but she has to give her publicist enough time to control the story. Fredrick won't be happy about that, but that's too bad, slimeball. I'm glad to play a part in this story, if only to get her out of this mess, too.

But once this ball got rolling, it was moving fast. Maddie and I are both playing our parts tonight and giving Oscar-worthy performances. Unfortunately, I wasn't able to talk to Harper about it, but the chances of her seeing a minor LA premiere are slim to none. While she follows celebrity gossip, this isn't her scene, and I doubt it will hit TikTok. I'll call her later tonight and explain everything.

———

After this shitshow of an evening, I'm finally back at the hotel. I shower and wash off the stench of perfume and vomit before I call Harper. Yep. Kelsey threw up on my shoes at the concert. I texted Fredrick to come get his problem and left. At least I have more time for Facetime with my girl. We'll get a good laugh over my horrible night, and she'll remind me that my world is amazing because she's in it.

I pick up my phone to call her and am sent straight to voicemail. I scroll through my missed notifications and see a missed call and voicemail from Harper. I can't wait to hear her voice, so I put it on speaker and hit play.

Her anger comes through the phone, loud and clear.

"What the fuck did I just watch, Julian? You know what? Don't bother answering."

Shit. I call her again. Straight to voicemail.

I text her.

> It's not what it looks like.

I wait for the bubbles to tell me she's responding. Nothing. It's late on the east coast. Maybe she's asleep.

I'm committed to one more appearance with Kelsey tomorrow, then I'm on the first flight back to New York immediately after. I need to explain everything to Harper, and we'll be fine. My NDA with Frederick specified Harper would be fully informed. Actually, she'll be included in all my future contracts. I want to be completely open with her, even about the Swedish Princess. I trust her implicitly.

> I'm taking the red-eye home tomorrow, and I'll explain everything.

> I love you.

If ever there was a time to hear those three words from her, now would be nice.

No messages from Harper this morning, but that's okay. I'll get through today and have her in my arms in twenty-four hours.

> Hey gorgeous! Can't wait to see you soon. I'll explain everything, and we'll get a good laugh from it. Love you.

My heart speeds up when I see the three dots start and stop. She's mad and has every right to be. Knowing she's awake, I call. Sent to voicemail. Yeah, she's pissed. To be honest, I'm a little turned on by her jealousy and fire. I'm glad she's possessive like that because I'm all hers.

I search online for footage from last night to gauge what she saw, and it isn't pretty. Shit. I'll make sure tonight doesn't look cozy at all. I can fix this. Just a little bump in the road. I mean, she all but told me she wasn't a "roll over" kind of girl. But I'm confident that once she gets the entire story and I'm able to kiss her, we'll be fine. No, better than fine.

Maddie and I met with Kelsey and she profusely apologized for last night and the incident with Cole. As I suspected, she's spiraling. We offered to help, see if we can renegotiate her contract, but most importantly, get her into treatment. Hopefully, the thirty days out of the spotlight will help clear her head and her situation. We need to get through tonight and then put our plan into action.

The event tonight is LA casual, allowing me to be stylish in jeans and casual shoes, which is great because my dress shoes got ruined last night. It also means the ladies are rocking shorter dresses and flaunting more skin. When it comes to perceptions tonight, I've got to be extra vigilant.

It's time for the show. Kelsey and I walk the carpet as friends.

We aren't giving couple vibes, ensuring the only touching is that of a gentleman escorting a lady. Of course, I can't control what they write, but I can do my best to make sure the pictures don't support their narrative.

More pictures. More reporters. I wish Harper was here. I imagine her in a sexy sequined dress, low back, fuck me heels. She'd put these women to shame with her natural beauty. I can't help but smile at the cameras because I'm thinking of her.

Kelsey ducks out after a few pictures to get ready for her set. "Good luck," I tell her. "I'm cheering for you." She really is a sweet girl. Unfortunately, she's caught in the ugly world of LA and the music industry.

I walk the last half of the red carpet by myself. Stop, smile, move on.

"Julian, Julian, over here!" they yell at me. I smile. Hand in my pocket. Nod, move on. Over and over.

"Julian, care to comment on your romance-writing career as JB Moore?" a voice yells over the crowd. My smile falters for a half-second before I compose myself and keep walking. I laugh it off and shake my head, working to keep my face neutral.

What the fuck? How did he know?

I duck into the restroom, press send, my call going straight to voicemail. Again.

"Well, you did it, and I really shouldn't be surprised." My voice is full of venom. "Hope you feel better now that you've gotten your revenge. Congratulations, gorgeous. I never thought you could be so fucking hideous. To think I thought I loved you. And I know for sure you didn't love me." My rage devolves to despair, and I choke back my emotion. "I shouldn't have trusted you," I say, all my life force drained. I disconnect the call and block her.

My heart shatters, but I splash water on my face and pull myself together. I'm in LA and have a performance to give. I'm a doting friend to Kelsey. I'll focus on helping her for now. That will be the one real thing I can do in a city full of fakeness. Now that my heart is in a million pieces, I can be fake too.

I remind myself I'm doing this to help Ashleigh and Cole. I dig deep to find the one good thing in this awful situation.

I should be grateful Harper's true nature came out before I got more involved with her. I can't be with someone I can't trust. Her betrayal cuts deep, but better to know now, I tell myself.

I try to stay positive, but it's tough when you're heartbroken.

CHAPTER
FIFTY-ONE

HARPER

———

His texts assure me it's not how it appears. After sleeping on it, I realize I trust him. My heart is in charge now. From day one, he's been faithful and keeps telling me things aren't always as they look. There's almost always a spin. While I can't imagine the spin of him acting like he's with a singer, I'll give him the benefit of the doubt for now. That's what you do when you love someone.

I put my phone on do not disturb so I can work on the last round of edits for our book. We agreed I'd finish it up since he's caught up with work, and we want to meet our deadlines. I take Noodle for his evening walk and pop in my earbuds to listen to my favorite podcast. That's when I see Julian's voicemail and hit play. He called me two hours ago. Maybe he got in early?

"Well, you did it, and I really shouldn't be surprised." I stop in my tracks at the hitch in his voice. His angry tone is one I've never heard before, and it scares me. I can practically feel the dagger in my chest. "Hope you feel better now that you've gotten your revenge. Congratulations, gorgeous. I never thought you could be so fucking hideous. To think I thought I loved you. And I know for sure you didn't love me. I shouldn't have trusted you." He says the last sentence as an afterthought, the hurt and heartbreak evident in his voice.

Loved? As in past tense? What is he talking about? What did I do? This is more than not responding to his texts. Noodle and I take the fastest walk on record, and I get home to call him. I didn't want to talk this out through text or a phone call, but I don't think I have a choice at this point. His message is dire.

I call him, and it goes straight to voicemail but doesn't allow me to leave a message. I text him, and it doesn't say delivered. Did he block me? Since I can't get in touch with the source, I resort to the internet to track him down. He's at a charity concert where Kelsey Hamilton is performing. He said she's a friend, and I believe him.

Julian looks amazing in his dark jeans, crisp white t-shirt, and blazer. My god, he's sexy. It's obvious why he's one of America's hottest bachelors. Julian is the total package. It's like he's made for the red-carpet world.

Although it's not the familiar goofy grin he has when we're together, his smile is convincing enough to deceive others into believing he's happy to be there. Then it happens. A reporter asks him about JB Moore. Shit. His smile slips, and his eyes narrow for a split second before smiling again. Unless you were actively searching for it, you would easily overlook his subtle transformation.

He's totally blowing off the person who shouted the question, shifting his attention to the venue entrance. He strides down the plush carpet with determination and disappears into the building.

I piece together the timeline. He called me seven minutes after that comment. Seven minutes to conclude it was me. Seven minutes for him to fall out of love with me because he thought I could hurt him that callously. Seven minutes to think that I'd betray his secret. Seven minutes to give up on me. On us.

Seven minutes. It's disheartening that he easily ended us so quickly, but what truly disappoints me is his lack of understanding about who I truly am. Did he miss my description of Charlotte? She's a fighter. She doesn't let go easily. It's not about revenge. It's about going down swinging. I refuse to let him end us that easily.

He kept saying he wanted to know everything about me. Well, Julian Decker is about to learn his lesson when it comes to me. How dare he declare I didn't love him. I regret not saying the words, but I'll be damned if he discounts my feelings for him to something less than what they are. Love. Love of the deepest, purest, most passionate nature. I love him down to my core. I'll have to prove it to him.

I take a deep breath and put my anger and heartbreak aside. I pull out my notebook and put the pieces together. I have a problem to solve. A puzzle. Step one: Find the leak. Prove it wasn't me. Step two: I'll get him to love me again. But one step at a time.

I force myself to listen to his message and write it down word for word. I need to address every sentence, every thought, every nuance. He's not the only one who was doing a deep-dive character study into the person they love. I was paying attention too.

According to Julian, only three people know his secret. His editor has known for years, and she wouldn't say anything. She has nothing to gain from it. The NYU writing program has our real names, but they wouldn't release that information, and certainly not to the paparazzi. So that leaves me. And in his mind, I have something to gain. Revenge. Only I don't. Because I didn't tell a soul. Not even during the bachelorette party, when the girls asked me questions about my writing. I stayed vague, never sharing his secret. It's his. I would never. But someone did. If I'm going to fix us, I'm going to have to solve this, and soon, before the damage is irreparable.

CHAPTER
FIFTY-TWO

JULIAN

————

"Well, the good news is, your book sales are ten times what they were last week," Casey Samuels, my editor, says. She's doing her best to cheer me up, but I'm not sure it's possible. Am I upset about my unmasking? A little. The response in the last two days has been mostly positive and encouraging. My friends and family are supportive, if not a little angry I didn't tell them. I'm a fool for doubting their reaction would be anything but positive.

The ongoing group chat is typical Decker chaos wrapped in love and support of one another. I scroll through the chat while Casey keeps talking and encouraging me to own my work. Between the two, my spirits lift.

CHANCE

How do you have time to write books when you spend so much time reading them? Well done, hermano.

ALEXANDER

I shouldn't be surprised with your Team True Love and all. BTW, Dani loves your books, and she gets pretty worked up after a particularly sexy scene, so thanks.

ASHLEIGH

First, Xander, ewww. I don't want to hear about that. But mostly, Jules, I adore your books. You know that because you've heard me gush about them. I'm not just saying that. When's the next one coming out?

ALEXANDER

Ash, you know that's how she got pregnant, right? Don't tell me I need to have the birds and the bees talk with you.

EMMA

Xander, I can't think of anything more horrifying. Please stop.

EMMA

Dani, control your husband. 🙄🙄

EMMA

Jules, I'm excited to read your next book. I'm kinda thinking a rugby player could be hot.

CHANCE

No way. Hockey players are way hotter. What do you know about rugby, anyway?

TREVOR

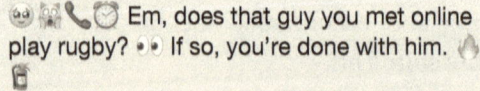 Em, does that guy you met online play rugby? •• If so, you're done with him. 🔥 📱

WAIT?! Emma is online dating. We can't be okay with that. I give her a question mark reaction. We need to come back to this.

DARCY

Is this why you were taking notes during book club? Were we your beta readers? I'm honored. Will you sign my copy?

I'm not surprised Darcy caught on to my heightened interest. She's perceptive and insightful.

COLE

You've encouraged me to lean into my music because of your own experiences. That's cool. You're a decent brother-in-law and even better mentor. 😅

I chuckle at that. I'm a fucking fantastic brother-in-law.

MATT

This explains all that time on your laptop in Mexico, doesn't it? You sneaky bastard. Well done.

DANI

Sorry, just woke up. What'd I miss?

———

"So, like I said, own it with pride," Casey continues. "Don't hide from it. Own it."

"You're right. I will. It's, well, it's not about the secret, really. It's how I was betrayed, that, well, you're right. Casey, I appreciate you. Thanks for reaching out." I don't really want to get into my feelings with Casey, even though I'm sure she'd be up to listening.

"Anytime. I'm so excited I can tell Joey now. He's going to flip, in a good way, of course." I can practically see her bouncing with joy. Yeah. This. Casey hasn't told her husband, the Carolina

Reaper's catcher, because she has professional boundaries. I know with absolute confidence she wasn't the leak.

"Hey, I'm getting another call. Thanks again and talk soon." I disconnect and click over.

Maddie dumped Fredrick and moved into her lavish Malibu beach house yesterday. I packed up my hotel room and moved into her guest room. My pity party relocated to Malibu, and now it's a party of two. They say misery loves company, so we're putting that to the test.

I've decided to stay in LA for a little longer. Honestly, I've been operating on autopilot since being destroyed two days ago. Madelyn's been there for me, despite her own relationship issues. Besides, the California sunshine is nice, and I'm not ready to go back to the cold of New York. Granted, LA's cold in its own way. Hell, it's probably the most heartless place I know. Heartless. I feel it.

Am I licking my wounds? Absolutely. Because New York is a reminder of Harper. It's a city of feeling. Passion. And my current state prefers no feeling at all. Maybe I'll open a west coast office of the agency since no signs of recovery are in sight.

"Hey, Mads. Are you going to be home tonight?" I push down my sadness and try to make myself sound normal, practically chipper. I'm afraid it falls flat.

"No, and neither are you. We're hitting Nobu, and I have to go to some club premiere, and you'll be on my arm. Let's give them something to talk about." She knows I'm heartbroken and is trying to cheer me up the only way she knows how. She's a good friend. Would pictures of us together be a huge middle finger to Fredrick and Harper? Sure. But I don't want to hurt Harper. I want to try to forget her. Move on. I tried the happily ever after approach, and it didn't work. Shallow and meaningless are the only relationships I can handle. Romance novels are pure fantasy.

"Not sure I'm up for it," I tell her while searching the empty refrigerator. Another strike against the LA scene. They don't really eat at home, if they eat at all.

"Too bad. I need some cheering up, you need some cheering up, so let's cheer each other up. Come on, be a friend," she whines.

"Fine," I mumble. "But I'm not going to enjoy it."

And I don't.

CHAPTER
FIFTY-THREE

HARPER

———

I shouldn't have put a Google alert on my phone because it's constantly popping off, but I need to keep track of Julian while fixing this mess. I'm still blocked, so I've resorted to cyber stalking. It seems he was out with Madelyn Reynolds last night, and they were all over LA. He's smiling, but not having fun. I've seen his genuine smiles, memorized them, cherished them, and these don't qualify. Not even close.

He told me Madelyn Reynolds is a friend, and I will myself to believe that's all they will be, even if she's recently single. Some internet stories imply she broke off her engagement for Julian. Understandable because he's so lovable, but they can't be romantically involved. Because he loves me. Present tense.

It's hard to watch him sliding back into his public life so effortlessly, after he shared how lonely it was before me. Unfortunately, he's relapsed back to his old ways because it's comfortable. But it's empty and he'll do anything to avoid pain. Clearly, because I'm watching the proof of his avoidance on TMZ.

"What the hell is all this?" Zac asks as he enters the living room from his morning skate. Arranged on the coffee table are two laptops, a whiteboard leaning against the window, and several notebooks scattered around. I'm in full-detective mode. I'm considering buying a corkboard and red yarn to tie it all together, to be honest.

"Just trying to solve a crime." I pull the pencil out of my messy bun, and my hair falls in my face.

"Should I be looking for a chalk outline?" He looks over his shoulder, and I give him a maniacal laugh when Noodle barks at him.

"Not yet."

He sits on the couch and leans down to rub my shoulders. I'm sitting on the floor in day-old yoga clothes, my glasses crooked on my nose, and my hair unbrushed. I must be a sight.

"Is Decker out with Madelyn Reynolds? Fuck, she's hot." He leans closer to get a better look at the gorgeous actress, her arm draped over his shoulder, dancing at some club. There's space between them, so at least she's not grinding up against him. I wouldn't blame her if she was because he can use those hips. Those hips. I sigh. And thoughts like that get me off task. Need. To. Focus.

"Yep." I shudder and lock my emotions away. They aren't helping right now.

"I don't know how you aren't losing it right now. Tell me you aren't going to snap or breakdown." His concern is touching, endearing even. But I don't have time to break down. Time is of the essence.

"Nope. I'm going to fix this." I'm determined. I'm going to solve this, make him talk to me, and if he doesn't want me after that, well, then I'll fall apart. But not now.

Zac slides down from the couch and joins me on the floor. He puts his arm around me and squeezes. "And I thought Decker was the crazy one. You guys belong together." I nod my head in agreement. We do. We absolutely do.

Another side hug, and he gets up and heads to his room. "Let me know how I can help. I'm going to go read for a bit."

That's not how Zac usually spends his down time, but maybe my chaos is infringing on his video-game space. "What are you reading?"

"Some sappy book by a guy I know. It's insightful." I can't help but laugh.

My phone vibrates with an incoming call.

"Hey, how ya' doing, Harps?" Lawson's voice is caring but cautious. He's worried about me.

"I'm okay." And I am. For now. "Kind of focused on solving this mystery of who leaked Julian's information, so this whole thing can be fixed."

"He still blocking you?"

"Yeah, I don't like it, but I understand. I'm a little disappointed he doesn't trust me, but I get that, too." And I do. I stayed in my head, waiting for the perfect time to confess my feelings. And that time didn't come. If I'd been more open instead of trying to live out some fairytale, maybe we wouldn't be in this mess.

And if I hadn't been angry and left that damn voicemail, we wouldn't be here either. It's important I own my part in the story.

"Hey, you didn't betray him and leak it, so don't beat yourself up."

"I'm not, really. But I've got to get him to talk to me. Has he talked to Chance?" I'm not proud, but I'll use every resource and contact I have to gather intelligence about what I'm facing.

"Short texts, that's all."

"Does Chance think I'm the bad guy?" I wince at the thought. His friends are fiercely loyal, but I'd like to consider them my friends too. Losing them is a one-two punch.

There's some mumbling in the background, and Lawson is back. "No. Listen, we'll be playing in LA Friday, and he plans on knocking some sense into him."

"Tell him I appreciate it. I need him to talk to me. Just talk. Once we do that, he can decide about me." I'm convinced that once we talk and I solve the mystery of the leak, it will all be resolved.

"From where I'm sitting, the apology should come from him." The slight edge in his voice lets me know I'm always his number one. I appreciate his support, but I don't want him angry with Julian. At least not yet.

An email notification chimes, and I open it quickly. "YES!" I jump up and do a happy dance. Noodle barks at my sudden change in demeanor.

Zac runs into the room. "What? Everything alright? Is this where you lose it?" Panic fills his face, and I cackle. I'm sure I look unhinged.

Lawson is also panicking. "Harps? You okay? Harps?" His distant voice is coming through the phone.

I pick it up and talk to Lawson. "I'm fine, but I've gotta go. I've got to go!"

I reread the email from Professor Daniels, rush to get ready, and go for an in-person meeting at NYU. It seems he has the answer I'm looking for, and hopefully the solution to my problem.

CHAPTER
FIFTY-FOUR

HARPER

———

Chance's Facetime with me is a grim update. He tried to convince Julian to talk to me, to hear me out. He wouldn't do it. My alleged betrayal cut deep.

"I appreciate the effort. I just need him to listen. Maybe I'll rent a billboard in LA?" It's been days since Chance talked to him. He won't share much with me about their conversation, but I'm assured he's safe. And heartbroken. Although, his pictures around town with Madelyn Reynolds tell a different story. *Things aren't always as they appear,* I remind myself.

"Doubt that will work. I even tried evoking the spirit of Team True Love and, well, it wasn't pretty." Chance is telling me straight, and I appreciate it. "How are you holding up?"

"Exhausted. I've never worked so hard in my entire life. But it's worth it." I've been writing for sixteen hours a day and I'm drained, physically and emotionally. But I'm focused on the task at hand.

I'm so tired, my brain takes a second to process what he said.

"Hey! That gives me an idea," I squeal. "Thanks Chance, you're the best friend Julian could ever have!" I'm so excited I pace around the disheveled apartment, Noodle scrambling to the safety of his bed.

"Um, thanks? What'd I do?"

"Can I ask a favor?" I bat my bloodshot eyes at him and poke out my bottom lip. It doesn't take much to look pathetic these days.

"Maybe?" He hesitates. Julian's lucky to have him in his corner. I feel awful asking him for this favor, but my desperation leaves me no choice.

"Can we call an emergency meeting of Team True Love? I have an idea, and I need their help."

"Do you mind if I ask them first?" Again, I appreciate Chance protecting his best friend. He's trying to balance what Julian wants versus what he needs. Because sometimes, we need our friends to take the lead for us when we can't think for ourselves.

"Of course. Let them know I didn't betray him, but I know who did. You believe me, don't you?"

There's a pause, and Chance's expression turns hard, like he's facing an opposing player at puck drop. "Harper, do you love him? He says you never told him. Is that true?" I'm a little stunned by his question. Would I be going to all this trouble if I didn't?

His question deflates me, the air leaving my lungs like a punctured balloon. The bitter taste of regret coats my tongue. Why didn't I just tell him? I close my eyes and take a calming breath.

"It's true. I never told him. But Chance, I love him with all my heart and soul. I didn't say those words because I was waiting for a mundane moment to tell him. I wanted him to know it wasn't in response to his declaration of love or because he whisked me off to Italy or fucked me senseless. I wanted to say it because I love him in the uneventful times too. But with Julian, there's never a moment that isn't dazzling and spectacular. I was waiting for an ordinary moment which doesn't exist when you're with an extraordinary man." I shrug, and a tear slips down my cheek. "So, yeah, I never told him."

Chance sniffles and wipes at his eyes. "That's fucking beautiful. I'll set up the meeting. My friend needs to hear that before he fucks it all up." Chance sniffles again. "Watch for my text. But be prepared, because Team True Love is a fierce bunch."

I put on my game face, ready to take on this battle. "That's what I'm banking on." I need them to all be in fighting mode, because Julian is worth fighting for.

An hour later, I have a link for a video call tomorrow evening. I've got a lot to do to prepare for the meeting of Operation Team True Love on Steroids.

CHAPTER
FIFTY-FIVE

JULIAN

————

Maddie and I sit on the beach watching the sunset in silence. We're kindred spirits these days. Both heartbroken fools. Even though Fredrick was a total douche, she loved him. That's the thing about Maddie. She loves fast, and she loves hard. That explains why she's been engaged so many times. Unfortunately, guys in her circle are like sharks looking for their next meal. Maddie is a big catch, and people often take advantage of her. She needs someone like me to look after her. I'm considering expanding the Decker Agency beyond sports to include actors like Maddie who need help, guidance, and protection, too.

So even though Fredrick was a horrible person, and this breakup is a good thing for her, it still stings. I feel for her. If she feels a fraction of the pain I'm feeling, she's a stronger person than me because I'm a shell of a man.

I'm the tinman functioning without a heart, the scarecrow without a brain, and don't have an ounce of the lion's courage in me. Maddie is my Dorothy, the eternal optimist, telling me it will be okay. She's been down this yellow-brick road before, and even though it sucks, there's hope at the end. If only there was a wizard who could fix me. Fuck. Twelve days in LA and I'm thinking in movie metaphors now.

We've stayed busy, because in LA, you can always find someone clamoring for a piece of you. But our cheerful facade and partying are merely a front to hide the pain. Tonight, we decide to face the pain head on. Stay home. Watch the sunset. Get drunk and numb it all. And vow to move on tomorrow. New book. New chapter.

"Do you really think she did it for revenge?" Maddie asks.

I shrug my shoulders. I don't want to accept it, but there isn't another logical explanation. It had to be her.

I miss her so much I consider forgiving her. But my heart and head are at war. Is this how it feels when your partner cheats and you decide to work it out? The problem with that? You can't have total trust again. You'll always have a fragment, a sliver of doubt, questioning their honesty. I can't live that way.

"Are you going to keep writing?" I enjoy it, but never as much as when I was collaborating with Harper. I've never felt more alive. Maybe it was the process. Maybe it was her. Either way, I'm not sure I want to write a book as a solo author again. I'm still unsure how my romance writing will affect my business. Will athletes still want to work with me? My agency. In a world where testosterone reigns, this side gig is not typically associated with masculinity. And while my head says I shouldn't allow other's judgement to matter, my heart cares. Another head and heart conflict.

"Dunno. I can't imagine writing a happily ever after, that's for sure."

"Sometimes you're grateful for the happily for now, you know." Maddie pulls her knees up to her chest and rests her chin there. As we sit on the sandy beach, she brings the bottle of wine to her lips and takes a long, satisfying swig. I can't let her drink alone, so I put my bottle of bourbon to my lips and take a generous gulp. Heartbreak drinking doesn't deserve glasses.

"That was Harper's take on our book couple. She didn't want to imagine their story past the last page, and I wanted to know they were forever." We battled back and forth on that point, and I gave in because I was happy in the now with her. I was willing to give her way a try. Look where that got me.

"Forever is a lie they sell in Hollywood." Her snarky, drunk philosophy sounds wrong coming from the champion of love. Although, she's got a point. I've lost my one great love. Forever.

———

"Rise and shine, sleepyhead," Maddie's chipper voice calls out. How can she be so cheery and bubbly when my head is swimming and my mouth feels like cotton? Last night I passed out on the couch, never finding the strength to make it to my bed. "I made you coffee, turned on SportsCenter, and charged your phone. You need to face today like a boss. New chapter, remember?"

"What happened to you?" This is the Maddie of our youth. The bright, fun, outgoing girl who commands a room. Not the sad actress on the beach from yesterday. And while I'm happy to see she's bouncing back, I wish she'd do it somewhere else. I'm not there yet.

"Nothing. Just starting a new chapter. Isn't it exciting? It's like I can reinvent myself again." She claps and hops on the counter, her legs swinging off the edge.

"Not really. I have writer's block," I mumble and pull the throw blanket over my head. I tune out her laughter and concentrate on getting my thoughts in order. There's an interview with Logan Swindell on in the background. It's a fluff piece, and he eats those up. I hear him say something about reading a book, and I sit up. Logan never reads.

"Where's the remote?" I feel around for it in the cushions.

"What?" Maddie asks, confused.

"The remote!" She picks it up and tosses it to me. I hit rewind to catch what I missed.

"What do you do to relax between games?" the female reporter asks.

"I'm like any other guy, really. I go out with friends, binge watch Netflix, and read," Logan answers. Why is he lying? There's nothing to gain with this. What's he up to?

"Really. Any book recommendations?" she asks.

"Well, I just finished this book by Priscilla Jenkins and JB Moore that came out yesterday. Couldn't put it down. And the ending? Chef's kiss."

"We'll add book reviewer to your impressive resume," she jokes. Her flirty laughter fills the room.

Did I hear that correctly? Harper finished our book and published it? She was working on it, but I would've thought with everything that happened she wouldn't have the heart to finish it. Well, apparently, she wasn't too heartbroken to work. Good for her. I'm not surprised. She cared more about the project than she cared about me.

I'm still trying to wrap my head around the fact Logan read a book. Especially that book.

"Is that the book you were writing with Harper?" Maddie asks.

"Yep. Guess she got it done. She's driven, that's for sure. Leave it to her not to miss a goal." The bitterness doesn't sit right, and I swallow it down. "I'm going for a run."

After a long run and an extra-hot shower, I sit down to face my workday. With the time difference, it's already late afternoon in New York, so I have a full day's worth of emails to respond to. There are the usual contract approvals and list of potential new clients. Nothing out of the ordinary until I open an email from a client telling me how much he loved my book.

My family group chat is all a twitter about the book, too. Did they all read it? Even Alexander?

Well, good for her. At least Harper can say she's published now. And surprisingly, I'm not angry about it. Maybe Maddie's right. New day, new frame of mind.

During our daily check-ins, Patrick hasn't mentioned JB Moore, which is making me a bit suspicious. He asks if I can go to the LA basketball game tonight because one of our clients, Derrick Johnson, needs some face time with me. Sure. Why not? I'll take Maddie. She likes those courtside seats. The focus in this city is more on being seen rather than the actual game, and I can work with that.

At halftime, the courtside reporter stops Derrick on his way to the locker room. "Derrick, you're on fire tonight. What's giving you the extra motivation and energy?"

"Man, I'm reading this romance book about a hockey player, and I'm hoping they'll write one about me next. It's LA, and I'm auditioning, baby!" The crowd goes wild as he bounces on his toes in a circle, his hands in the air encouraging the cheers.

Maddie laughs and bumps shoulders with me. I do my best to control my eye roll. The Jumbotron could flash to us any second, so I need to remain neutral.

"Seems I need to read this book and see what all the fuss is about," she teases.

"Don't bother," I mumble.

After the game, we go home, and I turn on the TV. I need comedic relief, so I find one of the late-night shows. Caleb Lyman, star safety for the Lonestars, is telling a humorous story about team travel and away games. I'm doomscrolling on my phone while he chats with the host about fans waiting outside hotels and fire alarms being pulled.

"No, really, that happens. Last night, I was in my hotel room reading this romance novel about a hockey player and his dog walker, and the fire alarm went off. I thought for sure it was because of the hot scene I was reading. I was definitely invested."

The host laughs and holds up a copy of the book as the

camera zooms in. "You heard it here first, folks. Caleb Lyman loves a hot romance."

"And my wife likes it when I read them too," Caleb adds. "It brings us together. Like the couple in this book. The ending was not what I expected. But it makes you a believer in forever love, that's for sure."

"We'll be back and play a game that will cool you off, Caleb," the host says, and the show cuts to an ad for acid relief. Which is exactly what I need right now because my stomach is rolling.

Forever love? That's not the way it ends, but if you aren't used to the genre, you might think a happily for now is forever.

Maddie comes in from the terrace, a bounce in her step. "I've got an audition for a Broadway play. I've always wanted to do Broadway. Tomorrow, I'm going to New York, and you're coming too. We're on this journey together. This new chapter is looking up!"

"I don't want to go," I mumble, sounding like a petulant toddler.

"I don't care what you want, you don't have a choice. I need to pack." Her tone is emphatic, and I know better than to argue. She'll win, so why bother fighting? She turns and goes to her bedroom.

And with that declaration, I'm going home.

CHAPTER
FIFTY-SIX

HARPER

PRISCILLA: You did a great job telling Charlotte's story, but you were wrong regarding her motivation. I fixed it. Sorry I didn't run the final draft past you. I'm sorry. For everything.

I hold my breath and hit enter.

Account not found

Well, fuck.

CHAPTER
FIFTY-SEVEN

JULIAN

———

We're dressed in hoodies and dark sunglasses, the LA version of a discreet disguise. Still, we have to fight our way through hordes of photographers and curious onlookers. I have my arm around Maddie to protect her from the paparazzi, who are pushing and shoving to get the money shot.

Once we're finally on the plane, we both relax. I'll never understand how she lives in this constant chaos and public scrutiny. Maddie rummages through her bag, pulls out her headphones, and a familiar book.

"Not you too?" I roll my eyes and sigh. I can't win. She responds with a shrug and a smile.

The woman across the aisle from me is reading it too. Tears stream down her face as she reads the last few pages. "Beautiful," she says to herself as she closes the book and hugs it to her chest.

"That good, huh?" I ask her.

"Yes. You probably think I'm being silly, but the way she

loves him. Fights for him. It's so romantic." She closes her eyes and continues to hold the book close.

I'm not sure what she's talking about because Charlotte doesn't fight for Gavin. He apologizes and does a traditional grand gesture, and they live happily for now. She's not the first person to mention the ending and, well…

What if? No. The mere thought of reading this book feels like unlocking a chest full of memories that I've struggled so hard to keep sealed. I fear that once opened, I won't have the strength to put them back in. I've made progress. Baby steps but progress, nonetheless. I only think about her eighty percent of my waking hours now. I'd hate to back slide.

Maddie twists in her seat, leans against the window, and pulls her legs until she's a compact ball. She's focused on her book and not in the talking mood. I get it. Me either.

I close my eyes and my mind drifts to Harper. Fuck, I miss her. Maybe I'll reach out and make amends. We can still be friends, right? Maddie and I are friends after being lovers. It's possible. But I never loved Maddie. Not like I loved Harper. My blood runs cold when I try to convince myself my love is past tense. I love Harper. I'm not sure I ever stopped. Or will.

I need something to focus on for the next five hours, so I'm not daydreaming about my shattered love life. I stare at the woman across the aisle for longer than is acceptable. Thank goodness her eyes are closed.

I lean across the aisle and tap her on the shoulder. "Excuse me, but do you mind if I borrow your book?"

CHAPTER
FIFTY-EIGHT

HARPER

————

My video call with Team True Love was awkward at first. They were quiet and allowed me to tell my story. And then Cole and Ashleigh added some context to what started the entire series of events. And when I heard that, I broke down in tears. Things aren't how they appear.

I knew Julian loved his family, but he was willing to fall on the sword and sacrifice himself for them. It makes me love him even more. After everything was said, we hung up. Two hours later, Ashleigh calls.

"Your story is a romance, not a tragedy. We want to help, especially since I started this mess. He deserves it. You both deserve it."

And that's how I became the leader of Team True Love 2.0. The plan? It's complex and bigger than the core Team True Love can handle. They tried to get him to listen, talk. But he shut down. So now we're on to Plan B. Team True Love needs rein-forcements.

It's been a week in the making and isn't quite a grand gesture, but more like an elaborate *hey, can we talk* kind of thing. Bigger than a billboard in LA. Desperate times call for desperate measures, after all. After a meeting at The Decker Agency, I launched the plan. I'll never be able to repay Patrick and Team True Love for their marketing strategies and contacts. I have no idea how many favors had to be cashed in, but when we reached out for help, everyone said yes. People's extraordinary actions on Julian's behalf, their unwavering loyalty and dedication to him, speak volumes about his exceptional character.

————

My Google alert goes off, signalling Julian's name is on the internet again. Cyber stalking him isn't healthy, but I feel like my clock is ticking. This is my last thread to him. The thought alone brings a lump to my throat and a sting to my eyes, but I can't afford to wallow in my sadness. There's work to be done.

Every photograph with Madelyn Reynolds is another punch to the gut. They've been spotted all over LA. She's broken off her engagement, and one report says they're living together. Ashleigh assures me they're only friends. So were we. Until we became more than friends.

With a deep breath, I click on the link. They're both dressed casually in hoodies, baseball caps, and sunglasses. Julian has his arm around her as he ushers Madelyn into the airport. Protective. Caring. Determined. Totally Julian. The headline says they're going on a romantic getaway. I can't help but think of our trip to Italy. He was like this with me, too. My heart sinks. I fear my time may be up. My lip quivers, tears slip down my cheeks, and this time, I let them flow.

————

When Zac wakes up from his pre-game nap, I'm curled up on the couch, muttering to myself, and clutching Noodle for dear life. Noodle struggles from my grip and runs to Zac. "Hey buddy, where's our girl?" Noodle runs back to me and whines.

"Traitor," I mumble.

Zac stands at the end of the couch and stares at me while Noodle yaps at him, demanding to be picked up. With Noodle securely snug in his arms, they both watch me, trying to figure out what's going on with me now.

"What are you looking at?" I snap. "Leave me alone."

He moves with lightning speed like he's blocking the game-winning shot and kneels beside the couch, tenderly pushing my hair away from my face and behind my ear. The tears threaten again. "Hey, hey, what happened?"

I only shake my head. I don't want to say it out loud. My heart isn't ready to accept defeat, but my head is saying it's white-flag time. I've lost.

He takes my phone from the table and flashes it at my face to unlock it, and I cry a little harder. It's reminiscent of the first time I bumped into Julian at NYU when he did the same thing. Zac looks at the phone and sees the website with the happy couple running away together.

"It's not what you think. Guarantee it. Listen, go take a shower, get cleaned up, and come to my game tonight. We're playing Boston. It'll be a good distraction for a few hours, and you can give out Harvard's number until your heart's content." I consider his offer and silently nod my head. He's right. It's time to move on and abandon the mission. I lost.

I sit up and take my phone from his hand to send a text to Team True Love 2.0.

> Great effort, but I'm afraid it didn't work. I appreciate each and every one of you. Julian's lucky to have you in his corner. 🩶

Harper left the chat.

CHAPTER
FIFTY-NINE

HARPER

———

Zac and I arrive home and walk to our door in companionable silence. The Havoc's loss was brutal, and he's pissed. Understandably so.

We come to an abrupt stop when we find a person in a hoodie, their face obscured, sitting on the floor beside our door. Next to them is a pathetic, wilting bouquet, looking like it was rescued from a dumpster, its once-bright blooms now mutilated.

The mumbling sounds vaguely like *she loves me, she loves me not*, as they continue to mutilate the flowers. It's like the nonsensical ramblings of a crazy person, and to be honest, it's a bit frightening. Zac positions himself in front of me, with his arm extended behind him, holding me back and protecting me.

"Jesus, man, you know this isn't a good look, right?" Zac says to him.

I try to move around Zac so I can see what's going on. The man jumps up, and his hood falls down around his shoulders. "Home. Yes. Game. Here." I steel myself at the sound of Julian's voice. His string of random words makes about as much sense as him sitting in the hall looking like a deranged homeless person.

I've spent the day accepting defeat. Maybe he's here to demand surrender. If I'm lucky, we can sign a peace treaty and move on.

Zac directs his attention to Julian, then gives me a quick glance, checking to see if I'm okay. I'm in shock, but he must decide I'm not in danger. "Look, I'm not leaving. We've both had a pretty shitty day. But I'll give you some privacy." Zac unlocks the door and turns to look at me. "I'll be in my room if you need me." Then he puts his hand on Julian's shoulder, and they lock eyes. "For a moment, you made me believe love was real." He shakes his head in disappointment and enters the apartment, leaving the door ajar.

Julian and I stand in the hallway in awkward silence. His eyes take me in from head to toe. I'm dressed in Zac's jersey and a pair of jeans, my hair in a messy bun. No makeup. Nothing fancy. But the way he's looking at me? It's unsettling. Compared to the flawless Hollywood women he's been hanging out with, I'm painfully aware of his critical gaze.

Of course, I do the same to him. He's a mess in a hoodie and jeans, his usual put-together look nowhere to be found. He's a long way from the red carpets he's been rocking lately. His hair looks like he's run his hands through it so many times it doesn't know which way to go. There's even a flower petal or two caught in his curls. But when I lock onto his blue eyes, they look sad and weary. I get it. Me too.

My heart wants to lash out, but my head says, what's the point? When I speak, it's flat. Distant.

"What are you doing here? Aren't you supposed to be on some romantic getaway?"

He seems genuinely confused. "What are you talking about?"

"You and Madelyn? Airport? Getaway?"

One corner of his mouth lifts slightly. "We were coming here. To New York. She has an audition."

"Oh." *Things aren't always as they appear,* my heart whispers. *Shut up,* my head shouts. It's been weeks. *Finally,* my heart sighs. *Why now?* my head questions.

I look down, and his eyes track mine. He takes in the mess on the floor, and it must trigger him. His arm shoots out, and he shoves the messy bouquet at me. "These are for you. Sorry. I was nervous." I don't need his nervous apology. Or the flowers.

I take the remaining flowers from him. They're wrapped in torn paper, and the tattered bow is destroyed. They look exactly how I feel. "Thanks," I respond with a shrug. "I'm sure they were lovely." Why is he nervous? I'm sure he's broken up with women before.

We stand in silence until Noodle wanders out of the apartment. He walks around Julian's legs, signaling he wants to be picked up. Julian scoops him up and snuggles him. "Hey buddy, I missed you."

He missed the dog. That's the last straw. "Why are you here, Julian?" He's blocked me and ignored his friends' pleas to talk to me. I'm confused. Tired. Heartbroken. Defeated.

"I missed you." He looks at me, his eyes pleading with me to believe him.

I've been working my way through the stages of grief today and I've shifted from denial to anger. "But you blocked me, ignored me, shut me out. But most of all, you didn't trust me. Missing me is kinda on you." I lash out.

"You're right. That's totally on me. And I'm sorry, Harper. It's unforgivable. And I'm not making excuses, but I was caught off guard, and you had talked about Charlotte being a revenge kind of girl and, well, no excuse. I was wrong, and I'm sorry. So fucking sorry." His eyes search mine, seeking something. Answers? Forgiveness?

"I'm not Charlotte."

"I know." He lowers his head in shame.

I can see where he might be confused. At first, to him, Charlotte was me. But as he got to know her as a character, she came into her own. "I suppose that's the problem with being a muse. It can get confusing about what's real and what's not."

"You are the most real person in my life. You didn't give up on me. Even when I was too stubborn to get out of my own head." He reaches out and then drops his hand back to Noodle. Great, this is the let's-be-friends portion of the conversation.

I bow my head in defeat. "It wasn't me. I didn't tell anyone." That's all I wanted to say this whole time. He probably still believes I betrayed him, but at least he's heard the truth. Now he can close this chapter and go back to Madelyn.

"I know."

I raise my eyes to his. My heart feels lighter knowing he doesn't hold me responsible. "You do?" Is that why he's here?

My wide-eyed look of surprise brings the ghost of a smile to his lips. "Yeah, I'm not sure how it got out, but I don't care. It wasn't you. You'd never hurt someone on purpose, especially someone you love."

"You think I love you?" I say with a scoff and more sass than I feel. I waited for the right time to tell him, and well, it never came.

"I know you love me. Without a doubt. Hell, the entire world knows you love me. Because you do, right?" His hopeful gaze causes the protective barrier I built around my heart to crumble into dust.

"Guilty." I shrug. Leave it to him to steal my love proclamation. "By the way, charges are pending for Professor Daniel's assistant."

She held the first meeting with Julian and did some unsanctioned research. When the secret leaked, I reached out to Professor Daniels, and he did some digging. They fired her, and the school is considering charges for breach of confidentiality. He has been extremely helpful during this time and is an honorary member of Team True Love.

He gives a half shrug. "Don't care."

"It was all my fault. I was jealous. If I'd only listened to you.

You've told me over and over things aren't as they appear." I've spent a lot of time accepting my part in this series of events. I shouldn't have left that message. I should have answered his calls. So many things I should have done differently if I wasn't tired and reactive. And jealous. It's still hard for me to grasp that this kind, generous, beautiful man loves me. Or loved me?

Now he's looking at me like the cat that ate the canary.

"I like that you were jealous." He's coming back to life before my eyes. His smile lights up his face, a rosy hue warming his cheeks, eyes twinkling with joy. With growing confidence, he straightens, his shoulders broadening as he takes control of the moment, our encounter now fully under his sway.

We've been inching closer, like two magnets that can't ignore their pull. Noodle gives a little yip, and we both laugh as he struggles to get down. Julian leans down and places him on the floor. He wiggles and walks away.

"I read the book on the flight here." He closes the gap between us. The flight. The one with Madelyn, I remind myself. I take a step back, and his smile falters. "What?"

I'm shaking my head, trying to figure out what to say without sounding like a jealous harpy. "Madelyn," I mumble.

His grin returns as he steps closer. "Oh, she loved it. Couldn't put it down. She might use the final profession of love as a monologue at her audition tomorrow. Since she wouldn't part with her book, I borrowed a copy from a nice lady on the plane. She's a big fan, by the way. She gushed over the ending. I was intrigued when she said things that didn't match my memory of the story." He shrugs. "Besides, it's trending on BookTok, and I needed to see if it really lived up to the hype."

Of course it didn't match. Since Julian wouldn't talk to me, I rewrote parts of the book to have Charlotte talk for me. I changed their conflict to mirror ours. The aim was to make it recognizable to him as I shifted from being his muse to becoming the main character in the story. Charlotte's words and actions? Mine. All mine.

The changes included Gavin blocking Charlotte and moving out of his apartment, giving her no way of reaching him. She was desperate to share her side of the story. To tell him how much she missed him. How her heart ached for him. How he's her one. How much she loves him. That maybe instalove is real after all. She hadn't said those important words to him before the misunderstanding, and he deserved to hear them.

Charlotte fought for their relationship. She dug her claws in and wouldn't let go of him. Them. She used everything at her disposal, and then some, to convince him to talk to her. She even created a hashtag that went viral.

Of course, writing her point of view went against the assignment, and Professor Daniels wasn't happy. But I needed Charlotte's voice to say the things I couldn't. And then pray Julian would read them.

"Sorry I didn't run the changes by you."

I watch Julian's self-assurance strengthen. "I liked them. The writing is full of passion, sensuality, and provocation. Charlotte is a fucking warrior, and I couldn't help but root for her. For them." His eyes smolder. He really liked the changes?

Changing the tone was challenging, but I treated it as a relentless writing sprint, the words pouring forth out of my intense emotion. They say keep your audience in mind when you write. In this case, I wrote this book with one reader in mind. Julian.

"Yep. She's a fighter. I told you that. She'll move heaven and earth if she has to. Especially when her future's in jeopardy. Even if there's another woman."

"Her tenacity might be her hottest character trait. But there was never another woman. When you love someone that much, there's only room for one." The gravel in his voice kick starts my heart. *Things aren't always as they appear*, my heart sings. *Damn right, they're not*, my head cheers.

"What was your favorite part of the book?" I cock my eyebrow. "The steamy sex scenes?"

This time, I inch a little closer, my hand resting on his chest. Every fiber of my being longs to touch him, and I can't wait a second longer.

He chuckles. "They were hot, but not my favorite part." He places his hand over mine. I can feel his heart racing. Letting the remaining flowers fall to the floor with a soft thud, I gently place my hand on his shoulder, my fingers tracing the curve of his neck.

"Oh, you liked the grand gesture where she worked with his teammates to get his attention?" Life imitating art, so to speak.

There's a familiar gleam in his eye.

"That was entertaining." He chuckles at the absurdity of it. "And an interesting twist. I can't imagine how she made that happen, but then, with her determination, nothing should surprise me." His other hand reaches up and cups my face. I close my eyes and lean into the warmth of his hand. I relish the feeling of his touch against my skin, and feel my heart piecing itself back together.

"Then what's your favorite part?" I ask expectantly as I search his stormy blue eyes.

"The happily ever after." His lips crash into mine, and with that touch, he rights my world. I kiss him, feeling the warmth of his smile against my lips. The dam of my sadness bursts, and a rush of exhilarating happiness and joy floods through me, a feeling so intense it vibrates in my bones.

The kiss ends, the silence broken only by the heavy, uneven rhythm of our breathing and the frantic pounding of our hearts. I cling to him tightly, not wanting to lose him again. I can admit when he's right and I'm wrong. He was actually right about quite a few things this time. But just one thing matters now.

"It's my favorite part too."

WHAT'S NEXT FOR THE DECKER CONNECTION?

Get ready for Sully Decker's romantic holiday novella!

Sullivan Decker's children are living their happily ever afters. It's what he wants for them - the kind of love he and their mother shared. It's been fourteen years since his beloved wife died and the loneliness is catching up with him.

Spending the holidays at his mountain retreat, this silver fox meets a woman whose nasty divorce has left her cynical about love.

Through a series of mishaps, fate gives them the push they need to consider the idea of love a second time around. And just because there's snow on the roof, doesn't mean there's not a fire in the furnace. He is a Decker man, after all.

ALSO BY CHERYL CAMPBELL

Trouble at First: Ashleigh and Cole

The Decker Connection series starts with Ashleigh and Cole 📖

All Ashleigh Decker wants this summer is to be the social media intern for the Savannah Pajamas. Is that too much to ask? She's off to a great start until she meets a player who is nothing but trouble.

This summer league is the perfect opportunity for Cole Davidson to impress the MLB scouts. His dream to play first base for the Carolina Reapers is within his grasp. An added bonus? A beautiful intern who steals his heart.

The only problem? She's hiding her identity. Her father is the owner of the Reapers, and her overprotective older brother is the General Manager. Can Ashleigh keep her secret and the guy without jeopardizing his career?

Sliding into Home: Matt and Darcy

Overwhelmed doesn't begin to describe my life. I'm in over my head remodeling a multi-million-dollar beach house. It's the only thing standing between me and college graduation. Then the guy I've crushed on since middle school offers to be my assistant. Did I mention he's my brother's best friend? Yep. Matt Hartman, swoony boy next door and professional baseball player, is working side by side with me this fall. It takes everything I have to keep my feelings for him contained, until, well, I don't. Can I put his friendship with my brother on the line for a relationship with me?

I've hit more milestones this year than most do in a decade. I graduated from college, got drafted into Major League Baseball, played on a triple-A team in my hometown, and now, for the first time in my life, I'm enjoying my off-season. But am I? When I'm presented with the opportunity to help Darcy Davidson with her senior project, I gladly volunteer my services. It's something to fill my time, and besides, my best friend's sister needs help. That's all it is, right? Then why do I want to be so much more than her assistant?

Living the Suite Life: Alexander and Dani

Stress and pressure come with the territory when you're the youngest General Manager in the MLB. Add in my self-appointed role as the protector of the Decker Connection, my tight-knit group of siblings and friends, and it's no wonder they say I'm grumpy.

I'm facing down a public relations nightmare after one of my players assaults someone at a local food festival, and this PR problem is about to push me over the edge. Then I meet this full-of-sunshine, rainbows from storm clouds, heart-full-of-kindness, single mother, and I'm in more trouble than I ever imagined. There's absolutely no saving me from falling now.

LET'S CONNECT

Cheryl loves connecting with readers and talking about the Deckers. Join her in the conversation. Follow for sneak peeks and behind the scenes fun.

And don't forget to leave a review on Amazon 😃

Cheryl Campbell Facebook Cheryl Campbell Author

Cheryl Campbell Instagram @Cheryl_Campbell_Author

Cheryl Campbell TikTok @cherylcampbellbooks

CherylCampbellbooks@gmail.com

Want to hear The Final Draft playlist? Check it out on Spotify.

The Final Draft Spotify Playlist

www.ingramcontent.com/pod-product-compliance
Lightning Source LLC
Chambersburg PA
CBHW050020120726
47903CB00006B/1849